HALFHYDE ON THE YANGTZE

Whistle and I'll Come
The Kid
Storm South
Hopkinson and the Devil of Hate
Leave the Dead Behind Us
Marley's Empire
Bowering's Breakwater
Sladd's Evil
A Time for Survival
Poulter's Passage
The Day of the Coastwatch
Man, Let's Go On
Half a Bag of Stringer
The German Helmet
The Oil Bastards
Pull My String
Coach North

Featuring Commander Shaw:
Gibraltar Road
Redcap
Bluebolt One
The Man From Moscow
Warmaster
Moscow Coach
The Dead Line
Skyprobe
The Screaming Dead Balloons
The Bright Red Businessmen
The All-Purpose Bodies
Hartinger's Mouse

This Drakotny . . .
Sunstrike
Corpse

Featuring Simon Shard:
Call for Simon Shard
A Very Big Bang
Blood Run East
The Eros Affair
Blackmail North
Shard Calls the Tune

*Featuring Lieutenant St Vincent
    Halfhyde, RN:*
Beware, Beware the Bight of Benin
Halfhyde's Island
The Guns of Arrest
Halfhyde to the Narrows
Halfhyde for the Queen
Halfhyde Ordered South
Halfhyde and the Flag Captain

Featuring Donald Cameron:
Cameron – Ordinary Seaman
Cameron Comes Through
Cameron of the Castle Bay
Lieutenant Cameron, RNVR

Non-fiction:
Tall Ships – The Golden Age of
    Sail
Great Yachts

HALFHYDE ON THE YANGTZE

Philip McCutchan

WEIDENFELD AND NICOLSON
LONDON

ONE

Darkness loomed, as did the enclosing banks of rock little more than one hundred and fifty yards on either beam, rocky banks that led into the gloom and danger of the narrow gorges through which the river ran for part of its course upstream from Shanghai. In the Chutang Gorge and in the Wu Gorge the channel narrowed at times to a mere hundred yards, and the British gunboats, steaming at slow speed in line ahead behind their leader, were frequently brought beam on to the rushing, turbulent waters of the Yangtze Kiang. Halfhyde sweated despite the cold of the night: to be brought to grief in this wild land, to take a shoal, to smash in the side of any of the gunboats, would be to ask for death. Heathen bandits would not be far away, bandits who had already shown hostility to the naval force pushing through from the East China Sea. Ancient guns had been let off, and some of the seamen had been wounded, and one had died. The British were not wanted up the Yangtze; some of the attackers had not in fact been bandits but uniformed soldiers of the old Empress-Dowager.

China was a closed land ever inimical to foreign devils, a cruel, harsh land of extreme poverty for all below the rank of mandarin, a land that knew well how to torture. The navigation of its rivers required a knowledge and an expertise very different from that demanded by the deep, open sea, and no Chinese had been found willing to pilot the flotilla through to Chungking, nor for that matter any of the British pilots of the Shanghai and Hong Kong pilotage, themselves not familiar with the Yangtze apart from the waters around its mouth; while the Senior Officer, Captain Watkiss, was no more help than a haddock. Lieutenant St Vincent Halfhyde, as he watched and prayed and used his engine in split-second decisions to keep the ship on a straight course as the water took her, found his mind turning in fragmented moments to the change in his orders after his arrival in Hong Kong. He had been in temporary command of a torpedo-boat destroyer for delivery to the China Squadron and had entertained hopes that he might be allowed to remain in command of *Daring*; but this was not to be, as he had been told within an hour of his arrival thirty-six days out from Portsmouth.

*   *   *

The commander of the Hong Kong dockyard, Commodore Renshaw, was a ponderous officer, lantern-jawed and darkly lugubrious, with a habit of reaching behind himself to scratch his bottom as he walked up and down, a nervous tic the frequency of which was indicated by the slight soiling of the backside of his white uniform trousers even though they would have been fresh upon his body that morning. He seemed unable to keep still; and Halfhyde, seated, found his eyes moving from right to left and back again as though he were watching a game of lawn tennis in England. Renshaw nodded from time to time as Halfhyde made his routine report upon the voyage from Portsmouth and then proceeded without delay to an exposition concerning Halfhyde's future employment.

'A situation has arisen,' he said carefully. 'Not unprecedented, but serious. It's a pity you're not familiar with Chinese river navigation, but in the circumstances it can't be helped.'

Halfhyde coughed. 'May I ask where you acquired the information as to my lack of river experience, sir?'

'By cable from the Admiralty,' Renshaw answered, scratching. He paced. 'As an intelligent and practical officer, you will no doubt quickly accommodate yourself. I am ordered to reappoint you from the *Daring* immediately. You are to take command of the river gunboat *Gadfly*. There has been sickness in the flotilla – this is a wretched station, Halfhyde, full of disease, as you're probably aware.'

'I am, sir. I've served out here before, though not upon the rivers.'

'Yes, quite. Now, both the Captain and the First Lieutenant of *Gadfly* are sick with the typhoid, and the flotilla is to leave as soon as possible for Shanghai. Thus I have also to fill the room of your First Lieutenant.' Renshaw ceased his pacing for a moment and stood in front of Halfhyde, staring down at him. '*Daring* must spare her First Lieutenant as well. How do you find Lord Edward Cole?'

'A capable officer, sir,' Halfhyde answered. Lord Edward had initially proved languid, but a charge of dynamite in the right place had worked wonders, and the aristocratic young officer was becoming used to having his beautifully tailored uniform soiled and to being sent for whilst in mid gin in the wardroom when matters required his attention; and had also resigned himself to being addressed by his Captain as 'Mr Cole'. 'I shall find him acceptable as my First Lieutenant in *Gadfly*, if that's what you're asking.'

'I am, yes. I'm glad of your remarks, Halfhyde.'

'I am glad to be able to offer them, sir. May I ask what the orders are for *Gadfly*?'

Renshaw said, 'I prefer to leave that to your Senior Officer, Halfhyde. A touchy man, with whom you have sailed before. To be precise, Captain Watkiss.'

He might have known, he told himself as he left Renshaw to scratch and took a *ricksha* back to the dockyard steps. Casting around through his telescope from his bridge just after arrival in the port, Halfhyde had observed a boat waiting at the foot of some steps descending to the water of the naval dockyard opposite the Kowloon side. Around this boat hovered a number of sampans bearing chattering Chinese, men, women and children. And down the steps an officer had been proceeding to embark in the boat: an officer of rotund shape, wearing a highly curious but well-remembered rig of white Number Ten tunic and overlong white shorts that ended just below the knee and obscured the tops of the white stockings. A telescope was beneath the left arm, and below the gold oak-leaves fringing the cap a monocle flashed back the sun's fire. As Halfhyde watched in incredulous astonishment at seeing Captain Watkiss once again, the latter's voice was heard loud and clear across the water.

'You there, cox'n. Clear away those damn dagoes!

3

I'll not have them impeding my boat and that's fact, I said it.'

That earlier sight of Captain Watkiss had held foreboding. Now the foreboding had come to pass; the future, whatever it might be, would be filled with tantrums and contradictory orders and sheer stupidity largely nullified for its perpetrator by the extraordinary luck that seemed to protect Captain Watkiss from court martial. It was not, of course, luck alone: Watkiss had useful connections in the form of two sisters, one married to the First Sea Lord and the other to the Permanent Secretary to the Treasury – these sisters no doubt being the reason why Commodore Renshaw had been walking warily and avoiding treading on Captain Watkiss' corns by pre-empting a captain's right to expound his orders. Watkiss could be a rude man when he felt his dignity assailed. Reaching his galley, Halfhyde was pulled out across the harbour towards the *Daring* in her temporary anchorage in Victoria Harbour. Once aboard, he apprised Mr Cole of his new appointment.

'I *say*, sir!' Mr Cole responded, beaming.

'What?'

'It's awfully good news really. I'm awfully interested in China. I imagine we'll be going up a river?'

Halfhyde said sourly, 'I imagine so, Mr Cole. Have you ever served under Captain Watkiss?'

Cole pursed his lips and screwed up the flesh around his eyes. 'Er ... no, sir, actually I haven't.'

'Then you may find him interesting also. I suggest you pack your gear without delay, Mr Cole, and inform the sub-lieutenant that pending the appointment of a more senior officer I wish to hand over the command to him at once. I repeat, we are ordered to join the *Gadfly* as soon as possible. In the terms employed by Captain Watkiss, that means ten minutes ago.'

Halfhyde turned away, leaving his First Lieutenant to puzzle over his words. Poor Cole was eager but not too bright: Half-hyde's mind went back with a degree of irritation to his first meeting with Lord Edward Cole upon joining the *Daring* in Portsmouth dockyard. The ship had looked dirty and the gangway staff had been inattentive, keeping him waiting while the brougham hired to bring him from his lodgings cost hard-earned money by the minute. When Lord Edward had appeared on deck and had seen the two gold stripes of a lieutenant of less than eight years' seniority, he had greeted the newcomer as 'old boy'. Frigidly, Halfhyde had identified himself as Cole's new Captain and thus as entitled to be addressed with respect as his previous Commanding Officer even though the latter had had the advantage of the extra half stripe of a senior lieutenant. He had added, 'Do I make myself clear?'

There had been a hurt look. 'Yes, sir, indeed.'

'I'm glad. I'd be obliged to be shewn to my cabin, and once there I'd like a word with you, Mr Cole.'

'Actually—'

'I know what you're about to say, Mr Cole, and that is a matter I shall discuss with you in private.'

'Oh. Yes, sir.'

The First Lieutenant had turned away and Halfhyde had followed. Once inside his cabin Halfhyde had ostentatiously shut the door and faced his second-in-command. 'I have some things to say. The first is this: I am aware from the Navy List that you are Lord Edward Cole, but from now until I leave the ship in Hong Kong you will be addressed as Mr Cole like any normal First Lieutenant. The second is this: the ship's a damn disgrace and will be cleaned from truck to keel before we leave Portsmouth. I've already noted lines hanging judas over the side, the ensign virtually at the dip, and potato peelings outside the galley. In the absence of your Captain, Mr Cole, you run a slack ship. That will cease.'

'Yes, sir. I'm awfully sorry.'

'You'll be sorrier if matters don't improve rapidly. The peerage doesn't count with me, Mr Cole, I care only for efficiency and good seamanship. Prove yourself, and I shall forgive you your family connections.' There was a smile lurking about the corners of Halfhyde's mouth now. 'Tell me, Mr Cole, did you have an ancestor at Trafalgar?'

'Er ... no, sir, I didn't.'

'*I* did,' Halfhyde had said with relish. 'Daniel Halfhyde, gunner's mate in the *Temeraire*. A common seaman.'

'Did you really, sir?' The eyes, wide already, had widened further. 'Oh, I say, I think that's awfully... awfully...'

'Awfully what, Mr Cole?'

'Awfully sporting, sir.'

Today, ten thousand miles east of Portsmouth yard, Halfhyde thought about that comment and grinned to himself as his servant, Able-Seaman Bodger, packed his master's gear along with his own bag and hammock: Halfhyde had been able to secure permission from the Commodore to bring his own servant in place of the Chinese locally-enlisted rating who would normally attend upon gunboat officers. Bodger had served with Halfhyde for a long time and was irreplaceable. Within half an hour of returning aboard, Halfhyde with his two companions was being pulled by *Daring*'s galley's crew round Kowloon Point to the warship anchorage. Halfhyde's first sight of the river gunboat flotilla was depressing. Four curious vessels, tiered like wedding cakes as to their decks, short and tubby and looking most remarkably unwieldy and unseaworthy, each with a single thin funnel sticking pencil-like through the layers of the cake. Aboard the leader, HMS *Cockroach*, a capless figure reclined in a deck chair beneath an awning, reading a bulky volume bound in red leather. This was Captain Watkiss; he did not look up as Halfhyde was pulled past, but had evidently noted his passage all the same. When the boat from *Daring* came alongside *Gadfly* and Halfhyde embarked and identified himself to a midshipman standing by with a piping party, he was at once handed a signal reading: GADFLY FROM SENIOR OFFICER. YOU ARE TO REPAIR ABOARD IMMEDIATELY.

*   *   *

'Ah, Mr Halfhyde once again. You might have reported quicker.'

'I—'

'Oh, don't start off by arguing, Mr Halfhyde, I detest argument as you should know. You argued with me when I commanded the Fourth TBD flotilla, and again when we were in South America, until I was nearly on the sick list. I really don't know why the Admiralty's wished you on me again, damned if I do.' Captain Watkiss looked vaguely unwell, as though China failed to suit him. He had a flabbier aspect than Halfhyde remembered, although their sojourn together in Chilean and

6

Uruguayan waters had not been so very long ago, and his skin was damp and yellowish ... Captain Watkiss went on, eschewing further words of welcome, 'My flotilla will leave for the mouth of the Yangtze at four bells in the afternoon watch. Is *Gadfly* ready to proceed, Mr Halfhyde?'

'I don't know, sir.'

Watkiss placed his monocle in his eye. His tone was incredulous. 'Did I hear you say you *don't know?*'

'You did, sir. The reason is that I was scarcely aboard before you sent for me—'

'I call that impertinent.'

'I apologize, sir,' Halfhyde said coldly. 'Be assured that my ship will, in fact, be in all respects ready for sea whenever required. May I know the orders, sir?'

'Yes.' Captain Watkiss, although the interview was taking place in the privacy of his cabin, lowered his voice as if instinctively and looked portentous. 'There is a most important task ahead of me, Mr Halfhyde, most important, and I fancy the Admiralty considers it fortunate that I happened to be here in Hong Kong. I dare say it explains why I was appointed to the command of a damn gunboat flotilla,' he added with a touch of angry pettishness, 'since nothing larger could make the passage, but never mind that. Will you kindly remove your blasted feet from before my legs, Mr Halfhyde, there is no room to swing a cat.'

Halfhyde moved his legs; he had the strong impression that Captain Watkiss found his appointment demeaning, and it was certainly true that his cabin was little bigger than a cupboard. When commanding *Venomous* in the Fourth TBD Flotilla he had solved his problem of space by removal of a bulkhead so that he could take in his First Lieutenant's cabin in addition to his own, but *Cockroach* was so constructed that he was unable to expand without dockyard assistance, and that would have called for Admiralty permission. Looking caged, Watkiss expounded. It appeared that the flotilla was under orders to enter the Yangtze and proceed up river to Chungking with the utmost despatch.

'A terrible voyage, Mr Halfhyde. The Yangtze is fast-flowing and filled with gorges. Damn dagoes along the banks, too.'

'Dagoes, sir?'

Watkiss shifted irritably. 'All foreigners are dagoes, Mr

7

Halfhyde, I've told you that before. And I don't like them, don't like them at all. Not honest, and murderers to a man. Pirates, that's what they are out here Chinaside, and that's fact, I said it. Well, we shall have to brave them, that's all.'

'In the interest of what or whom, sir?'

'Of Her Majesty, basically. Surely that's obvious?' Captain Watkiss bent forward, then twisted backwards to make sure no one was eavesdropping outside the square port of his cabin. 'Mr Halfhyde, be so good as to pull up the jalousie.'

Halfhyde reached out to pull up the slatted shutter. When he had done so Watkiss went on. He said, 'There's been trouble in Szechwan province, I'm damned if I know quite what, I'm a simple sailor after all. I expect to be given further information by Commodore Marriot-Lee commanding the China Squadron off Foochow, under whose orders I am to come.' He sniffed. 'It's some kind of rebellion, of course – the dagoes are always rebelling, dreadful bunch. If only everyone could be British, but of course I suppose they can't be. To escape slaughter, a number of British traders and their wives have taken refuge in Chungking, one of the treaty ports if only a blasted river one. I am ordered to bring them out aboard my flotilla, and this I shall do. There's one important thing: word has been put about that my flotilla's leaving Hong Kong for the treaty port of Foochow, so the dagoes won't know we're bound for Shanghai and the Yangtze, do you understand?'

'Until we reach Shanghai, sir.'

Watkiss stared. 'What do you mean, Mr Halfhyde?'

'They'll know then, sir.'

'Oh, that's not the blasted point, is it?' Watkiss bounced angrily in his wickerwork chair. 'We shall have pulled the wool over their eyes for a time at least, and it all helps.'

'No doubt it does, sir,' Halfhyde said sardonically. 'These British traders ... where are they taking refuge?'

'In Chungking, Mr Halfhyde. I said that.' Watkiss looked long-suffering.

'So you did, sir. My question was meant to be a narrowing one. In what building are they to be found?'

'In the British Consulate,' Watkiss answered. 'Traders are always a confounded nuisance, but there we are. Trade, they say, follows the flag. I know where *I*'d sooner be. Traders are not gentlemen.' He sounded much put out, though Halfhyde guessed that the beleaguered Britons would prove to be not so much traders as respected company officials, bankers and so on, but of course they were not gentlemen either.... Watkiss went on, brandishing his telescope as though it were a sword or cutlass, 'We shall cease for a while to be sailors, Mr Halfhyde, and shall become soldiers. We shall form landing-parties, with gaiters, rifles and side-arms, to fight through to their succour!' He waved an arm and struck the exhaust steam pipe for the steering engine, which led through his cabin to make it hot and stuffy when at sea. 'Oh, God damn!' He was about to add further comment when a somewhat timid knock came at the frame around his door-curtain, which he had forgotten to check earlier when he had checked the port, and a face came through bearing a deferential look. It was a face Halfhyde recognized: Mr Beauchamp, a senior lieutenant, proud possessor of a half stripe between the two thicker ones on his shoulder-straps. Poor Beauchamp, who had evidently not managed to avoid another spell of drudgery as Watkiss' First Lieutenant....

'Go away, Mr Beauchamp, can't you see I'm busy?'

'Sir—'

Watkiss brandished his telescope. 'Are you deaf, Mr Beauchamp?'

'No, sir. An important matter—'

'Oh, God damn—'

The voice grew louder in desperation. 'Your ice-box, sir.'

The Senior Officer's face reddened dangerously. 'Yes, Mr Beauchamp, what about my ice-box?'

'No ice has come aboard, sir. I'm very sorry, sir. Your lettuce has become limp.'

'My lettuce has become limp, has it?' Watkiss said in a hiss. 'Why am I to be plagued continually by my blasted ice-box? My cheese – my vegetables – every blasted ship I've ever commanded! A boat is to go inshore at once, Mr Beauchamp, go with it yourself, and demand ice from the Fleet Paymaster who can damn well carry it personally if he can find no one else for the task. I think you know Mr Halfhyde?'

'Of course, sir.'

'Good. He's to command *Gadfly* and will take second of the line. I've been studying seniorities in the Navy List. He's my

9

senior Commanding Officer and thus will be second-in-command of my flotilla, Mr Beauchamp.'

Beauchamp's face was a picture of hurt pride. 'Sir, I am a senior lieutenant, while Mr Halfhyde is—'

'Yes, yes, yes, I know, I'm not blind, Mr Beauchamp, but you are unfitted for command and I won't have you in that capacity. In any case, the appointment is an Admiralty one.'

'Sir—'

'Go away, Mr Beauchamp, and find ice.'

'But—'

'If you linger, Mr Beauchamp, I shall place you in arrest.'

Sliding the curtain dispiritedly back into place, the leader's First Lieutenant departed. Watkiss gave a sigh and dabbed sweat from his face. Hong Kong in summer was deplorably hot, quite viciously so, and it smelled too. Too many dagoes with too many children. 'I don't know why I have continually to be plagued, Mr Halfhyde. Plagued with detail ... command's hard enough as it is, and Beauchamp's not fit to put a woman on her back, let alone take over from me in an emergency. I hear your First Lieutenant in *Daring*'s joining you.' He lifted a hand and tapped the red leather-bound volume he had been reading on deck earlier; Halfhyde saw without surprise that it was *Burke's Peerage*; on a shelf above Watkiss' desk rested its sister volume, *Burke's Landed Gentry*. 'Lord Edward Cole ... a good family, that goes without saying, of course. Military, not naval, which is a pity, but still. Father's Field-Marshal the Earl of Frensham, don't you know.' Had Captain Watkiss been standing, Halfhyde thought, he might well have bent the knee.

'I was aware of that, sir, but must stress that I am not overawed by birth. However, Mr Cole has proved himself to my satisfaction so I can forgive the rest.'

Captain Watkiss seemed to be about to boil. '*Mr Cole?* God damn it, he's Lord Edward!'

'Not aboard my ship, sir,' Halfhyde said firmly.

'Your ship or not, Mr Halfhyde, he is to be properly addressed as Lord Edward, and that's an order.'

'One, sir, that I shall not be obeying. Aboard my ship, he will continue to be Mr Cole for all duty purposes, and if you care to sail for the Yangtze with one of your commanding officers in arrest, then I think both the Commodore and the Admiralty will ask for a medical board to examine your sanity.' Halfhyde got to his feet, bending his lanky frame from the deckhead. 'If there is nothing further, I propose to repair aboard my ship to make ready for sea.'

*   *   *

Full bunkers had already been taken by all the gunboats and a signal from the Commodore-in-Charge had indicated that replenishments would be made available from the cruisers of Commodore Marriot-Lee's China Squadron off Foochow and that these would be lightered off to the flotilla upon arrival. Sharp at four bells in the afternoon watch the executive signal came from the Senior Officer in *Cockroach* and formal permission to proceed was given by the Queen's Harbour Master. With the White Ensigns drooping in the windless air, the flotilla weighed anchor and formed into line ahead for the northward passage to Shanghai and the Yangtze Kiang: *Cockroach*, *Gadfly*, *Bee* and *Wasp*. From his navigating bridge Halfhyde watched Captain Watkiss bouncing on his heels, importantly, his stomach out-thrust against the after guardrail as he stared astern at his junior ships, seeking faults. When the bouncing stopped, up came the telescope and upon its heels the signal of complaint: *Bee* was too far to starboard, and *Gadfly* was making too much smoke. The name of the engineer was to be signalled by flag hoist. Captain Watkiss was on form; and Halfhyde ground his teeth at his ill fortune in being once again projected into a special situation with his tiresome Senior Officer. It seemed as though the Admiralty was unable to get the curious partnership out of its mind; success, at any rate of a sort, had attended their previous joint performances in Russian waters, in Spain, and in South America, and now they were neatly labelled though in this current case their proximity had been fortuitous. Halfhyde wondered how Captain Watkiss would bounce to victory this time; his knack of considering himself ever victorious was an enviable one.... In the meantime the Chinese were far from being fools, and already the word could be going through to Chungking that the foreign devils – that was how the 'dagoes' would be thinking of Captain Watkiss – were sending towards Shanghai what might be a relief force. If ever they got there ... Chungking lay 1,325 miles, no less, up river from the East China Sea, and although it was undoubtedly accessible by steamer, and the Yangtze had more than enough actual depth of water to take the shallow-draft gunboats built expressly for river service, no naval vessel had yet, to Halfhyde's knowledge, made the passage of the rapids in the Ichang gorges.

TWO

The Commodore commanding the China Squadron was lying with his heavy cruisers in the Pagoda anchorage twelve miles below Foochow on the Min Kiang; and as Captain Watkiss brought his flotilla within signal range of the flagship a little more than two days' steaming out of Hong Kong, a message came from the Commodore ordering him to report aboard whilst his gunboats took bunkers. The leader's signal to the flotilla, fluttering from Watkiss' halliards, bringing the gunboats to anchor, was accompanied by a semaphore message to Halfhyde, who, as second-in-command, was to join his Senior Officer aboard the first-class cruiser *Undaunted*. As soon as *Gadfly* had got her cable, Halfhyde was pulled across the blue water towards the flagship, passing the coal lighters on the way. The arrival of Captain Watkiss took place within two minutes of his own. Watkiss came importantly up the ladder with his telescope beneath his arm and Mr Beauchamp behind him. Salutes were exchanged as the shrill notes of the boatswain's calls died away; and then Commodore Marriot-Lee led the way below to his quarters. Gin was poured, and his servant was dismissed. Marriot-Lee got down to business immediately thereafter. Word, he said, had reached him from Chungking that all the foreign consulates except the British had been entered and sacked and that the British Consulate itself was under seige by the mob. The building was defended by the weapons of those who had taken refuge and of the staff, and, although so far no actual attack had come, such was to be expected at any moment.

'Your task will be a hard one, Watkiss.'

Watkiss screwed his monocle into his eye. 'No doubt. I am equal to it, however.'

'Of course. But you'll stand in need of every man you can muster to fight through to the Consulate, and you'll not be able to leave your ships untended. Therefore I propose to detach my marines to your assistance – fifty men, with a lieutenant and three NCOs, who shall be split up between the ships of your flotilla.'

Watkiss looked flattered; the presence of marines would add much to his importance, curious though they might be aboard river gunboats with their khaki-drill foreign service tunics and pipe-clayed belts. He said, 'I am most grateful, sir. Yes, Mr Beauchamp, what is it, pray?'

'Accommodation, sir,' Beauchamp said. 'We are pressed for space as it is, and—'

'Thank you, Mr Beauchamp, space will be found.'

'But—'

'I said space will be found and there is no more to be said.' Rudely, Watkiss turned his back upon his First Lieutenant and addressed Marriot-Lee. 'It is my understanding, sir, that I come under your orders rather than those of the Commodore-in-Charge at Hong Kong. Am I to have *carte blanche* whilst detached from your immediate vicinity?'

'Not exactly,' Marriot-Lee said, frowning. He prowled the day-cabin, large shoulders hunched and hands clasped behind his broad back. 'Whilst the overriding consideration is and must be the relief of the Consulate and the evacuation of Europeans—'

'Europeans, sir? Are they not all British subjects?'

'No, they're not. There are some French and Americans with them.'

'Americans?' Captain Watkiss seemed taken aback. 'What the devil are *Americans* doing there, sir, may I ask?'

'Advancing their country's interest, as we do ours. But to return to my point: there are diplomatic considerations also to be taken into account, and I must stress their importance. China is in a state of transition and there are many conflicting interests at work in Peking and throughout the land – it's a long and involved story and indeed few people in the West understand the Chinese and their aspirations, but for our present

14

purposes it's possible to summarize very briefly, Watkiss: cables from Whitehall, passed to me by despatch vessels out of Shanghai, indicate the concern of Her Majesty's government that friendly relations should be maintained with the Empress-Dowager and that a war should not be provoked by hasty action.'

'Hasty action, sir?'

Marriot-Lee spread his hands and sighed. 'Whitehall is Whitehall, Watkiss. Any action can be considered hasty in retrospect if matters go awry – I think you understand well enough. Care and circumspection will be needed, and a regard for "face" will be most important. Be assured you will have my full moral support so long as matters have been handled correctly.'

'And your physical support, sir?'

Marriot-Lee nodded. 'So far as that is possible. Obviously I can't take my squadron into the Yangtze, but upon your return to Shanghai you will find me lying off the river mouth to afford full protection – and if necessary I shall put landing-parties ashore for your support. You should be able to reach Chungking in eight days from the time you weigh from here, Captain, and upon the assumption that your negotiations for the relief of the Consulate take two or three days, I shall expect your return to Shanghai in, let us say, eighteen days from now.'

* * *

'I shall be obliged if you'll accompany me to *Cockroach*, Mr Halfhyde.'

'Aye, aye, sir.'

'I propose holding a conference of all commanding officers,' Watkiss went on as he stepped into his boat behind Halfhyde. The bowman and sternsheetsman bore off the *Undaunted*'s great steel side with boathooks and the boat was headed towards *Cockroach*, with Halfhyde's boat following astern. Watkiss was in a fractious mood, muttering about blasted Americans and why they couldn't take refuge in their own consulate or legation or whatever.

'According to the Commodore, it's been sacked,' Halfhyde pointed out.

'Oh, don't argue, Mr Halfhyde,' Watkiss said with forbearance. He added, 'I don't like Americans.'

'No, sir?'

'No,' Captain Watkiss stated flatly. 'Dreadful people, as bad as Australians. Same thing really – colonists. They write to one another as Mister, not Esquire, not that any of them are gentlemen I admit. That's just one thing.' He paused. 'Did you notice the Commodore's reference to negotiations, Mr Halfhyde?'

'I did, sir.'

'If I'm to negotiate, why send marines? I'm pleased enough to have them, of course, I don't deny it. But marines don't negotiate!'

'Negotiations are best conducted from a position of strength, sir.'

'Yes, yes, I take your point,' Watkiss said sagely. He lapsed into silence, and stared balefully back at the *Undaunted* and Marriot-Lee's broad pennant – broader, as a commodore, than his own thin one. Halfhyde, who knew Captain Watkiss like the back of his own hand, could follow his thoughts with ease: possibly this forthcoming task, if successfully carried out, would lead to promotion and honours. But as ever there were the snags, both obvious and hidden. The obvious ones – navigation, possible land fighting, and the physical evacuation of the besieged persons – were on the whole less lethal than the hidden ones. Post Captains of Her Majesty's Fleet bore immense responsibilities and because of this held their heads ever ready for the chopping block, scapegoats to a man, scapegoats for the wretched politicians who never had to make instant decisions for life or death like Post Captains. One mistake and the buggers had you by the short hairs, and this time the Americans, with their history of rebellion against the crown, were seemingly involved, which made it far worse ... and, as ever, the orders were vague enough to cover Whitehall whilst at the same time leaving the unfortunate sailorman as exposed as a whore's charms.

Captain Watkiss' boat came alongside *Cockroach* and to the wail of the piping party the Senior Officer stepped across to the quarterdeck of his low-freeboard command, wishing he had the dignity of a ladder to climb. Signals were sent to *Bee* and *Wasp*, and the commanding officers reported aboard the leader. The conference, which was really a monologue, was held in the small wardroom, and Captain Watkiss announced his detailed orders for the passage of the Yangtze. Charts and land maps were flourished, and the Admiralty Sailing Directions for the area were studied closely. The Yangtze was not a pleasant prospect and they would be much open to attack should the dagoes prove hostile. Mr Beauchamp at this point manifested a wish to make a point, and Watkiss sighed.

'Yes, what is it now, Mr Beauchamp?'

'If the – the Chinese prove hostile, sir, what about the Commodore's warning? Do we return fire with fire, sir?'

'I shall issue my orders on that point when it arises, Mr Beauchamp,' Watkiss said, letting his monocle drop to the end of its black silk toggle and ride his stomach. 'Now, the question of provisions. The Commodore is sending across fresh meat and vegetables with his marines, and woe betide you, Mr Beauchamp, if my ice-box is without ice again. I propose to delay off Shanghai only long enough to take a pilot, but there will be time for any deficiencies to be made good whilst we're hove to, so long as you smack it about, Mr Beauchamp, and don't dilly dally. As to the marines, who will be sent across at any time now, I wish them to remain out of sight whilst off Shanghai and all the way through the Yangtze. They must keep strictly to the alleyways – their effect will be the greater when they march through the mob in Chungking, if they are not seen before and reported ahead. Yes, Mr Halfhyde?'

'The alleyways will be close and uncomfortable, sir—'

'Oh, balls and bang me arse, Mr Halfhyde, I don't give a fish's tit for discomfort, they're men, are they not, not mice? They can put up with it, surely.' Captain Watkiss stood up and hitched at his over-long shorts. He looked like a tub in a table-cloth. The conference was over and the commanding officers returned aboard their vessels. As soon as the Royal Marine Light Infantry detachment with the meat and vegetables had arrived from the flagship and had been distributed throughout the flotilla, Captain Watkiss hoisted his sailing signal and they continued north for the Yangtze. Another two and a half days saw them off Woosung, where delay set in: Halfhyde, watching from his navigating bridge, saw an

17

exchange taking place between Captain Watkiss and some men in a sampan, with Captain Watkiss dancing up and down in apparent anger. Soon after this came the signal to anchor and the Senior Officer was seen proceeding inshore in his own boat. After two hours he returned and another signal went to each of the gunboats: YOU ARE TO REPAIR ABOARD IMMEDIATELY.

Captain Watkiss, as his commanding officers mustered, was almost incoherent. He brandished a fist towards the shore, and the tail of a tattooed serpent emerged in matt colours from his cuff.

'The buggers won't provide a pilot. I met with a flat refusal – damned impertinence! A lot of grinning dagoes . . . they seemed to be enjoying it. A mealy-mouthed lot, can't stand 'em. Well, they're not going to beat the British Empire, damned if they are.' Watkiss puffed his chest out. 'I shall pilot the flotilla through myself and balls to them.'

*　　*　　*

They proceeded in line ahead through the estuary of the Yangtze, moving slowly past Woosung. Since the altercation with the Chinese pilotage, certain changes had been made in the command structure of the flotilla; they had been made, in one respect, with reluctance and bad temper: Mr Beauchamp had been despatched, to his immense pleasure, and never mind his Captain's earlier expressed opinion as to his capabilities, to take command of *Gadfly*. The sole reason for this was that Halfhyde could be released to accompany Captain Watkiss upon the bridge of *Cockroach*. Captain Watkiss, aware of Halfhyde's previous service in the waters off China, had decided to make close and personal use of his expertise.

'My river expertise is non-existent, sir,' Halfhyde had stated.

'Never mind that.'

'But the open sea is a very different matter—'

'Yes, yes, yes, I'm not a fool, Mr Halfhyde, but you *know China* – that's important.'

'Not in river navigation, sir.'

Watkiss stamped his foot. 'Kindly don't damn well argue, Mr Halfhyde, but transfer your gear and your command at once.' Halfhyde had obeyed, able to read between the lines well enough. The transfer made, it turned out to be Halfhyde's task to take the flotilla through into the narrows of the Yangtze; Captain Watkiss, and never mind his indicated intention to act as pilot, uttered no word at all as the ships nosed in to head upstream for Nanking and beyond. At least, not until they had left the estuary, when a sampan was seen to be crossing their course from the direction of Tsingkiang.

'Take care not to run the damn thing down, Mr Halfhyde. It has the right of way.'

'Be assured I shall come round to starboard if I see fit, sir, but at present I do not.'

'On your head be it, then, Mr Halfhyde.' Watkiss paused, and brought up his telescope. 'They're trying to attract attention, I fancy. There is a passenger, and an arm is waving. Possibly it's a pilot after all – the buggers may have seen sense! Reduce speed, Mr Halfhyde, if you please, and we shall parley.'

Halfhyde passed the orders down and the way came off *Cockroach*. They drifted; the sampan came alongside and Watkiss called down: 'Are you a pilot? Oh, blast these people who can't speak English.' He lifted his voice and essayed pidgin: 'Makee go-go up river?' A deplorable coolie in the sampan nodded vigorously, and grinned. Watkiss mopped at his face with a large handkerchief. 'Good – thank God! Come aboard ... get him aboard, Mr Halfhyde, and turn the hoses on that blasted sampan if it doesn't stand away afterwards.'

The manoeuvre was duly completed. A portmanteau was hoisted aboard and the sampan passenger was brought to the Captain's presence. Watkiss waved ahead pompously. 'Makee go-go. Makee go-go plenty safe or I'll have your guts for garters, damned if I won't. And take that grin off your face.'

The grin stayed, even widened. The head-dress, a Chinese-style straw hat like a shallow tent, was removed and at once the face looked quite different. The man said, 'Sorry, Captain, but it's case of mistaken identity, I guess. I'm no pilot so I can't help, but I'd like passage up to Chungking—'

'Are you an American and not a Chinee, my dear sir?'

'Sure thing. From the—'

'Mr Halfhyde, have this person removed back to his sampan.' Captain Watkiss turned his back with dignity and moved to the opposite wing of his bridge, but the nasal voice followed to torment him.

'From the United States Legation in Peking, Captain, though not directly. I have full authority to board your craft in anticipation of a lift up river, and this authority I have in writing from the United States Legation, countersigned by Rear Admiral Hackenticker of the United States Navy—'

Captain Watkiss turned with a face like thunder. 'Whose edict does not run aboard Her Majesty's ships of war, Mr whoever you are—'

'Bloementhal, Captain. I'm a trade attaché at—'

'I'll not have grocers aboard my ship.'

'I'm no grocer any more'n I'm a pilot, I guess. And my authority's signed by one of your British diplomats as well. Take a look.' Mr Bloementhal reached beneath his Chinese coolie dress and delved around in a webbing belt attached to his stomach. He brought out a folded sheet of paper and handed it to Captain Watkiss. The document bore the embossed heading of the United States, an eagle with spread wings Watkiss fancied it to be, together with the official rubber stamps of both the American and the British Legations and various signatures, one of which was that of one Cecil de Champneys Harcourt-Fotheringay to which was added KCB. It appeared well authenticated, and its gist was that Mr Clay Bloementhal was required to make contact with one of the persons currently taking refuge in the British Consulate at Chungking, no reason for this being stated.

'I suppose,' Captain Watkiss said ungraciously, 'I have no option but to give you passage.'

'Thank you, Captain.'

'Where is Rear Admiral Hackenticker?'

'In Peking,' Bloementhal said.

'Thank God. Mr Halfhyde, watch your course, I have no wish to ground in the entrance to the Yangtze.' Captain Watkiss bounced up and down on the balls of his feet, bad temperedly. 'What a nuisance Americans always are,' he said, and turned away again. *Cockroach* moved on along the river, with the wider waters of the estuary dropping behind, taking the unfamiliar passage at slow speed. Behind came *Gadfly*, with Mr Beauchamp glorying in command, however temporary his unexpected elevation might prove. If he could handle it success-fully he might yet achieve a permanent ship of his own. And he wished Halfhyde all the luck in the world in his close proximity to Captain Watkiss, whom might the gods destroy.

*   *   *

Captain Watkiss had been down to his cabin and had returned looking portentous as the day began emerging into night. 'He's in *Burke's Landed Gentry*,' he announced to Halfhyde.

'Mr Bloementhal, sir?'

'Of course not!' Watkiss snapped. 'Sir Cecil Harcourt-Fotheringay.'

'Ah.'

'Whoever heard,' Watkiss muttered disparagingly, 'of an American in *Burke's*? The point is this, Mr Halfhyde: I don't trust Bloementhal, even though Sir Cecil appears genuine. I've never heard of Rear Admiral what's-his-name and Bloementhal doesn't look like a diplomat.'

'Not even a trade attaché, sir?'

Watkiss lifted his chin and scratched, in the fading light, beneath it. 'Well, of course, there's that, I agree. Trade's trade. No doubt the less well-connected men are seconded to deal with that sort of thing.'

Halfhyde bent to the binnacle and took a cross-bearing of looming leading marks. He straightened after passing a helm order to the quartermaster. 'May I ask why you don't trust him, sir?'

'Not American enough,' Watkiss answered promptly. 'Not particularly nasal for one thing. A little, but not enough.'

'They aren't all nasal.'

'Yes, they are.'

'I'm afraid I must disagree, sir.'

'Kindly don't be impertinent, Mr Halfhyde, I detest imper-tinence and argument, simply detest it. Americans are nasal. And twang, twang too, or an abominable drawl, depending upon which part of America they come from. Bloementhal's neither. Further, he drinks coffee not carffee, and I don't like it.'

'Yale or Harvard, sir, tend to reduce the extremes.'

Watkiss shifted irritably. 'Oh, balls, Mr Halfhyde, once a Yank always a Yank, and I should know, I served once upon the America and West Indies station and encountered a number of Americans. They were unmistakable.'

'Do you imagine he's a Chinese in disguise, sir?'

'No. I'd not go so far as that. But he's to be watched, Mr Halfhyde, watched like a hawk when we reach Chungking. He may be a renegade Englishman in the pay of the American Legation, do you not see – and may attempt to make capital out of the unfortunate British position in Chungking.'

Halfhyde raised his eyebrows. 'In what way, sir?'

'I have no idea, how could I have? Time will tell.'

'The Americans are perfectly friendly, sir, and well disposed towards us.'

'Oh, nonsense, Mr Halfhyde, you are not very well versed in the ways of diplomacy, I fear.' The Captain raised his nostrils and sniffed. 'What an appalling smell, quite poisonous. What is it?'

'Rotting vegetation and excreta, I imagine, sir. We're well within the confines of the biggest public convenience in China, otherwise known as the Yangtze Kiang, and the Chinese—'

'What filthy people. Thank God we're British, Mr Halfhyde, and that He saw fit to make us so. I—' Watkiss broke off sharply: all hell seemed to have erupted ahead of them as the river narrowed still further. From both banks came explosions, noisy and fiery in the darkness, and the acrid smell of gunpowder drifted down on the light wind from the west. 'Bandits, Mr Halfhyde, dago bandits firing upon us!'

'I think not—'

'Sound for action, Mr Halfhyde, at once.'

'Sir—'

'Kindly obey my order, blast you, or I shall place you in arrest.'

Halfhyde raised his voice and shouted back angrily, 'I shall not sound for action, sir, since it is not necessary. The Chinese are merely chasing away devils by the use of fire-crackers.'

'Oh. Why?'

'Possibly there's a religious festival in progress.'

'How damn silly,' Watkiss said. He thrust his stomach

22

against the forward guardrail of the bridge and glared out at the childish nonsense. Such primitive people. Immediately astern, the acting Captain of *Gadfly* was in a quandary: the sounds from the shore were clearly warlike, and the Senior Officer had expressly warned his commanding officers of bandit activity likely to manifest itself. Beauchamp fingered his chin uncertainly. Captain Watkiss did not appear to have gone to action stations, but he, Beauchamp, was in command of his own ship and was duty bound to take prudent action as seemed fitting; and he sought his First Lieutenant's advice.

'Firing, Lord Edward. I think we should be prepared.'

'Jolly good idea, sir.'

'You agree, then?'

'Yes, sir!'

'Pipe action stations, if you please, Lord Edward.'

'Aye, aye, sir.' Within seconds the boatswain's mates were shrilling throughout the gunboat and the men of the Royal Marine Light Infantry were trundling out from the close confines of the alleyways, glad enough of some fresh night air and never mind the stench. The three-pounder quick-firing guns were trained this way and that; and then *Cockroach*'s reaction was heard in a stentorian bellow from Captain Watkiss. A searchlight outlined the wilting figure of *Gadfly*'s captain on his bridge. Mr Beauchamp was a blasted idiot, any fool could tell that the Chinese were scaring devils and the moment the flotilla reached Chungking Mr Beauchamp would be placed in arrest for exposing his marines to the enemy.

THREE

Nanking – noisy and smelly, its waterway crammed with all manner of craft – was passed; not without difficulty as vessels bearing whole families complete with livestock barged across Captain Watkiss' course. Throughout the flotilla, on the Senior Officer's signalled order, the hoses were manned to keep dirt and disease away.

Days later, Hankow came up and was left astern to fester like Nanking. On into the Central China plain ... cottages were seen, thatched, filthy and semi-derelict yet sheltering inordinately large families. Grandfathers, sitting cross-legged and phlegmatic on the bare earth, surrounded by swarms of children, stared from wizened yellow faces as the strange vessels passed by.

'Nothing else to do, Mr Halfhyde, but fornicate.'

'Some people are born lucky, sir.'

Watkiss sniffed. He paced his small bridge, two bouncing steps one way, two the other. Time passed. One more day and there loomed ahead, past Ichang, the first of the three narrow gorges through which the flotilla must pass: the Hsiling Gorge, deep between gigantic bluffs with enormous mountains reaching to the skies. Along the terraced banks caves could be seen, inhabited according to Captain Watkiss by God knew what desperate bandits.

'Have a care now, Mr Halfhyde, the waters are narrow and the river fast. As the level of the bed alters and we take the rapids, you will find a need for more speed from the engine if we are not to make sternway. There is a man relieving himself at the water's edge. How filthy.' Captain Watkiss turned, hearing a step on the ladder: Mr Clay Bloementhal, in a sharkskin suit of gleaming white. For the last day or so the American diplomat had been busy with bottles of whisky, but he now appeared recovered. He rubbed his hands briskly and gave a wide and friendly smile as the *Cockroach* came below the high sides to enter a world of gloom and rushing water, a world enclosed by rock tinged with blue and purple and green as though rising above a loch in distant Scotland.

'Good morning, Captain.'

'Good morning, Mr Bloementhal, you have not been invited to step upon my bridge—'

'My apologies, Captain.'

'Go away, if you please.'

'Captain, I have to say—'

'No, you have not, Mr Bloementhal, and I repeat my request which will become an order if you do not obey it immediately, d'you hear? My ship is entering a gorge and will remain in it for how far, Mr Halfhyde?'

'Eighteen miles, sir.'

'For eighteen miles, Mr Bloementhal, eighteen miles of immense danger, and after that there will be more gorges. When my flotilla is safe, and not before, I shall send for you.' Captain Watkiss turned his back and placed his monocle in his eye. Behind him the American blew out his cheeks and lifted two fingers in an insulting gesture before descending the ladder to the upper deck. The British were painful, their navy officers especially, they had a fixed idea they were God. Worse, really, than British diplomats who were smoothly polite even though they had perpetually lifted noses and disdainful airs. This Watkiss, he was in for one hell of a shock when he reached Chungking, if ever he did ... Mr Bloementhal lurched and struck his backside heavily against a guardrail as something odd happened to the *Cockroach*, which had somehow come broadside on to the rushing Yangtze waters and appeared to be moving back sideways towards the East China Sea beyond Woosung with her bows pointed at a family group outside a cave. On the bridge Captain Watkiss was frantically gesticulating with his telescope, and Mr Bloementhal heard his shouts.

'Mr Halfhyde, you are in dereliction of your duty, how dare you! Bring her back on course, man!' There was a brief pause.

25

'Jesus Christ, Mr Halfhyde, I am about to be struck amidships by that fool Beauchamp!'

* * *

Aboard *Gadfly* Lord Edward Cole, not waiting for his captain, had acted with commendable swiftness. He had put his engine astern and his helm to starboard; with the engine gathering sternway, the ship's head came round to starboard with the helm and *Gadfly* scraped past Captain Watkiss' stern, removing a coat of paint but little else. When *Gadfly* had passed in safety, Halfhyde brought *Cockroach* round against the stream and once again headed westerly, bows first, for Chungking.

Watkiss mopped at his face. 'Thank God for our deliverence, Mr Halfhyde. You must use more care in future.'

'I was avoiding shoaling water, sir, and boulders.'

'I dislike excuses, dislike them intensely, Mr Halfhyde, as you should know by now.' Watkiss prodded his telescope into Halfhyde's stomach. 'I suppose you realize what's happened, don't you?'

'All's well that ends well, sir.'

'Oh, balls and bang me arse, Mr Halfhyde, have you no eyes in your head? Look!' Captain Watkiss pointed ahead with his telescope, which shook with his anger. '*Gadfly*'s ahead of me, and there's no sea room to overtake, what with your blasted shoals! That fool Beauchamp's in the position of leader!'

The moment it was safe to do so, Captain Watkiss ordered *Cockroach* back into her rightful position at the head of the line, sweeping past *Gadfly* without so much as a glance in her direction. Leaving the Hsiling Gorge, the flotilla entered the Wu Gorge. The water was deep and clear but the great rock sides shut out the sunlight. Far above the little gunboats fishermen's huts were perched precariously on the precipices, and hawks flew overhead. Emerging from the Wu Gorge, the vessels, as another night's darkness came down, moved into the last of the gorges, the Chutang, where pagodas and temples on the crags stood out sharp against the night sky; and it was here that the long anticipated attack came when ripples of rifle fire were seen along the cliff tops and bullets smacked into woodwork and ricochetted off metal bulkheads and stanchions. Prudently,

Watkiss refrained from manning his guns, which in any case could not possibly have elevated enough to be of any use; and throughout the ships the sailors were piped to remain in cover and to return the rifle fire only when a target could be identified. Some of the Chinese bullets found their marks: aboard *Cockroach* two of the ship's company were wounded, luckily in their fleshy parts; and from *Wasp* a petty officer, hit fatally in the head, went overboard, his body drifting away downstream. Aboard *Bee* the quartermaster had suffered a wound in his hand, and the ship's head had paid off to starboard. Like the leader earlier, the gunboat had been taken by the fast flow of the river and swung broadside on to be laid against the rock wall of the gorge. *Wasp* had been ordered to send a line across and pull her clear, and the armed Chinese above had taken full advantage of the resulting situation. Before the two vessels were safely under way again, their upperworks had been peppered and the woodwork and canvas dodgers looked like colanders; and six more of their companies had been taken below wounded to be tended as best possible by unskilled men. After the passage of the Chutang more attacks came, and the gunboats' searchlights picked out the uniforms of the Empress-Dowager's army. Watkiss passed the signal for maximum speed, and the flotilla began to draw away, but not before a Chinese had thrown himself into the water ahead, and then, with a curved knife clenched between his teeth, had used sinewy arms' to haul himself aboard amidships whence he had made a dash for the ladder to the navigating bridge. Behind him came a petty officer armed with a cutlass, which he swung as the Chinese got a foot upon the rungs. The blade, wielded forcefully, sliced straight through the neck and lifted the severed head upwards to roll bloodily across the bridge planking and stop at Watkiss' feet, where it glared up at the foreign devil as though still possessed of life. Watkiss stared at it, for once speechless. Halfhyde bent, picked the thing up by the hair, and dropped it overboard. He called down to the cutlass bearer.

'Hoses, Petty Officer Boyne. At once. Chinese blood can carry Chinese disease for all I know.'

The ships steamed on, clear now of attack, at any rate for the time being. With the gorges behind them, Captain Watkiss prepared to leave the bridge. 'You also, Mr Halfhyde. Sleep is important, and the sub-lieutenant can take over, but I am to be called at once should anything untoward seem likely to occur.'

'Mr Bloementhal, sir—'

'Where?' Watkiss swung this way and that, as though unwelcome Americans might manifest like wraiths from any point of the compass.

'Not present in fact, sir, but if you remember, he wished words with you.'

'I shall send for him when I want him, thank you, Mr Halfhyde.' Watkiss turned his back and descended the ladder, making for his cabin. Reaching it he found that Bloementhal, as though by some alchemy summoned as a result of Halfhyde's reference to him, was using the bulkhead outside as a resting post: Americans had no backbone.

Bloementhal smiled. 'Busy now, Captain?'

'Not busy, but tired. I intend to turn in for a spell.'

'I thought ship captains were always on duty.'

Watkiss glared. 'You thought right, Mr Bloementhal. They are. Nevertheless, they are also human, and need sleep.'

'Duty first, Captain. I won't keep you long.'

Watkiss fumed, giving a low hiss from between his teeth; Americans were such pushful people and if he didn't give the fellow audience now, he would most probably be waiting when he woke up, and the knowledge of his presence outside his cabin would prevent sleep. Besides, Captain Watkiss still had his suspicions: the fellow had said duty, not dooty. Let him talk and he might give something away.

'Oh, very well then,' Watkiss said irritably. 'Come into my cabin.' He stepped through, followed by the American. Below decks the heat was stifling, and the electric fan switched on by Watkiss' servant made little difference. Watkiss lowered himself into his wickerwork chair and motioned his unwelcome visitor to be seated also. Bloementhal hitched at his trousers and sat. Like Halfhyde he was tall, and took up a good deal of room. Watkiss placed his monocle in his eye and said, 'Well, what is it?'

'It would save time, Captain, if you would tell me what you already know.'

'About Chungking?'

'The situation there, yes.'

28

'Nothing.'

'Nothing at all?'

'That is what I said, Mr Bloementhal. I know my orders and nothing more.'

'Your orders being to bring out all Europeans – this much I also know, Captain. It's not going to be easy.'

'The officers and men of Her Majesty's Fleet are not deterred by difficulties, Mr Bloementhal.'

'Indeed not,' Bloementhal said earnestly, and at, once became more American in Watkiss' eyes. All Americans were earnest. 'No offence intended, Captain.'

'I trust not. What do you wish to tell me? I repeat, I have been many hours upon my bridge, and I wish to sleep while I can. It's not much to ask,' Captain Watkiss added on a note of angry pettishness.

'I'm sorry, Captain. What I wish to do is just simply to inform you of the diplomatic background so that when you meet with the Chinese authorities, as you will, you won't put your foot in it.'

Americans were also rude. And perhaps after all he *was* a genuine American: he had said meet with – Americans always used unnecessary words. He went on at some length and most of it, in Captain Watkiss' opinion, was rubbish. When at last the American had gone and left him in peace, Watkiss undressed and turned into his bunk. The night passed peacefully: no alarums or excursions. After breakfast next morning, Watkiss sent for Halfhyde to come to his cabin.

'Bloementhal, Mr Halfhyde,' he said. 'Blasted fellow kept me awake half the night. Kindly deflect my fan away from me. Air blowing upon one spot leads to neuralgia. He said nothing of much importance, the gist being what I already knew – that war must not be provoked.'

'Nothing more pointed than that, sir?'

'Well. Yes, there was something. There's a squarehead there, a Hun. I dislike Huns ... this is an important one, I gather. Count Hermann von something, Furstenberg, that was it. He sounds well-connected, but apparently he's not to be trusted.'

'Is he one of the people in the Consulate?'

Watkiss shook his head. 'No. He's friendly with the Chinese

29

authorities ... there's a lot of jiggery-pokery going on between him and the local mandarins, and apparently the Empress-Dowager's involved – not directly, but through intermediaries. According to Bloementhal, there's a treaty in the air. The Huns want to get a footing ahead of the blasted Russians, and it's not going to suit the United States whichever of those two concludes an agreement with the Empress.'

'And us, sir?'

'D'you mean Whitehall?'

'Yes. Will a treaty with the Germans or Russians be unwelcome to Whitehall as well?'

'That's scarcely Bloementhal's business, Mr Halfhyde, is it? Frankly, I don't know, but I would assume any such agreement to be possibly against our British interest, and I have no doubt that is why I was selected to lead our mission.'

Halfhyde stared. 'Our mission, sir, is surely to cut out the Europeans and sail with them to Shanghai – that alone, with no outright involvement in diplomacy suggested or desired?'

'Circumstances alter cases, my dear Halfhyde, do they not?' Watkiss said with dignity. 'I am resilient and shall not be found wanting if my services should be required beyond the expressed orders.'

Halfhyde offered no comment, but reflected that his Captain's total dislike of foreigners was likely enough to cause any diplomatic situation to deteriorate sharply. Watkiss' effect would be like that of a bull in a china shop, and he would best be confined to the straightforward duty of rescue and removal. Watkiss, however, having had time to ponder, and as a result having thought himself into expansion of his duty, was starting to preen; and in that lay much danger.

*　　*　　*

'Captain, sir.'

Lord Edward Cole's tones, coming down the voice-pipe from the navigating bridge, woke Mr Beauchamp from pleasant dreams of confirmed command. He seized the voice-pipe and applied the flexible tube to his ear. 'The Captain speaking,' he said.

'A signal from the Senior Officer, sir.'

Respectfully, Beauchamp sat up in his bunk. 'Yes, Lord Edward?'

'*Cockroach* has Chungking in sight, sir, and reports sounds of gunfire. As a matter of fact, sir, I can hear them myself.'

'Yes. You should really have informed me earlier, Lord Edward, but never mind. I shall come to the bridge at once.' About to replace the voice-pipe, Beauchamp heard further sounds and put the thing back against his ear. 'What was that?'

'I said it's awfully exciting, sir.'

'Yes, indeed, very.' Beauchamp clambered out of his bunk and dressed quickly, sweating into his white uniform the moment it met his body: the nearer they came to Chungking, the hotter grew the temperature. Chungking was a nasty place, Mr Beauchamp had always heard, desperately hot and very, very rainy. As yet unshaven, he proceeded to his bridge and returned the salute of his First Lieutenant. He heard the gunfire, something rather heavy interspersed with the sharper crack of rifles. He fancied he heard yells, and undoubtedly he saw the smoke of fires as though the whole city was being sacked. A wateriness came to his stomach; as Lord Edward had said, it was exciting, but within the next fifteen minutes or so he, Beauchamp, was going to be put to the test; the test not of battle but of possibly being ordered by Captain Watkiss to take his ship alongside the wharf, a manoeuvre for which he had never yet, as a commanding officer of very recent appointment, been wholly and personally responsible. To make a shambles of it would be disastrous and Captain Watkiss would not mince matters afterwards. However, his anxieties were to be relieved: in due course another signal came from the leader, general to all ships, indicating that they were to anchor in the stream upon the executive signal from *Cockroach*. To bring a ship to an anchor was easy.

Mr Beauchamp pulled at his jaw. 'Watch for the executive, Yeoman. Lord Edward, pipe the cable party, if you please, and then stand by on the fo'c'sle.'

'Aye, aye, sir.'

*   *   *

31

'I don't like the look of it, Mr Halfhyde.' Watkiss lowered his telescope and steadied his white-clad stomach against the forward guardrail. 'I've half a mind to beat to quarters,' he went on, as though commanding a sailing line-of-battle ship. 'But I shall not. We must not exacerbate the dagoes.'

'Suppose they attack, sir?'

'Oh, they'll not do that! They'll not take the risk of firing upon the White Ensign, Mr Halfhyde, that's fact, I said it. Of course, once we go ashore, it's a different matter and we'll have to be ready for 'em – but the buggers won't try anything against the British flag.'

'I don't see the difference between attacking British uniforms and attacking the British flag, sir.'

Watkiss clicked his tongue. 'Oh, balls and bang me arse, Mr Halfhyde, if you can't see the difference that's your misfortune, not mine. I'm lying off in the stream precisely because they won't dare attack and I intend to handle all this with tact and diplomacy. Where's that man Bloementhal?'

'Below, sir.'

'Good. Probably can't tear his bottom away from the heads I shouldn't wonder. Listen to that din.'

Halfhyde listened: somewhere, and it was probably the British Consulate, was under heavy attack. He remarked as much to the Captain, who gave a sage nod. 'Yes, you may well be quite right, Mr Halfhyde. I had formed the same conclusion. I think I'll make a signal.'

'To whom, sir?'

'I wish you wouldn't always think of the difficulties,' Watkiss said irritably. 'I suppose they have a mayor or something, a headman, or possibly there'll be a Chinese general, I really can't be expected to know. Yeoman!'

'Yessir?'

'Make a signal by lamp: "General from Senior Officer of gunboat flotilla. The fighting is to stop instantly or I shall bombard the town."' Watkiss turned impatiently upon his First Lieutenant. 'Yes, what is it, Mr Halfhyde, and if you're going to say the dagoes won't understand English I shall reply that *I* certainly can't speak Chinese. Someone will pick up my signal and someone will translate it.'

'Sir, I—'

'Kindly don't argue with me, Mr Halfhyde, I detest argument and consider it insubordinate.'

Halfhyde shrugged; he had been about to draw the Captain's attention to an inconsistency between the wording of the signal and his expressed intention of using tact, but really it was not worth the waste of breath. The yeoman of signals began clacking out the message on his Aldis lamp and peering vainly through the smoke for an acknowledgement, and Halfhyde, alternately watching his chart and the leading marks upon the shore, announced that *Cockroach* was now coming up to her anchorage.

'Executive, Mr Halfhyde.'

'Aye, aye, sir.' The flag hoist was brought down on the halliards, giving the executive signal to the ships astern, and simultaneously the slips were knocked away upon all the fo'c'sles and the anchors went down with a rush and a splash into the murky waters of the Yangtze. As they did so a tremendous explosion came from beneath the *Gadfly*, a vast spout of water shot skywards and dropped back in drenching spray, and the gunboat began to settle gently in the water. Captain Watkiss, blown flat and dripping with filthy water, scrambled to his feet, his face redly furious. He shook both fists in the air, one towards the shore, the other towards the sinking *Gadfly*. No heavy gunfire, so much he knew, had been directed at the ships by the Chinese.

'That fool Beauchamp – he must have dropped his blasted anchor smack on a blasted bomb or mine!'

FOUR

'You are a damn disgrace, Mr Beauchamp, a *damn disgrace!*'

Beauchamp was like a jelly, a jelly that wrung its hands. 'There were no casualties, sir. All hands have been brought off—'

'But not by you, Mr Beauchamp – by the rest of my ships' companies!' Captain Watkiss shook a fist in Beauchamp's forlorn face. 'I repeat, you're a damn disgrace to the service and the Queen and you've lost me a valuable ship—'

'But I wasn't to know, sir! It was – it was wholly fortuitous. You could have done the same thing yourself, sir.'

Watkiss opened his mouth and closed it again. Then he said, 'That's impertinent, Mr Beauchamp, the facts are that when there is a mine or bomb on the river bed, *you*, not I, have to go and drop your blasted anchor on it and detonate it. Nevertheless, you have raised a valid point: there may be others in the vicinity. We must all walk warily. How loathsome dagoes are. We might all blow to kingdom come at any blasted moment. Mr Halfhyde?'

'Sir?'

'Warn all hands throughout the flotilla: nothing is to be cast overboard and when boats are lowered, they are to be lowered gently. If there should be wind enough to cause us to drag our anchors, God help us all. Mr Beauchamp?'

'Yes, sir?'

'You may consider yourself in open arrest for hazarding and losing your ship. I shall ask for court martial proceedings on our return to Hong Kong.' Captain Watkiss called to the yeoman of

34

signals. 'Has there been any acknowledgement of my signal, Yeoman?'

'No, sir.'

'What a useless lot foreigners are.'

* * *

All the COs came aboard for a council of war called by Captain Watkiss. Together with Halfhyde and Lieutenant Sankey commanding the marine detachment, they assembled in *Cockroach*'s wardroom, cramming it to capacity. From the head of the table Captain Watkiss surveyed his subordinate commanders with the aid of his monocle, and began a dissertation, which was interrupted by the arrival of Mr Bloementhal.

Watkiss stared rudely and said, 'I am in conference with my officers, Mr Bloementhal, and shall be most obliged if you'd make yourself scarce.'

'I must remind you, Captain, that I'm concerned in—'

'Diplomatically. Not militarily.'

'The two go hand in hand. I must insist on a seat at your conference, Captain.'

'You will insist on nothing, my dear sir, when aboard my ship. Kindly leave.'

Bloementhal shrugged and lifted his palms. 'If that's your order, naturally I have no alternative. But it'll be my duty to report to Rear Admiral Hackenticker, and,' he went on in a voice loud enough to drown some derogatory remarks about Rear Admiral Hackenticker, 'to my legation and yours as well, and if subsequently matters do not go as hoped, then the absence of my counsel will be noted in the highest quarters. However, you do not wish me to remain, so I'll go.'

'You will not leave without my permission,' Watkiss snapped, 'and it so happens I have changed my mind and require your presence. Kindly sit down.'

'No chair,' Bloementhal said sourly.

'Stand then. Now, gentlemen.' Watkiss cleared his throat, making an important sound of it. 'We all know what we have to do, and that is, to relieve the unfortunate people in the British Consulate, bring them back here and hold them safe.'

'Easier said than done, Captain.'

'Thank you, Mr Bloementhal, I am well aware of the difficul-ties of my task. If you'll allow me to proceed, I shall make known my plan of campaign. It is simple.' Lifting his telescope, Captain Watkiss pointed it through the scuttle on the ship's port side. 'Over there, so my chart tells me, is a wharf, currently obscured by the blasted drifting smoke. I propose to use that wharf as my assembly point. The entire ship's company of *Gadfly*, thanks to Mr Beauchamp, will be available for the landing-parties, and fifteen men from each of the remaining ships of my flotilla, together with your marines, Mr Sankey, will join me ashore to make up the complement. Rifles and bayonets, one hundred rounds of ammunition per man in car-tridge belts, gaiters of course for the seamen and stokers, petty officers to be armed with revolvers and cutlasses, officers with revolvers alone. Drums to be provided by the marines. Also fifes. You have fifes, Mr Sankey?'

'I have, sir. Four fifes, two drums.'

'They shall give heart to my men.' Captain Watkiss drew out a turnip-shaped silver timepiece and gazed at it for a few moments. 'It is now a little past five bells. At eight bells all hands are to be ready to land and the boats in the water. When all my commanding officers have reported their state of readi-ness, I shall make the signal to proceed inshore. This signal will be four long blasts from my steam siren. All boats will then head inshore, independently, for the wharf. One man will remain to tend each boat, the remainder will fall in immediately upon disembarkation ... yes, what is it now, for God's sake, Mr Halfhyde?'

'Two points, sir. One, the boats. *Gadfly*'s boats have been lost, and since we also have to land the marines—'

'Yes, yes, yes, what a fuss you always make, Mr Halfhyde, to be sure. I was about to add, had I been given time, that the boats will return for more men when they have shed their first loads. Your other point, Mr Halfhyde?'

'With great respect, sir, I've not yet finished with my first one. There will be a period of danger when an inadequate force is left to kick its heels on the wharf while they wait for the others to be put ashore.'

'Yes indeed, but *I* shall be there with them, and the dagoes will think twice before offering violence to a Post Captain of Her

36

Majesty's Fleet, Mr Halfhyde, so fiddlesticks. Your second point?'

'It can be left, sir.'

'Oh no, it can't, you've raised it, so kindly make it.'

'Very well, sir. The question of what happens if – when – we are able to bring the besieged persons off to the flotilla.'

'I'm glad you changed if to when, Mr Halfhyde, very glad. Well?'

Halfhyde said, 'I noted your earlier remark, sir, that they would be held safe.

'Certainly.'

Halfhyde coughed into his hand. 'There seemed to be an indication that you didn't intend weighing and proceeding at once to Shanghai, sir.'

'Precisely. Do you object, Mr Halfhyde, do you perhaps fear the animosity of the blasted dagoes?'

'No, sir. I am merely bearing in mind the orders from the Commodore.'

'Which are not your concern, *I* am the officer in command here. In any case, there's no need for decision at this moment and I think you are being premature in raising a stupid point just now, Mr Halfhyde. I may sail for Shanghai, I may not. Time will tell. The Commodore spoke, did he not, of a need for tactful handling? If I feel that my presence may be of help in a situation which is not yet clear, then I shall remain in Chung-king. What a damn nuisance you sometimes are, Mr Halfhyde, as bad as Beauchamp.' Captain Watkiss hoisted his long shorts and looked disdainfully towards the American. 'Have you lost your tongue, Mr Bloementhal? Scarcely a word has emerged from you after all the fuss you made about joining my conference!'

Bloementhal smiled; an oily smile, thought Watkiss, and somehow untrustworthy. 'My tongue's safe and sound, Captain. I wished only to be an observer at this stage.'

'Just to make sure,' Captain Watkiss asked tartly, 'that I didn't do anything wrong?'

Another smile. 'Your words, Captain.'

'I think you sound impertinent.'

'Sorry.'

The conference broke up, the officers going out on deck to

37

return to their commands and prepare the landing-parties. The sound of fighting was heard still, but more distantly; there was sporadic rifle fire and many yells and cries, and the smoke hung over all, filled with menace and with the red glow of the burning buildings. It was an angry and tricky situation but Watkiss had seemed confident; he always did. Halfhyde was not so sanguine. The might of Britain, of the British Navy, was respected throughout the world, it was true, and bombast could go a long way, but to place total reliance upon it could be unwise. The full strength of the landing-parties would amount to no more than a hundred and twenty officers, petty officers and men, the marines included. Such a force could and would give a good account of itself, but it would be opposed by a number of Chinese as yet unknown but which would all too likely amount to many thousands: Chungking contained a population of more than a hundred thousand souls and the rabble-rousers would presumably have been at work for some while. As Halfhyde looked out towards the teeming city he was assailed by raindrops. He shrugged; some heavy rain might well dampen both fires and hotheads, and if so would be welcome. He had turned away to have words with the gunner's mate in regard to the equipping of *Cockroach*'s contribution to the landing-parties when Lord Edward Cole ex *Gadfly* laid a hand on his arm.

'A boat coming off, sir. A sampan, actually.'

Halfhyde followed Cole's outstretched arm: there was indeed a sampan emerging from the rolling clouds of smoke, and it appeared to contain two passengers, both of them uniformed. As the sampan was propelled closer by a large Chinese wielding an oar, the passengers became identifiable; one was wearing the British naval foreign service uniform of a warrant officer, the other, despite the intense heat of Chungking, wore a blue uniform tunic, braided and buttoned to the neck, the sleeves bearing a thick gold stripe surmounted by a thinner one with a gold star above.

'Something tells me,' Halfhyde said with a grin, 'that Rear Admiral Hackenticker is approaching. I suggest you go and tell the Captain, Mr Cole.'

*   *   *

Captain Watkiss was bouncing up and down with anger: Rear Admiral Hackenticker, USN, who was virtually hidden by a heavy grey beard and was drenched in sweat, was bad enough. He appeared to think he was entitled to take command since he was the senior officer present and there were American citizens involved – but Watkiss felt well able to take care of that. Currently the chief trouble was the elderly warrant officer, ex-warrant officer strictly speaking since he was on the retired list and had no right to wear his uniform unless called out for service. Mr Bodmin, Boatswain, was not far off his eightieth birthday and was unquenchably garrulous. Moreover, he remembered Captain Watkiss as a midshipman some thirty years earlier.

'I knew ee, zur. That's that there Mr Watkiss I says to meself, I did, zur, on'y 'e's that there *Cap'n* Watkiss now, I says. I—'

'Yes, yes, Mr Bodmin—'

''Twas in the old *Princess Royal*—'

'Yes—'

'No, 'twasn't come to think of it, zur, 'twere the old *Racoon*, ship-rigged corvette she be, or were it the old—'

'Oh, really, Mr Bodmin, I can't blasted well remember, and I doubt if—'

'Mind, I'd not have known ee like if I hadn't been told you were aboard the *Cockroach*, zur. You be fatter if I may make so bold as to say so, zur.' Mr Bodmin gave a deep chuckle. 'A right young rascal you was in them days, zur, a right young scallywag, up to all manner o' mischief ... like puttin' purgatives—'

'Thank you, Mr Bodmin, that'll be all.'

'Like puttin' Gregory Powder in the Chief Boatswain's tea—'

'*Mr Bodmin!*' Captain Watkiss flourished his telescope. 'I have much respect for great age and much service, but you have gone on for long enough. What are you doing aboard my ship? What are you doing in Chungking – in China, come to that? Why are you wearing uniform?'

Mr Bodmin cupped a hand around an ear. 'Beg pardon, zur?'

'Oh, never mind, never mind!' Watkiss swung his stomach towards Rear Admiral Hackenticker. 'Possibly you can explain, sir?'

'I doubt if I can explain the old gentleman,' Hackenticker said briskly; he was a brisk man, sparrow-like in build but given added stature by the beard's full-hearted sprout. 'He kind of turned up at the wharf . . . said something about Chinese Customs—'

'Ar,' Mr Bodmin said, nodding his head vigorously. ''Er Marjesty's Chinese Customs, zur, after I left the sea. There be a Customs station in Chungking, zur, see?'

'You're the Customs man, then?'

'Ar, that I be, zur, and bein' as I were comin' out to one of 'er Marjesty's ships, zur, I come in my old naval uniform, zur—'

'Yes, yes, quite – misguided and illegal, but understandable. Why are you still at large?' When Mr Bodmin seemed uncertain as to his meaning, Watkiss elaborated: 'Why have the dagoes not impounded you along with the rest? I refer to the Chinese, Mr Bodmin,' he added.

'Ar, zur. Yes, zur. I be well known to the Chinks, zur, see. I married one o' 'em like. And besides, zur, them Chinks, they do respect the Queen's uniform.'

'Yes, indeed, you're quite right, Mr Bodmin, quite right, and it's the very point I've been making to my own officers.' Watkiss turned again to Rear Admiral Hackenticker. 'I understood you to say you'd arrived from Peking, Admiral. May I ask how and why?'

'Surely. How? Horse transport. Why? Diplomatic considerations, Captain.' Hackenticker twinkled through his beard. 'We don't have a Queen, but we do have a President, and the Chinks respect his naval and military uniforms like they do the Queen's, and—'

'You mean your government believes such affairs are better handled by the armed forces than by civilians?'

'Correct, Captain.'

Watkiss smiled, and clapped the Rear Admiral on a shoulder. 'We see alike, Admiral. I wish you'd make that plain to your Mr Bloementhal, who seems to believe he has a right to vet my military decisions.'

Hackenticker nodded. 'I've boarded you largely to talk to Bloementhal. I have certain information, and this information may affect your own movement decisions, Captain. May we go below?'

'By all means, but I must ask you to be brief, Admiral. I am proceeding to war stations within the next hour.'

*　　*　　*

Mr Bodmin, it seemed, had boarded purely upon Customs duty and was not connected with the war situation; he was fortuitous in that respect. Whilst Captain Watkiss closeted himself with Rear Admiral Hackenticker plus Lieutenant Halfhyde and Mr Bloementhal, Boatswain Bodmin tottered below decks, delighted to be once again aboard a British man-o'-war wearing the White Ensign. His duties as far as they concerned shipping took him mainly aboard sampans and junks and sleazy river steamboats officered by largely drunken persons rejected by the deep-sea trade. Not very pleasant people; Mr Bodmin was a lifelong, or almost lifelong, teetotaller, nonswearer, and largely non-womanizer although there had been sad lapses in the latter virtue. These facts he now retailed to Mr Beauchamp, who had come face to face with him on emerging from his cabin to visit the heads. Mr Beauchamp had enquired in some astonishment who he was; and Mr Bodmin launched again into his spiel.

'I knew that there Cap'n Watkiss when 'e were a snotty-nosed young shaver, zur.'

'Really?'

'Ar. I first went to sea, zur, when I were ...' Bodmin scratched his head. 'I dunno what I were. I were a foundling like, see, found in the town o' Bodmin in Cornwall ... that's why they called me Bodmin, zur. Outside they barricks in Bodmin, zur, in a shawl. They might 'ave christened me Cornish Light Infantry, zur, but they didn't ... it were their barricks, see, the Duke of Cornwall's Light Infantry they do be now, zur—'

'Ah, yes—'

'Anyway, zur, when I went to sea, it were back in '24 or '25 or thereabouts, when King William were on the throne, zur. I'd be about ten, I reckon. Them were the days, zur. Shellbacks we was, shellbacks, an' 'ard livers. 'Ard drinkers, many o' us, zur. But not me, oh no, zur.' Mr Bodmin sucked in his cheeks.

'No?'

41

'No, zur, not since I were four-and-twenty, zur, nor loose women neither, leastways ...' Mr Bodmin gave a cough and refrained from elaboration. He paused, brought out a highly-coloured handkerchief and blew his nose like a bugle. 'You looks like a gentleman, zur, like all naval officers o' course. I dare say you don't take alcohol, nor go with women, zur, nor curse, nor take the Lord's name in vain, zur, nor suchlike.' The old man looked somewhat startled as a frantic shout came from the upper deck, a shout directed at Mr Beauchamp requesting him to cease chatting like a blasted whore off duty and attend when his Captain called. 'What were that, zur?'

'Captain Watkiss,' Beauchamp explained, and then moved at the double towards the shout and the upper deck. 'You want me, sir?'

'Yes! Prepare to land! The situation is more serious than I thought. I shall need even you.'

'But I'm in arrest, sir!'

'No, you aren't, don't argue, Mr Beauchamp, I've changed my mind, but you'll be back in arrest in double quick time if you don't smarten up your ideas, Mr Beauchamp, and move. Tell Bodmin I want him. He may be Customs, but he's being commandeered.' Captain Watkiss turned away and bounced along his decks in his long shorts, his telescope held out like a lance. Action was imminent; his blood pumped strongly. He would show the dagoes who was master in their blasted country, and at the same time he would show the Americans what the British Navy was made of. It was a pity about that fool Beauchamp, who would be sure to let him down sooner or later, and Bodmin had one and a half feet in the grave and was no advertisement for smartness, but at least he would know the short cuts to the British Consulate.

*   *   *

'All ready, Mr Halfhyde?' Watkiss asked.

Halfhyde saluted. 'All ready, sir. Landing-party standing by under the gunner's mate, and all reports in from the flotilla.'

'Good. Four short blasts, if you please.'

Halfhyde reached up and jerked on the lanyard. A lot of hot water shot out but the siren gave only a tiny bleat. Watkiss

42

brandished his telescope. 'The damn engineer's in arrest! Try again.'

Halfhyde did so; the result was a little better, and four watery snorts emerged. Watkiss was furious; what would the wretched Americans think, but it would have to do for time was short. Rear Admiral Hackenticker had passed unbelievable news: the Russian Empire had now become actively involved and shallow-draught ships of the Russian Imperial Navy were understood to have left Port Arthur some days previously, bound south. It was not unlikely they might attempt to force a passage past Woosung and enter the Yangtze: it was imperative that the Europeans in the British Consulate should be extracted without delay and that they be sailed out of the Yangtze before the Russians entered. It was believed, Hackenticker had said, that the Russians meant to get their hands on the German, Count Hermann von Furstenberg, who was also to be brought out whether he wanted to be or not. Watkiss was damned if he could see why he should bother about Huns, but there it was: Hackenticker had been firm that the British authorities were in accord with the American and that what he brought were, in fact, orders.

Halfhyde followed his Captain towards the cutter, which was already in the water. The landing-party was embarked with Beauchamp, Cole, Bodmin and the gunner's mate. On deck waited Rear Admiral Hackenticker, plus Bloementhal, and Halfhyde foresaw a situation developing vis-à-vis Hackenticker: in the British Navy, junior officers entered a boat first, and disembarked last, the idea being that on neither occasion should juniors keep their seniors waiting. Captain Watkiss looked murderous as he took in the fact that Hackenticker was waiting for him to embark first. He clenched his sword scabbard like a vice and motioned Hackenticker to get aboard.

'After you, Captain.'

'You first, my dear sir.'

'You have the privilege, Captain.'

Watkiss' mouth opened, then closed again without utterance. Time could be short; Watkiss decided upon magnanimity and with a face like thunder embarked in the cutter, followed by Hackenticker. With no time lost the order was passed to bear off and the cutter's coxswain took his boat out into the stream, heading through the smoke for the wharf and the confused sounds of rebellion, war and riot. The heat, both natural and conflagration-induced, was appalling and Watkiss, pulling at the sweat-drenched neckband of his white tunic, wondered how Hackenticker could bear to be wearing heavy blues, but then Americans always dressed, like they ate, oddly ... and the stench was as dreadful as the heat. Captain Watkiss pulled out a handkerchief and held it to his nose. Every dead cat and dog from all China must have found its horrible way into the Yangtze to drift past Chungking, and other things too. Captain Watkiss, looking astern to watch the onward progress of the other boats bringing the landing-parties, saw some of the other things and felt his stomach heave. How anyone could bear to be a Chinaman was beyond him; he noted that Hackenticker was looking ill also.

As the *Cockroach*'s cutter came alongside, Watkiss was ready and executed a nimble manoeuvre, virtually leaping across the American's knees to get his feet upon the slippery steps leading up to the top of the wharf. Luck was with him: he remained upright, and climbed pompously as the others disembarked behind him. Smoke rolled across the wharf and in its eye-watering gloom figures could be seen – dagoes, flitting like ghosts. Watkiss took not the slightest notice of them other than to draw the only weapon he had brought: his sword. Out it came from its black and gold scabbard to be waved vigorously towards the foe, and after doing this Captain Watkiss disdainfully turned his back as the boats came in from the rest of his flotilla.

'Mr Halfhyde, the muster to be carried out speedily. Mr Beauchamp?'

'Yes, sir?'

'You are an officer, I suppose, but you shall take no command. You will bring up the rear.'

'Sir, I—'

'Kindly hold your tongue, Mr Beauchamp, or back you go in arrest and that's fact, I said it.' Watkiss gazed about, peering through the smoke. 'Where's that man Bodmin?'

'I be 'ere, zur.'

'Ah, Mr Bodmin. Take up your position in the lead with me, if you please. If your age is against fast movement, then two hands will be detailed to carry you and you shall lead the way from there.'

Bodmin protested. 'I be fully capable o' motion, zur.'

'Good, good. You appear senile to me, but still. Now, Admiral Hackenticker, you may take your position alongside me, but you'll kindly remember I'm in command throughout, under orders from the British Admiralty which in effect means Her Majesty.'

'Captain, I must—'

'Hold your – kindly do as I say, sir. This is no time for dispute.' Captain Watkiss moved away, putting his officers and men between himself and some Presidential pronouncement, taking it that Hackenticker was probably about to indicate that his orders too came from a high source. Within minutes of disembarkation the party from *Cockroach* was joined by the men from the rest of the ships.

Halfhyde reported: 'All mustered and correct, sir, and ready to proceed.'

'Thank you, Mr Halfhyde, I'm obliged. I do hope Mr Bodmin is as fit as he makes out. Move off, if you please.' Watkiss strode to the right of the line, which would lead out. Sword in hand, he advanced with Hackenticker and Bodmin as Halfhyde gave the nod to the gunner's mate. They marched stolidly into the smoke as the gunner's mate turned them into column and began to shout the step, one hundred and twenty bluejackets and men of the Royal Marine Light Infantry, the former smartly gaitered and with chin-stays down, their rifles with the gleaming bayonets held at the slope, the marines in their khaki-drill tunics, also with bayoneted rifles and with heavy ammunition boots that clanged on the ancient stone of China as they moved inwards from the wharf. They could, Watkiss thought with pride and emotion, have been marching upon a simple ceremony from the barrack hulks at Portsmouth, or upon the Hoe at Plymouth where Drake had finished his game of bowls before sailing out to smash the dago armada centuries before. The British tar was splendid, really splendid, and could never be beaten. To the British tar, there was no difference between a route march through Queen Street and Edinburgh Road and Commercial Road, out from the main gate of Her Majesty's dockyard through Portsmouth town, and an advance

45

to war and death in filthy China. The smell was worse now, much worse, like a million drains gone wrong. Bodmin must have a cast-iron stomach to manage to live in China, Watkiss thought as he moved on behind his elderly guide, who was miraculously mobile yet. Watkiss stared ahead as they left the proximity of the river and started to climb. Chungking, as had been noted from the chart, was a hilly place, and sweat began to pour in streams from all the marching men. Soon they came close to the fires: the Street of the Tailors, the Street of the Aphrodisiac Sellers, the Street of the Cobblers, the Street of the Prostitutes, all were burning. Captain Watkiss' voice came in a ringing shout: 'Mr Halfhyde!'

Halfhyde moved ahead. 'Yes, sir?'

'No enemy, Mr Halfhyde!' Watkiss waved his sword. 'No guts! They've seen our uniforms.'

'It could be a trap, sir.'

'Oh, nonsense, Mr Halfhyde, dagoes haven't the intelligence for that.'

'I'd not bank on it.'

'Oh, wouldn't you, Mr Halfhyde, well, I shall.' Captain Watkiss bounced on importantly, his eyes gleaming, his monocle jerking at the end of its toggle as it rode his stomach, his sword-point waggling dangerously about as he gesticulated. 'It's always the same, you know. You remember Sevastopol,' he said in reference not to the Crimean War but to something much more recent and well recollected by Halfhyde, 'when I landed with my men to cut out that old sea-captain what's his name from Prince Gorsinski? Why, the blasted Russians were like lambs – you've only to disregard dagoes and it utterly undermines their confidence in themselves. Utterly undermines it. What a stench.' Peering about suspiciously, he felt a hand on his arm, and glanced sideways. 'Yes, Admiral, what is it?'

'I think your Lieutenant Halfhyde's right, Captain.'

'Oh, nonsense,' Watkiss snapped, looking angry.

'We ought in my view to be ready for attack.'

Watkiss stared. 'Do you imagine for one moment that we're not, my dear sir? The British Navy is ready at all times, ready for anything that may happen.'

Hackenticker asked quietly, 'Ready for that, Captain?' He

pointed ahead, and the others saw it in the same instant: coming visible now through the clouds of smoke was a solid wall of Chinese, both soldiers and civilians, standing massively across the British line of advance. Watkiss gaped, but marched on. Halfhyde turned back along the line, calling orders for the men to stand-to and bring their rifles to the ready. In the rear of the line Mr Beauchamp fingered his jaw in much doubt: how was an officer in arrest placed for the use of his revolver? Could he shoot as a man of war, or would he be tried for murder as a civilian if he killed anybody? If he didn't, would he then be court martialled for the very grave crime of cowardice and giving succour to the enemy? From many angles at once, death stared Mr Beauchamp full in the face; and as he pondered and came to no conclusions at all, he felt some sort of presence behind his back, something fearful and filled with menace. He turned and glanced furtively over his shoulder, and saw more Chinese crowding in from the rear. Feeling his stomach turn to water he gave tongue, shouting up the line to Captain Watkiss.

'Sir, the enemy!' He was too far away; he left his place at the tail of the line and went ahead full belt to make his Captain aware of the creeping danger that threatened to squeeze the British force like a pair of nutcrackers.

FIVE

'Hold your tongue, Mr Beauchamp, I have other things to think about than lily-livers and fools, I am about to come under attack—'

Beauchamp's control broke. 'So am I!' he screamed.

'What?'

Beauchamp, his eyes wide and his face working, gestured violently towards the rear. 'We are being pincered and all you do is—'

'Kindly calm yourself, Mr Beauchamp,' Watkiss interrupted with dignity. 'What do you wish to report?'

'A large force closing in from the rear, sir!'

'I'll be damned! Why the devil didn't you say so before, Mr Beauchamp, you are utterly useless and a great trial to me. Mr Halfhyde, pass the order to halt, if you please, and to re-form with my for'ard half facing front, my after part facing to the rear, front ranks to kneel. And quickly.'

'Aye, aye, sir.' Halfhyde passed the order. The manoeuvre was completed within the minute, and Halfhyde returned to his Captain's side. 'What's your intention, sir?'

'To stand and fight, of course, what else?' Watkiss flourished his sword. 'When the enemy disperses, I shall continue towards the relief of the hostages. In the meantime, I shall fight as a square.'

'A square, sir?'

'Yes, Mr Halfhyde, I have in effect formed square, have I not, and what was good enough for Wellington is good enough for me. When ashore, we must adapt to land fighting, and the British square has never yet been beat. God damn and blast these filthy yellow swine, Mr Halfhyde, kindly get rid of *that* for me.' Watkiss jerked some vile-smelling object from his arm, an object that had flown through the air from the enemy ahead. This was only the first cast, the one that seemed to act as a signal, and a moment later the bombardment began. Stones, clods of mud, small dead animals, everything handy to the Chinese came flying; and simultaneously a murmur began, a murmur of hate and fury that rose higher and higher. Rear Admiral Hackenticker brought his mouth close to Watkiss' ear. 'I guess we should open fire, Captain,' he shouted. 'Will you give the order to your men?'

'No.'

'I think—'

'I am not concerned with what you think, my dear sir, I know my orders deriving from the Queen and I shall follow them. The dagoes are to fire first, or diplomacy will be shattered—'

'The heck with diplomacy!' Hackenticker shouted back, his face scarlet with anger. 'You'll kill every man jack unless you show fight!'

Watkiss glared. 'Sticks and stones can only break our bones, Admiral, not kill us. Mr Bodmin?'

'I be 'ere, zur.'

'I know, that's why I addressed you, I wish you wouldn't say that each time I open my mouth. Did you not say your wife was a da – Chinese woman?'

'Ar, she be that, zur.'

'And that you had influence with her fellow countrymen?'

'Ar, that I did say, zur.'

Watkiss bounced up and down. 'Use it, then, for God's sake!'

'Well ...' Mr Bodmin scratched his nose, looking dubious. 'What be I to say like, zur?'

'Oh, dear ... anything you feel may call the buggers off!'

'Ar. That be a 'ard task now, zur, but I'll try.'

'Yes, do.'

Mr Bodmin made his way ahead and stood a few feet in advance of the main body. He waved his arms, and the sounds of hate died a little as did the hail of filth and stones. He called out in Chinese, seeming voluble. He produced no effect of value: the verbal assault and the missiles picked up again, and Mr Bodmin was himself struck heavily on the chest by a chunk

49

of earth. He fell to the ground, his influence at an end, and was assisted back into the British lines by Admiral Hackenticker. 'He's proved quite useless,' Watkiss said angrily, and stamped his foot. 'Mr Halfhyde!'

'Sir?'

'Stronger measures are called for. I shall try to disperse the blasted dagoes bloodlessly. The men are to open fire over the heads of the mob, Mr Halfhyde, kindly see to that.'

'Aye, aye, sir.'

The order passed, the massed rifles crashed out ahead and astern. Watkiss gave them six volleys and became extremely bitter when the crowd sounds worsened and even more filth was cast. Ammunition was only being wasted, and Watkiss ordered the cease fire. He stared around at his tattered men: they were all covered in muck, their white duck jumpers and gaitered legs almost black, and many were streaming blood from cuts sustained in the bombardment, and there were many contusions and lumps – Watkiss himself had one like a hen's egg on his forehead, but was able to cover it up a little by means of pulling down the blue-puggareed white helmet which he was wearing for action rather than his gold-oak-leaved cap. He breathed hard; what was he to do now? He was not, in fact, short of advice; Rear Admiral Hackenticker was offering plenty in a loud, hectoring voice. The British were ninnies, and Watkiss lacked guts. The time had come to fight and by heck, if Watkiss wouldn't give the order, well, he would and be damned.

'Not to my men,' Watkiss snapped. 'They will not obey you. I shall see to that! I shall not break diplomacy. I am under orders, for the tenth time I think this is, to avoid bringing about a war.'

'What the heck d'you think you're in now, for crying out aloud?'

'Not a war. A civil disturbance.'

'Civil my arse.'

Watkiss turned his back. He seethed up and down, growing filthier by the second. Civil? *Was* it? There were uniformed men present in the mob, were there not? And it was more than a disturbance, more than a riot really, it was deliberate attack, a damned insult to the Queen whose representative he, Watkiss, was at this moment. He looked around for Halfhyde, but Halfhyde was not to be seen. Captain Watkiss reached a decision: diplomacy was important, naturally, but now it was a case of first things first; total failure and many dead would scarcely commend him to the Admiralty and never mind the damn diplomats, he was a seaman. He turned again upon Hackenticker. 'The situation's altered,' he said huffily, 'and it is clear that I must retaliate whatever your view may be, Admiral. I am about to give the order to open fire.'

'A shade too late, I guess.'

'What d'you mean?'

The American swept a hand around, sardonically. 'Look.'

Watkiss looked. Down side alleys to right and left more Chinese had closed in, while from the gaping windows of sleazy dwellings alongside yellow faces peered through above rifles and dirty bayonets. In rear the mob had moved closer and looked extremely menacing. And in front as well: the massed Chinese, moving forward like those in rear, chose this moment to part to left and right and into view trundled an ancient field piece, a muzzle-loading gun, probably of smooth bore and certainly of very heavy calibre, mounted on a gun-carriage propelled by coolies stripped to the waist and wearing blue calf-length trousers and straw hats.

'God damn!' Watkiss said, staring. The field gun would blow everybody to smithereens, so much was quite obvious, unless it blew up in its firers' faces when sent into action, which was a strong possibility but one on which a prudent man could not afford to bank. Watkiss must consider his gallant men, and did. 'I told you it was blasted stupid to open fire in such a situation,' he said to Hackenticker. 'I shall not now do so.'

'You'll surrender?'

'The British never surrender. No, I shall parley.'

Hackenticker grinned. 'With the gun?'

'I don't consider your attitude helpful, and I shall report as much when I reach Hong Kong.' Bravely, Captain Watkiss advanced, waving his sword belligerently. Having second thoughts about belligerency when parleying, he thrust the sword back into its sheath. He advanced smack into the mouth of the field gun, which he saw was in a deplorable state and might well have blown up, but never mind that now, the die was cast for good or ill. Halting, he called out in an imperious tone,

'Who's in charge here, may I ask?' There was no answer; the hail of muck and the catcalls in Chinese had stopped by now, and there was a heavy silence, full of threat. 'Damn them, none of the buggers speaks English. Mr Bodmin?' Bodmin failed to respond with his customary answer, and Captain Watkiss turned impatiently to find out why. Then he turned back again, having heard sounds from the Chinese mob, and found a person in uniform advancing upon him bearing an immense sword such as he believed the dagoes used for public executions.

'You head *serang*?' this person asked.

'I am not a *serang*, no. I am a Post Captain in Her Britannic Majesty's Fleet. If your query was designed to find out if I am the senior officer present, the answer is yes, I am. The Rear Admiral behind me is an American.'

The uniformed Chinese towered unpleasantly over Captain Watkiss and flourished his sword so close to Watkiss' nose that he stepped back a pace. Having thus been made to look foolish, Watkiss scowled; he was annoyed already at being correlated with a *serang*, who was a kind of Chinese boatswain, or alternatively a leading hand in an engine-room. In any case, he believed the person confronting him had not taken in the purport of what he had said, and he was flummoxed for what to say or do next, and where the devil was Bodmin? As Watkiss started once again to turn to look for Bodmin, an immense yellow hand, very bony, clamped hard on his shoulder and swung him back again. Watkiss immediately ordered the fellow to remove the hand, but his order was totally disregarded. Inappropriate words about placing him in arrest bubbled to Watkiss' lips, but, seen in time as absurd in the circumstances, did not emerge. Instead, scarlet in the face, he called out: 'Mr Halfhyde!'

'I be 'ere, zur,' a voice behind him said.

'Oh, it's you. I called for Mr Halfhyde, but never mind. Why didn't you come earlier?' Watkiss breathed hard. 'Tell this person who I am, if you please, Mr Bodmin, and what I have come for, which is, to obtain the release in the name of Her Majesty Queen Victoria of the Europeans held in the British Consulate, peacefully if possible, but if the buggers insist on opposing me, then *not* peacefully. Tell him that.'

'Aye, aye, zur.' Respectfully, Bodmin touched his cap-peak.

He spoke in Chinese to the uniformed person, who gave several nods of his head and a number of what Watkiss took to be grunts but which appeared to mean something to the former boatswain.

'Well, Bodmin, is it peace or war?'

'I be unsure, zur, just yet like.'

'Hurry up, then.'

'Aye, aye, zur. It be 'ard, zur, to 'urry them Chinks.'

'Balls, I haven't got all day. Tell him.that.'

'Aye, aye, zur.' Mr Bodmin turned back to his task and further exchanges took place while Captain Watkiss mopped at his face and looked forbearing. The whole thing was thoroughly undignified and the dagoes were appalling, quite impossible, dirty and unkempt, uniforms or not, and if this fellow was their commander then he had no business to be. He didn't look like a gentleman to start with, and presumably even in foreign armies the officers were expected to be gentlemen, in this case mandarins or such. Captain Watkiss began to suspect he was mere mob and had stolen his uniform from a dago officer slaughtered in some riot, that would be just like foreigners, untrustworthy buggers to a man. Captain Watkiss appeared to steam like an engine as the ridiculous parley continued, and he stamped his foot.

'Mr Bodmin, this is crazy.'

'Ar, zur.'

'Tell the man to remove that wretched field gun, and I shall march my force through his ranks.'

'I don't think that be wise, zur.' Mr Bodmin shook his head.

'Oh, balls to wisdom, Mr Bodmin,' Watkiss said wearily. 'It's action that's needed, not blasted wisdom, dagoes always respect thrust and I didn't ask your advice anyway so far as I'm aware. Do as ordered, if you please.'

'Zur—'

'Get on with it, blast you.'

'Very well, zur.' Mr Bodmin did, though not looking happy about it. The result was remarkable, really extraordinary; it caused Captain Watkiss to preen and hoist his sagging stomach up into his chest: the uniformed person grinned at Bodmin, then turned and shouted incomprehensible sounds at his ragged mob. As Watkiss watched, trying not to look astonished since what appeared to be happening was only what he had predicted, the field gun was once again set in motion by its blue-trousered coolies and hauled aside, while at the same time the mob ahead remained parted to right and left, evidently for the British sailors to march through.

Captain Watkiss immediately drew his sword again and flourished it. 'Well done, Mr Bodmin, what did I tell you! There's no substitute for determination, by God! What did that fellow tell his men?'

'I didn't catch it, zur, I'm afraid. I be a shade deaf, zur, at long distance like, since—'

'Yes, yes, never mind, Mr Bodmin, I seem to have settled matters very satisfactorily.' Captain Watkiss turned a pompous back upon the enemy to the front of his line of advance, and marched with drawn sword back to the group of officers, where he halted and once again mopped at his face: Chungking was murderous, and the smells were still there too. 'You see, Admiral Hackensticker—'

'Ticker. Hacken*ticker*. Not Hackensticker.'

'Oh, very well then, ticker. I apologize,' Watkiss said huffily. He was glad the American was only a very little taller than himself. That was one of the things about Halfhyde, too damn tall. 'You see, I expect, that I was right. It's no use shilly-shallying with the heathen Chinee, my dear sir, one must take the fight into their midst and never mind shot and shell—'

'I'll be darned!' Hackenticker said in amazement. 'If you'll pardon me saying so, Captain, it was me that—'

'If you wouldn't mind, there is now no time to be lost.' Captain Watkiss, seeing Halfhyde approaching, called out to him. 'Mr Halfhyde, you'll be so good as to form up the men for the march through the mob. Rifles at the short trail, ready for instant use if required.'

'Are you sure this is wise, sir?'

'Of course I am, or I'd not order it, thank you, Mr Halfhyde.'

'I smell a trap, sir,' Halfhyde said for the second time that morning.

'Oh, rubbish, there's no blasted trap, that's fact, I said it. I know these people,' Watkiss said with confidence, 'they go down at the first fence. Mr Beauchamp?'

'Yes, sir?'

54

'I'm putting you in charge of the fifes and drums, that's non-combatant enough. You can't do much harm. You've no objection, Mr Sankey, have you?' Watkiss asked perfunctorily of the lieutenant of marines.

'Well, sir, it's really my—'

'I thought not. Now, Mr Beauchamp, the fifes and drums. Play manfully. Mr Halfhyde, you will advance in column of fours at once. No quarter.'

'Aye, aye, sir.' Halfhyde passed the order to the gunner's mate and the seamen moved out once again behind the music of the Royal Marine Light Infantry and Mr Beauchamp. The sound, though thin for lack of numbers of musicians, beat off the war-torn walls of the primitive Chinese dwellings. They moved through the close-packed, smelly bodies of the mob and as they came past yet another Street of the Prostitutes the voice of Captain Watkiss was heard calling loudly over the fifes and drums.

'Sing, if you please, Mr Beauchamp. Show pride.'

'I can't sing, sir!'

'Yes, you can, if you try. "Heart of Oak". It's an order, Mr Beauchamp, and you will sing so as to be damn well heard.'

Beauchamp, scarlet-faced, sang. The high-pitched but yet stirring words drifted back over the ranks of grinning blue-jackets:

> ''Tis to glory we call you
> Not treat you like slaves,
> For who are so free
> As the sons of the waves?
> Heart of oak are our ships
> Heart of oak are our men,
> We'll fight and we'll conquer
> Again and again . . .'

'That's enough after all, Mr Beauchamp, you have no idea of the tune.' The shaky, tuneless voice sang on and Captain Watkiss seethed. '*Shut up*, Mr Beauchamp, you are making me look foolish in the dagoes' blasted sight!'

Beauchamp stopped; almost crying with vexation, he reflected that there was simply no pleasing Captain Watkiss.

*   *   *

Even Watkiss was amazed at the lack of interference, though he refrained from saying so, when behind the guidance of Mr Bodmin he halted his column outside the British Consulate, which was in fact surrounded by the Chinese so deeply that the naval force was entirely cut off from it. 'There you are, my dear sir,' he remarked to Hackenticker. 'I told you, did I not?'

'I'm a trifle lost,' the Rear Admiral admitted, 'as to who told who what—'

'Well, never mind, we're here and intact.'

'So what?'

Watkiss glared. 'I beg your pardon?'

Hackenticker indicated the mob outside the Consulate building. 'Do you now ask them respectfully to stand aside and let you in, Captain?'

'I haven't decided yet, I've only just arrived. Mr Beauchamp, you're as much use as a bishop in a brothel, you can't even sing. It was like a dirge, not a sound of British stalwartness. Mr Halfhyde?'

'Yes, sir?'

'What do you suggest now?'

'I suggest you ask to speak to the British Consul, sir, as a start.'

'Yes, I thought that too. Demand, not ask, why be puny? Faint hearts made no empires, Mr Halfhyde. Mr Bodmin?'

'Ar, zur?'

'Tell the dagoes in Chinese that I demand to speak at once to the British Consul.'

Bodmin pointed upwards. ''E be there, zur, at the window like. Why not just yell, zur?'

'Just yell?' Captain Watkiss stared. 'Just yell, like a common seaman? It's scarcely dignified, is it? I think you're impertinent, Mr Bodmin ... yet on the other hand ...'

'Ar, zur?'

'On the other hand, why bother with the blasted dagoes?' Watkiss pondered. 'Which is the Consul – the bald man with the eyeglasses?'

'No, zur, that be parson.'

'Well, which, then, for God's sake?'

'The thin gentleman, zur, the one with red 'air and a beard, zur, and riding boots.'

'Riding boots?'

''E always wears riding boots, zur.'

Watkiss clicked his tongue. 'Oh, bugger his boots, they can't be seen from here anyway, can they? Put me in touch with him, Mr Bodmin.'

'Zur?'

'You don't expect me to yell at a complete stranger, do you? Put me in touch, tell him who I am. Then I'll talk.'

'Aye, aye, zur.' Bodmin lifted his voice. 'Mr Carstairs, zur, I be 'ere with Cap'n Watkiss o' the Royal Navy, zur. Cap'n Watkiss, 'e do wish to speak to ee, zur.'

From the window a hand waved in acknowledgement and the red beard seemed to wag. A cultured voice floated down: 'Thank God!'

'I don't know about God,' Watkiss muttered angrily. Then he became aware of one of his officers, who was making an attempt to address him. He turned. 'Yes, Lord Edward, what is it?'

'I say, sir! It's awfully curious, you know, but—'

'Kindly be more precise, Lord Edward.'

'Sorry, sir. It's a most extraordinary coincidence, but isn't that Mr Carstairs up there at the window?'

'Yes!'

'Well, I was at prep school with one of his sons, sir. Awfully good chap, sir – Stinky Carstairs. I met his pater once in Eastbourne.'

'Really.'

'Yes, sir. Awfully funny coincidence ... all this way from Eastbourne, isn't it?'

'Yes, very. Well?'

Lord Edward gave a big smile and shifted his feet. 'Well, sir, I can speak to him for you if you like.'

'Why should I like? He's not a blasted Chinee, is he?'

'Oh, no, sir, certainly not, they're an awfully good family—'

'Hold your tongue, Lord Edward, damn you, and don't waste my time.'

'Awfully sorry, sir. It was just an idea. I thought if you had anything to say that you didn't want the Chinese to overhear, you see – I mean, it's awfully possible, isn't it, that some of them speak English, or anyway pidgin—'

'Yes.' Captain Watkiss was growing angry even though Lord Edward Cole was of the aristocracy and must be tolerated further than most officers of his junior rank. 'What the devil are you talking about, may I ask?'

'Latin, sir,' Lord Edward said cheerfully.

'*Latin?* Latin my arse, Lord Edward, don't be ridiculous.'

'Not ridiculous, sir. Mr Carstairs is a Latin scholar, you see. Stinky became one too as a matter of fact.'

'Did he really? And you, Lord Edward?'

'A smattering, sir,' Lord Edward said modestly. 'Rather more, actually. It was wasted aboard the *Britannia*, of course, but—'

'But now you've found a use for it. Smart thinking, Lord Edward, and I shall so inform the Admiralty from Hong Kong upon my return.' Captain Watkiss laid a friendly hand on Lord Edward's arm. 'You shall shout to Mr Carstairs, in Latin, that I have four, no, God damn that fool Beauchamp, *three* river gunboats in the port, and that the moment I secure his release and that of his companions, we shall return aboard my flotilla and stand by to sail for Shanghai. You shall add that speed is vital since the blasted Russians are believed to be about to enter the Yangtze—' Watkiss broke off as someone came round from behind to confront him. 'Yes, Mr Bloementhal, what is it, I'd forgotten you'd come with us. Make it brief.'

'I'll make it brief, all right,' Bloementhal said, sounding truculent. 'The information about the Russians is secret and is not to be yelled out for all and sundry to hear.' He turned to Hackenticker. 'Is that not right, Admiral?'

'Right! As I was about to tell Captain Watkiss.'

'Not right at all,' Watkiss snapped, and went on obscurely. 'If either of you think the damn dagoes speak Latin, you've never been to an English preparatory school, or public school come to that. Lord Edward will do precisely as I tell him, and that's fact, I said it.'

'Now look here—'

'Hold your tongue, Mr Bloementhal, and don't interfere with the execution of my duty or I shall make a special report upon you to the Admiralty, who will forward it to the White House. Now, Lord Edward. You shall add that my strategy is to be as follows ... Mr Halfhyde?'

'Yes, sir?'

'A discussion, if you please, as to my strategy.' Captain Watkiss brought up his monocle and placed it in his eye. 'Lord Edward, be so good as to shout in Latin to Mr Carstairs that I am in conference and will contact him shortly.'

'Aye, aye, sir.' Lord Edward Cole's aristocratic tones swept over the heads of the waiting Chinese mob towards the British Consul, merging from his introductory English, in which he spoke of Stinky and an establishment called St Donat's Academy, into Latin of weird construction.

Meanwhile Captain Watkiss conferred with Halfhyde, joined against Watkiss' intentions by Rear Admiral Hackenticker and Bloementhal. The latter especially riled Watkiss; Hackenticker was, after all, a seaman and within limits they spoke the same language. Watkiss detested all diplomats and never mind their nationality, they were a spurious lot, and slimy. Never honest, never open, dreadful upstarts, cads and bounders, quite impossible. There was a good deal of argument about the strategy to be adopted, and Bloementhal kept on shoving in his blasted diplomatic oar and vetoing, as it seemed, everything Watkiss proposed, saying it would lead to a confrontation and that it was the civil power, and not the military or naval, that was charged with the duty of conducting affairs between nations. In the end it was Rear Admiral Hackenticker who rounded upon his own countryman.

'Heck,' he said, 'you're beginning to sound like a one-man State Department. Hear this, Mr Bloementhal: right now this is a military situation that has gone way beyond diplomacy, and if we don't handle it right we're all likely to end up with our heads cut off and stuck up on those poles you see in Peking. Now, what I suggest is this: we allow Captain Watkiss here to shout at Carstairs, just the first part of his message. The strategy to be shouted later when decided upon. How's that for a start, gentlemen?'

Captain Watkiss, who did not like being allowed to do something by anyone, let alone an American, reacted badly to begin with and hot words rose to his lips; but he forced himself to retain them unsaid. The Queen, in the dangerous circumstances, would expect no less. Ignoring Hackenticker and Bloementhal, he spoke again to Halfhyde.

'Mr Halfhyde, in the past you have not been short of ideas and stratagems. Can you not produce one now, for God's sake?'

'Nothing very dramatic, I'm afraid, sir. The situation is against us and I can only repeat my earlier advice: ask—'

'Demand.'

'Demand, then, to speak to the Consul – privately.'

'Yes, yes. We've been into that, have we not? I—'

'With respect, sir, it would be more practical, really, to make your demand to the Chinese.'

'Why?'

Halfhyde said patiently, 'Mr Cole's Latin may well prove inadequate. The situation has gone beyond the campaigns of Hannibal and *forte buses in aro*.'

'Suppose the buggers refuse my demands, Mr Halfhyde? What then?'

'Then they'll perhaps put themselves out of court to Mr Bloementhal's satisfaction, and we can fight.' Halfhyde caught Hackenticker's eye, and the American nodded his agreement. 'I believe we can fight through into the Consulate, sir, if we take the Chinese by surprise with a sudden burst of rifle fire followed by a bayonet charge.'

'Yes.' Watkiss lifted his head and scratched beneath his chin. 'I can find no fault with that, Mr Halfhyde. I wonder what Mr Bloementhal has to say? No, I wouldn't bother to say it, Mr Bloementhal, since my mind's made up and I consider it my duty to enter the blasted Consulate – yours, too, since I understood your damn authorization chit to board the *Cockroach* said you were under orders to contact a certain person inside the Consulate. And what about that damn Hun – hey?'

Bloementhal answered surlily, 'What about him?'

'You spoke of jiggery-pokery – but perhaps that can wait, so never mind.' Captain Watkiss waved his sword. 'Mr Halfhyde, circulate discreetly among the petty officers and warn them to be ready for action. Lord Edward, you may withhold your Latin for the time being. Mr Bodmin, you will put me in touch immediately with the Chinese leader. Which is he, do you suppose?'

'That be him, zur.' Mr Bodmin pointed to a squat man with a curiously bulbous face, no hair and no ears, who was standing atop a pile of rubble to the left of the entry to the Consulate. 'Lim Puk-Fo, zur.'

'What happened to his ears, Mr Bodmin?'

'Ar, zur, they do say 'e be like that from birth, zur, but I dunno—'

'Well, never mind, speak to him.'

'Aye, aye, zur. What do I say like?'

'Captain Watkiss of Her Britannic Majesty's Navy wishes to talk to the British Consul.' Watkiss paused. 'One moment, Mr Bodmin. I must know to whom I speak. What is Lim Puk-Fo's standing? He's not in uniform like the last bugger I spoke to.'

'No, zur. 'E be a civilian—'

'Bandit.'

'Ar, zur, civilian bandit like. They be powerful people, they bandits, zur, uniforms or not. China, zur, 'tain't like Devonport—'

'Yes, yes, I'm aware of that, thank you, Mr Bodmin, just get on with it.'

Bodmin turned towards Lim Puk-Fo and cupped gnarled hands around his mouth. As he began to speak in Chinese the weather changed with the most astonishing rapidity; the few raindrops that had struck Halfhyde prior to disembarkation from the *Cockroach*, and had thereafter ceased, came back again, this time in sudden drenching fury: the smoke lying over the city had obscured the sky's increasing overcast and now the heavens opened without warning. Rain such as Captain Watkiss had never seen even upon the west coast of Africa sliced down with such force that, taking the ground, it bounced up some two or three feet, drenching all hands from below as well as above. In seconds the white uniforms were soaked through to the skin, and cold struck with the wet. Captain Watkiss stood like a small, fat waterspout while Rear Admiral Hackenticker pulled his blue tunic open and dragged it over his head. Men rubbed streaming water from their eyes and found their gaiters covered with mud brought up around them by the bouncing slivers of rain. The ferocious downpour seemed to inhibit thought and to disorientate the will, and all at once, in the middle of it all, the Chinese struck like demons. One moment they were apart from the British sailors, silent and enigmatic and withdrawn, the next they had become a howling mob that came out of the wall of falling water and were inextricably mixed in with the armed but helpless seamen and marines, wielding clubs and rifle-butts, exhibiting a terrible and intense determination and present in such numbers that the British force was overwhelmed within minutes without a shot fired.

As Captain Watkiss' force found itself helplessly pinioned by supple Chinese arms in a virtually bloodless victory, there came the sound of trumpets and of horses and through the wild torrent of water riders were seen, a strong guard of cavalrymen led by a bulky man in a spiked helmet and with the eagled flag of the German Emperor held aloft by a standard-bearer behind him.

SIX

Beside himself with fury, Captain Watkiss stamped a foot and the Chinese arm about his throat tightened. He gasped and choked. Evidently seeing the stripes of his rank upon his shoulders, the German officer rode towards him, pointing a cavalry sabre at his throat. The German spoke excellent English.

'You are a captain of the British Navy.'

'I am, blast you—'

'You are the senior officer, Captain?'

'Yes!'

'I apologize for your predicament. I am Count Hermann von Furstenberg.'

'Really. Kindly tell this man to release me or you'll be in trouble after I reach Hong Kong.'

The German smiled. 'I wish nothing but your welfare, Captain, and shall do as you ask, but if you move a step I shall slice off your head.' He gave a sharp order in Chinese, and Watkiss felt the grip around his neck slacken and fall away.

'What's the meaning of this?' Watkiss demanded as the rain continued with undiminished force. He glared around at his individually pinioned men, much surprised at the lack of bloody wounds; with the dagoes, that failed to make sense. 'Why have I been attacked?'

'Did you not expect to be?'

'Never mind what I expected,' Captain Watkiss replied angrily. 'Merely explain, that is all I ask! What is your involvement, Count von Furstenberg, pray tell me that?' He shivered; the wet cold feeling was dreadful and Watkiss believed he must take a fever. China was full of fever since it was so dirty, and there wouldn't be a decent British leech within a thousand miles.

The German said, 'I act for my Kaiser, and my Kaiser does not wish war. I am commanded from Berlin to deflect your sailors—'

'You knew I was hurrying to the succour of the Consulate, did you?'

'No, Captain, I made the assumption after certain intelligence reached me of your naval movements from Hong Kong. I sought instructions by cable from Peking. I was told only to stop you if you should come, and send you back to your gunboats without undue fighting.'

'You mean the blasted Chinese are in German pay?'

'You may make your own deductions, Captain, but should remember that the Chinese are not easily controlled and I have had much difficulty in preventing them slaughtering you. I offer no guarantee that their good behaviour will continue, and I advise you to be circumspect and accept your situation.'

'I shall do no such thing,' Watkiss declared flatly. 'I am here in the name of Her Majesty Queen Victoria and here I shall remain until I have carried out my orders from my Commodore.' He lifted his voice. 'Mr Halfhyde? Count von Furstenberg, kindly find Lieutenant Halfhyde and have him brought to me.'

'For what purpose, Captain?'

'I consider that my business, Count von Furstenberg, and you will kindly do as I say without further argument.'

*   *   *

Halfhyde was absent upon action of his own choosing: in the sudden confusion of the blinding rain and the mêlée as the Chinese advanced, he had seen a way more or less clear down a side alley alongside which he and Cole had been standing; and he had grabbed Cole's arm and hustled him along it. Their uniforms were so filthy as to be virtually unrecognizable, and speed had done the rest. The two officers had approached the rear of the Consulate garden unmolested, all the Chinese being engaged in the embattled front. They had scaled a wall and dropped smack through the rusted tin roof of an earth closet provided for the use of the coolies attached to the Consulate and thus placed out of sight from the building itself. Here they had lain low just in case any hostile eyes had spotted them and were waiting. When reconnaissance showed a clear field, Halfhyde decided to take the risk.

'Now, Cole.'

'A simple dash for it, sir?'

Halfhyde nodded. 'Possibly not so simple. The Consulate staff may have itching fingers on their triggers. We must run for our lives.' Ahead of his First Lieutenant, he came out from cover, letting go of his nose as he emerged. As it happened, no Chinese had penetrated into the grounds and the reason for this, a reason that Halfhyde had anticipated, became clear the moment they came in sight from the windows in rear: a stream of rifle bullets zipped into the ground close to Halfhyde's legs and a voice ordered the two filthy figures to halt.

They did so, raising their hands in the air as a precaution, and Halfhyde identified himself. 'Open up a door quickly!' he called. This was done; and Halfhyde and Cole entered the Consulate by way of the kitchen area. There were no Chinese servants to be seen, but European women were preparing a meal by the look of it; Halfhyde assumed, and this was later to be confirmed, that the Chinese staff had deserted en masse many days previously. The women, all of them haggard and many of them red-eyed, were a mixed bunch, many of them being, presumably, escapees from the sacked consulates: French ladies of fashion, voluble as they toiled at vessels containing soup and rice, English housewives and some formidable American ladies who looked as though they had recently come from opening up the West. Halfhyde was led by the man who had admitted him, a young man named Vosper who held the junior rank of consular-agent, to the upper reaches of the Consulate and into the presence of the Consul himself. The window shutters stood open despite the rain and Halfhyde, hearing mob sounds, looked down to see a movement of Chinese and British away from the Consulate, with Captain Watkiss waving his arms energetically in the air in apparent protest as he was tugged at by his detested dagoes.

Carstairs shook Halfhyde's hand. 'Welcome to my

65

Consulate,' he said with a smile. 'You're two more mouths to feed, but no matter – we'll be glad enough of you when the attack comes.' He turned to Lord Edward. 'So you're my son's friend – I remember you, of course.'

'Awfully good of you, sir.'

Carstairs, a friendly man, waved a hand and grinned. 'Not at all. Your Latin's atrocious, by the way.'

'Oh, I say, sir!'

'However, I got the gist as well as the gerunds, my dear fellow. Well, Halfhyde, what's the situation with your men below? I mean, it doesn't look too good to me.'

'It isn't, sir. I fear my Captain is being removed, and there's no knowing where.' Halfhyde looked sardonic as he went on, 'I fear something else: Captain Watkiss will consider Cole and I have deserted him in his hour of need, but such was not my intention, I assure you.' He paused. 'You spoke a moment ago of an attack. I'm here to get you out before the attack comes, and that means there's no time to lose.'

Carstairs shook his head. 'It's a brave thought, Halfhyde, but two can't possibly make an escort!'

'Well, as to that, sir, we shall see.' Halfhyde rubbed his hands together briskly, the light of battle in his eyes. 'There are things I shall need to know. First, how many persons have you here, men, women and children?'

'Forty-three men, twenty-four women, fifteen children of varying ages, most of them American – the children, that is.'

'I see. And rifles and revolvers?'

'Enough for all the adults. Foreigners in China need to be armed, and all of them brought their arms.'

'Then we shall have a fighting chance, sir. Next, I would be obliged if you would inform me fully of the diplomatic situation in Chungking, and of where a certain Count von Furstenberg fits into the picture, and as to why a Mr Bloementhal from Peking was to contact a person inside your Consulate. And I would be most grateful for brevity.'

*   *   *

Captain Watkiss bounced balefully along the sodden Chungking streets under the continuing downpour, in the tight

66

clutches of two large Chinese bearing curved swords the edges of which, he felt, might at any moment cleave his neck. That they were razor-sharp he knew, for that had been demonstrated: his monocle had been ripped away and cast into the air with its black silk toggle dangling. As the toggle streamed down and fell, one of the swords had flashed in the air and cut it in half, cleanly and instantly, despite the almost total lack of bite that it offered. Yes, the swords were sharp . . . not that Watkiss was afraid of death, of course: Post Captains of the fleet were never cowards. Watkiss felt obliged to make this stiffening point to Beauchamp, who was being herded along beside him.

'We are of the Navy, Mr Beauchamp. Remember that.'

'Yes, sir.'

'We are not to be scared from our duty by dagoes.'

'What's our duty now, sir?' Beauchamp asked.

'Yes, Mr Beauchamp, it would take you to ask that, would it not?' Watkiss said disparagingly. 'Our duty is to Her Majesty, Mr Beauchamp, and it will be resumed the moment we are back aboard my flotilla!'

'I see, sir.' Beauchamp paused. 'What do you intend to do, sir, after that?'

'Why, bombard the port, of course! Blow blasted Chungking to smithereens with my three-pounders! What else?'

'Yes, I see, sir,' Beauchamp said politely, 'but Count von Furstenberg will have that in mind, will he not?'

'Possibly,' Watkiss snapped. 'But do you suggest that I should refuse my duty because a blasted Hun may have my intentions in mind, Mr Beauchamp?'

'Oh no, sir—'

'Good. Now hold your tongue and save your breath for the future. Since Halfhyde has seen fit to desert me,' he added with extreme bitterness, 'you'll have to become my First Lieutenant again and much will depend upon you. Do well, Mr Beauchamp, and possibly the past can be forgotten.'

'Oh, thank you, sir!'

'Don't congratulate yourself too soon, Mr Beauchamp.'

They slogged on, back along the streets towards the wharf in abject defeat. The taste of it was horrid but Watkiss considered he had had no option. Count von Furstenberg had with him a strong detachment of cavalry and a piece of horse artillery, while the Chinese hordes were nothing short of legion. Von Furstenberg had been all too precise: refusal to retreat would mean slaughter. It would have been hard, no doubt, to explain away to his blasted Kaiser but in fact he had *carte blanche* and could probably have come up with excuses, lying ones of course, but still.

Watkiss glowered about himself, feeling half drowned. There was one thing about the rain, it held the smell of Chungking down a little. He looked ahead at his marching men; the damn Hun was being correct, certainly, they had not been deprived of their arms – yet was that a good thing after all? Von Furstenberg would say in Berlin that he had received Captain Watkiss' surrender and had been magnanimous enough to take the British word that the rifles would not be used. Captain Watkiss was damned if he regarded himself as having surrendered; he had merely agreed to relinquish his ground under duress and that was quite different. But the Admiralty would have to see his point, or he, Watkiss, could face much trouble for retreating whilst still armed. There was only one ray of sunshine: Hackenticker and Bloementhal were also in retreat, though they could scarcely, of course, be said to have surrendered since they had no armed force of their own with them. A momentary regret struck Captain Watkiss as he seethed along: why the devil hadn't he allowed Hackenticker to take command?

'Mr Beauchamp!'

'Yes, sir?'

'The dagoes are crowding the seamen and marines.'

'Yes, sir.' It was true: the retreat was being extremely well shepherded and the naval force was being pushed tight together to the detriment of their marching.

'I don't like it, Mr Beauchamp, but I suppose there is nothing I can do about it.'

Beauchamp almost wept with relief: he had visualized a direct order for him to keep the Chinese clear and knew that his total inability to do so would not be considered an adequate excuse for failure. The retreat continued, as did the terrible rain. Mangy dogs cowered in the lee of broken buildings and one or two of them barked at the British as they went by. There was less smoke now, since the rain had largely put out the fires, or had at least stopped them spreading. As they came down in

68

clearer air towards the wharf, Beauchamp saw the Yangtze and the three remaining gunboats of the flotilla: the water-level, he noticed, had already risen an appreciable amount. Then something unexpected happened. As the armed Chinese soldiers, assisted by the pressure of the mob, turned the head of the marching column of seamen and marines directly for the wharf, Watkiss and Beauchamp, together with Mr Bodmin, Rear Admiral Hackenticker and Mr Bloementhal, were brought to a halt in the rear by their individual escorts and held fast. As his men marched away, leaving him behind, Captain Watkiss protested vigorously until he was given a blow on the forehead that tilted his white helmet, now grey from the rain, backwards. As he gasped with pain and shock, he became aware that one of the dagoes, the dago Lim Puk-Fo, was speaking to Bodmin; and a few moments later Captain Watkiss was himself addressed somewhat sheepishly by the Customs man.

'Zur, zur – they do say they want ee to remain.'

'Do they? What for?'

'An 'ostage like, zur, I reckon. All of you gentlemen, zurs. And they say, zur, that if the gunboats open fire on the town, then they'll chop off your 'ead, zur.'

Watkiss stared. 'Mine?'

'Ar, zur, that's what they do say, zur.' Mr Bodmin stood as though awaiting orders. They came like a torrent. Mr Bodmin was to reason with the blasted dagoes and point out that both Her Majesty and the Emperor of Germany would be displeased and that vengeance would strike Chungking like a typhoon. Mr Bodmin was further to point out, in case his plea should fail, that the seamen and marines and the junior officers had all marched away and that Captain Watkiss had been given no opportunity to pass orders that they were not to open fire. When they discovered that their Senior Officer was being held ashore, they might very well open fire and the dagoes would be hoist with their own petard. Mr Bodmin did his best, but the plea was not accepted in its first part, only in its second: the British head *serang* could send one of his fellow hostages aboard with the ships' companies to take charge and ensure that no hostile act was committed.

Watkiss breathed hard down his nose. 'It'll have to be you, I suppose, Mr Beauchamp.'

Beauchamp tried not to look too happy. 'Yes, sir. You may rely on me, sir, I assure you.'

'I hope so, Mr Beauchamp, I hope so indeed. Bear in mind constantly what is at stake.'

'I will, sir!'

'Why not,' Hackenticker asked, 'let me go, Captain? I—'

'My dear sir, you shall *never* take command of my flotilla! Off you go, Mr Beauchamp. Do your duty.'

'I shall, sir.' Released, Beauchamp saluted and turned away for the wharf, holding himself back with some difficulty from going fast. Captain Watkiss' final words rang in his ears like a knell: *do your duty*. There had been a hint of pathos; Beauchamp's duty was also to his threatened Captain, and his threatened Captain had sounded much as though he were reminding him of it. Beauchamp, however glad he was to hasten his feet from Chinese soil, was a conscientious man and knew he could face a conflict of duties: presumably Her Majesty's interests had to come before those of Captain Watkiss. Indeed, Captain Watkiss would have been the first to say so himself ... wouldn't he? Mr Beauchamp's thoughts, as he caught up with the seamen and marines, became tinged with bitterness: Captain Watkiss would be quite likely to place him in arrest for saving his life if he failed to do it in accordance with Queen's Regulations and Admiralty Instructions.

*   *   *

In the Consulate, the preparations were in hand for a break-out and the flight to the gunboat flotilla; and Carstairs had spelled out the overall situation to Halfhyde as requested. As Watkiss had been advised by Bloementhal, the Russian and German Empires were competing for treaty rights in the great land mass of China and along her coasts, and at the present time the Germans appeared to be in the ascendant thanks to the nefarious efforts of Count Hermann von Furstenberg who was well accredited to, and well received by, the ancient Empress-Dowager of China in Peking. Both Germany and Russia were, Carstairs said, taking advantage of the current situation in Chungking and Szechwan province.

'The rising, sir?'

'Yes. They're hoping to extend it from Szechwan throughout China to the detriment of British trading interests – then they, or rather one of them, will step into the vacuum. Meanwhile, we're the hostages.'

'For what purpose?'

Carstairs shrugged. 'Partly to put the wind up our nationals, both British and American, in the rest of China. Partly to show the world that the Chinese have no more time for us, and that we're henceforward unwelcome. We're to be the pawns, is what it comes down to – bargaining pieces. If Britain and America back out of China, we'll be released unharmed.'

'Yes, I follow. Are you all, in fact, unharmed?'

'Yes. There have been no attacks beyond simple harassment designed to keep our heads down, as it were. Mind you, we're not all too healthy ... the food's been short, so has the water, and the strain's been pretty immense on the women and children.'

'Quite. And Bloementhal, sir?'

Carstairs said, 'Bloementhal was under orders to make contact with one of my protégés, as you know—'

'May I now ask which one, sir?'

'Of course, and if I knew, I'd tell you – but I don't. I was advised by cable that Bloementhal was on his way, but no mention was made of whom he was to contact.'

Halfhyde nodded. 'Then may I suggest the time has come to find out? There's a need of speed in case attack should come before we leave—'

'I doubt if it'll come as fast as you fear, Halfhyde. As I said, we're the pawns. Our use is not finished yet.'

'Perhaps, but the sooner the better nevertheless, then they've lost their pawns – and I for one wouldn't trust the mob not to take the bit between its teeth and jump the gun.' Halfhyde paused; in point of fact, and most oddly, the mob sounds had died away. He moved to the window and looked down. The roadway was relatively empty now. Shrugging, he turned back to the Consul. 'I suggest questioning, sir. Questioning of all in the Consulate, to find out who is Mr Bloementhal's contact, and why. I think we must have the answers before we move out.'

*   *   *

71

Mr Bodmin was marched away with the other captives, protesting about being treated thus when he was married to a Chinese woman and therefore part of the family, as it were, of China.

'It be uncivilized, zur.'

'They're an uncivilized people,' Watkiss snapped. Amongst other indignities, they had snatched away his sword.

'Ar, zur, they're not – not really. Their civilization's as old as the 'ills, zur—'

'Kindly don't argue with me, Mr Bodmin, I detest argument, detest it. The Chinese are uncivilized.'

'Well, zur,' Bodmin said doubtfully, 'if you says so. I'm an uneddicated man, zur, not like the gentry—'

'Yes, yes.'

'O' course, the old woman, zur, the wife that be, she'll be all right, she 'as ninety-seven relatives livin' in Chungking alone, zur—'

'Good heavens! As I once remarked to Mr Halfhyde, the Chinese have little else to do ... but never mind. Ninety-seven in-laws, it's unbelievable. Don't keep lurching into me, Mr Bodmin, I don't like it.'

'Sorry, I'm sure, zur.'

The downpour was not slackening one iota, it was quite appalling, and Watkiss hoped without much conviction that Beauchamp would handle his flotilla in a seamanlike way if the Yangtze should rise to unacceptable limits. With this in mind, he enquired from Bodmin what the maximum rise and fall had been in his experience: the charts and Sailing Directions were not always, in Watkiss' view, to be wholly trusted.

'Ar, it be bad, zur, bad.' Mr Bodmin shook his head.

'Yes, but *how* bad?'

'Why, zur, last year 'twere, zur, the river rose ninety-seven feet above low-water mark, zur.'

Watkiss was aghast. 'Goodness gracious, Mr Bodmin, you're confusing your navigation with your in-laws, surely!'

'No, zur. 'Twere a whacking great coincidence I'll not deny, zur, as I remarked to the old woman at the time, but the figures be dead correct, zur, in both instances, I'll take my solemn Bible oath on it.'

Captain Watkiss blew out his cheeks and sent up a prayer for his gunboats, only too certainly to be hazarded by that fool

Beauchamp if the worst should happen. Beauchamp, poised ninety-seven feet above low water, would be lethal. They trudged on surrounded by the Chinese guns; behind them, Rear Admiral Hackenticker and Bloementhal maintained a morose silence. Not long after Watkiss' chat with Bodmin, the awful march ended and they moved thankfully out of the rain into shelter of a sort. Extremely dirty and smelly shelter, but relatively dry and clearly very secure: shelter was the city gaol, a foetid place which they were evidently to share with criminals, and Watkiss protested at such treatment.

'I am a Post Captain of Her Majesty's, Her *Britannic* Majesty's, Fleet. Mr Bodmin is an officer of Chinese Customs. There is also a Rear Admiral of the United States Navy I should add. Mr Bodmin?'

'Ar, zur?'

'Tell the buggers.'

'They do know already, zur.'

'Tell them again.'

It was of no avail. Each of the three, plus Bloementhal whom Watkiss had not felt worth mentioning, were pushed unceremoniously into a kind of cage, a filthy place with iron bars around it. There were other similar cages, with other occupants, common criminals, thieves and murderers no doubt . . . Watkiss was aghast. There appeared to be no lavatories: the evidence of this lack was only too apparent. Some of the prisoners were lying flat on plank bunks, on their backs, with eyes staring upwards. Opium, no doubt – disgusting! Watkiss believed he could smell opium, which the wretched dagoes took like afternoon tea. He seized the bars in a rage and shook them, and once again reminded his gaolers of his rank and authority, but it was quite useless and when Hackenticker had the blasted cheek to murmur something about a monkey in a zoo, he let go of the bars and sat down on a plank bed and sulked. His mortification was complete. There was just one consolation: a gaol was an official place, therefore he was being treated officially and was not in the hands of, for example, pirates. That was something, if not much. Watkiss groaned aloud and put his head in his hands. Somebody, only God knew who, must get a despatch through to Commodore Marriot-Lee, who would soon be lying with his first-class cruisers off Shanghai . . . or to the Commodore-in-Charge in Hong Kong, who would alert the Empire by means of the underwater cable ...

* * *

The occupants of the Consulate were questioned separately, one by one, in the Consul's office. Carstairs did the questioning, with Halfhyde and Cole present but not taking part. All but the children were questioned, although it was thought unlikely that a woman would be Bloementhal's contact; and in the end it was the last person to be interrogated who turned out to be the one: perhaps the most unlikely of them all, the bald man with the eyeglasses whom Mr Bodmin had earlier pointed out to Captain Watkiss as 'parson', the Reverend Marchwood Erskine, missionary to the heathen, a citizen of Great Britain from Worthing in Sussex, member, as he said in a curiously hoarse voice, of a breakaway group from the established Church of England known as Jacob's Tabernacle. This, Halfhyde gathered, was a sect much concerned with propagation of the gospel; in a word, evangelists.

Carstairs, who knew Erskine well enough, was greatly surprised and said as much. 'What's the connection with Bloementhal?' he asked. 'I'd not associate you with diplomatic activities, Mr Erskine, nor with Americans come to that.'

The Reverend Marchwood Erskine, wrapped in dignity and black clothing that must have been as hot as Hackenticker's blues, cleared his throat. 'Bibles,' he announced in his hoarse tones.

'*Bibles?*' Carstairs seemed more surprised than ever.

'Not an unnatural commodity for my cloth, I think?' The eyeglasses were removed and polished and replaced before Erskine went on again. 'Bibles spread the word, Mr Carstairs, and the good Lord knows the Chinese people need the word. I do His work.'

'Yes, of course, I'm sorry.' Carstairs paused, tapping his desk and looking baffled. Halfhyde felt the grip of impatience: time could be all too short. 'That doesn't quite explain the connection, Mr Erskine, does it?'

'No, I realize that.' The parson was enunciating with much care, as though he might make mistakes, not diplomatic ones,

74

but ones of speech, and Halfhyde, bearing in mind the extra-ordinarily hoarse voice, like a coffee-grinder, suspected whisky. Mr Erskine, though steady in his seat, was, Halfhyde believed, a little tight. Erskine went on, 'In all the circumstances I feel I have no option but to make disclosures that perhaps I should not. Indeed, having started, I must go on, must I not?'

Carstairs nodded. 'It would be appreciated, certainly.'

'Very well, then.' Hollowly, the clergyman coughed before proceeding. 'Mr Bloementhal happens to be a friend of mine, a good friend. I was first introduced to him when I was in his country, don't you know, for a conference of American Taber-naclers, of which he is one. Yes, we became good friends . . . and in due time Mr Bloementhal made me a proposition. To be brief, he made the point – and it was a valid one I believed and still believe – that Bibles could, had they a mind to, tell more than the word.' He peered around through his eyeglasses which, catching the light, magnified fishlike pale eyes. 'To put it into other words, Bibles can carry messages if they're in the proper hands. *Secular* messages.'

'For Mr Bloementhal?'

'Precisely, Mr Carstairs, for Mr Bloementhal and the American State Department,' Erskine answered with a touch of con-descension. The State Department was much more important than a Consulate. 'I felt that this was by no means wrong, nor inconsistent with the cloth. The Americans are not our enemies, and the maintenance of peace is always a Christian's deepest wish. So I was prepared to act as an agent as it were and, I confess, a *paid* agent.'

'Good heavens!'

A pained expression crossed the clergyman's face. 'You do not, I think, quite understand. Being employed mainly upon God's work, I naturally saw to it that all money received was handed as soon as possible to the Tabernacle funds except when it was more appropriate to pass it to the Anglican Bishop in Peking. I—'

'Yes, I take your point – very worthy.' Carstairs paused. 'Have you messages currently in your possession, Mr Erskine?'

'Yes, indeed. For Mr Bloementhal.'

'Who is not here, but is somewhere else in Chungking. I think perhaps the time has come . . . Bloementhal may be in danger of

75

his life, may be dead already for all I know.' Carstairs leaned forward. 'I am going to suggest, Mr Erskine, that the time has come to break a confidence, and hand the messages to me.'

Erskine rubbed at his jaw. 'It's unethical. Very, very unethical.'

'I agree, of course. But it could be vital. The messages may have some bearing upon our current problems, and could even assist Bloementhal himself.'

'Yes, yes.' Erskine looked grave, and gave a sudden involuntary belch that seemed possibly to confirm Halfhyde's diagnosis. 'Yes, indeed, you may be right, Mr Carstairs. I know you, and I trust you. Yes, I shall pass the messages and ask God's forgiveness if I should transgress.' He lost no time; at his feet lay a black leather bag, into which he delved. Bibles were seen, and the neck of a bottle of John Haig, the latter being quickly pushed out of sight again. From between the leaves of a volume from his religious stock, the clergyman brought a sheet of rice-paper; from another, another sheet ... again and again. The consular office began to look like the scene of a paper-chase.

SEVEN

Food was brought to the prisoners, horrible stuff that turned the stomach: a nasty substance akin to thin porridge, with black bean husks floating in it like dead beetles. With this was water in a dirty earthenware pot, water that smelled foul and was a risk to drink, but after a while thirst overcame discretion and they drank – the porridge-like substance had a content of salt that had increased the thirst. Captain Watkiss, sitting on the wooden bed, felt very ill and tried to fix his mind on rescue. He would not, of course, be left to his fate; the China Squadron under Commodore Marriot-Lee, whilst not able to negotiate the Yangtze on account of draft, would bombard Shanghai, or anyway threaten to, unless the prisoners were at once released. That would make the dagoes sorry they had ever laid hands upon a Post Captain! But, as ever, the other side of the coin loomed large: there would be no bombardment unless and until word could be got through as to what had happened in Chung-king. Time might produce a reaction, certainly – when no flotilla steamed back down the Yangtze questions would be in the air, and revenge, but Captain Watkiss believed that death might well strike him before that happened. There were times when the sword of Admiralty was dreadfully slow to leave its sheath ... and always he had to bear in mind that Post Captains, though important, might not be important enough to send the Empire to its war stations. The wretched Lord Salisbury, smug and safe in Number Ten, Downing Street, might be over-cautious ... and although Watkiss felt convinced that Her Majesty would, with her customary vigour, berate her Prime Minister for namby-pambyism, it was a sad fact that Her

Majesty was always much more stirred by sad happenings to her soldiers than by the sufferings of her fleet.

'Mr Bodmin?'

'Ar, zur, I be 'ere.'

'I know, that's why I addressed you. What do you suggest, with your knowledge of the dagoes?'

Bodmin scratched his head. 'Why, I dunno, zur. They be unpredictable, they Chinks. A funny lot they be, zur.'

'Yes. Is there any way of getting a message through to Hong Kong or Foochow?'

'I dunno, zur.'

Watkiss clicked his teeth and instinctively reached for his missing monocle with a groping hand. 'For a former boatswain, you seem somewhat useless, Mr Bodmin. Suggest something, for God's sake!' He came up with an idea of his own. 'Your wife, perhaps?'

Bodmin demurred. 'Ar, no, zur, no. The old woman, zur, she be no use at that sort o' thing. She be a Chinee, you see, zur. She wouldn't act against her own country, zur.'

'Oh, nonsense, she's British now, having married you.'

'She don't see it that way, zur.'

'Damned disloyalty.'

Watkiss brooded: no doubt Mrs Bodmin would in any case take time to reach Hong Kong on foot and could be waylaid by bandits en route. He glared at the two Americans, sitting side by side on the bed opposite and throwing dice between them which was typical of the casual attitude of Americans.

'May I ask what you're doing, Admiral?' Watkiss asked.

Hackenticker looked up. 'Throwing craps.'

'Craps?' Watkiss fumed. 'At a time like this?'

'Your Francis Drake played bowls on a similar occasion.'

'Oh, nonsense, there's no parallel at all! What about the United States Navy, will they take no action – or your President?'

Hackenticker shrugged. 'We're pawns, Captain, pawns in an international power game. We just have to be patient—'

'Patient!'

'And wait developments. My guess is, they won't kill us. We stay here till the game's won or lost, then they release us. In the meantime, we throw craps. Care to join us?'

78

'Oh, hold your tongue!' Watkiss snapped. He wrapped his arms around his thick body and gloomed. Stalemate at least was in the air, probably checkmate. There was, in all truth, nothing to be done about it and Hackenticker was right. *Force majeur* was *force majeur* and that was that. He tried to think of happier times, great days on the broad and stormy ocean, commanding his flotilla, or stalking his bridge as Captain of a great battleship steaming out of Plymouth Sound to the splendour of the band of the Royal Marine Light Infantry beating out *Rule, Britannia* ... but the dreadful present kept intruding into pleasant fantasies: the horrid noises from the other cages, and the evil smells, and the murderous looks as the Chinee convicts manifested enmity towards the white devils. That, and the drumming rain upon the gaol-house roof as the downpour continued without a moment's remission and indeed seemed to be increasing so that Captain Watkiss pondered with dread upon what the stupid Beauchamp would be doing now with his flotilla as the waters of the Yangtze rose and lifted the gunboats upon its swelling bosom. Then, suddenly, something smote him that should have been obvious much sooner: Count von Furstenberg.

'Mr Bodmin, and I know you're here so you needn't say so. Call the guard.'

'Zur?'

'In Chinese, call for the guard.'

'Aye, aye, zur. Might I ask why first, zur, then I'll know, see?'

'Oh, very well! I wish to speak to Count von Furstenberg at once. This is the official gaol, so he'll know we're here, and he's been guilty of the most damnable duplicity ... I shall tell him so, and demand our immediate release unless he is willing to risk war between the British and German Empires.'

'Ar, zur, but 'e'll know that already like, zur—'

'Hold your tongue, Mr Bodmin, and do as I say.'

*   *   *

Out upon the Yangtze there was indeed a most remarkable surge of water already as the heavens remained open and the headwaters, swollen earlier by much rain in their vicinity, rolled downriver to Chungking. Inexorably the gunboats rose

79

and tugged strongly at their cables and Mr Beauchamp, nervously fingering his jaw upon *Cockroach*'s bridge, ordered the paying-out of more cable and sent signals advising the other two vessels to do likewise. Steam had been maintained upon the engines ever since arrival, so no extra decision was called for in that respect. Beauchamp paced the bridge, drenched even through his sou'wester and oilskins, his stomach turning over in response to his anxieties as to what to do next. He had only so much cable; if the waters rose much more, the cable would be straight up-and-down between the anchor shackle and the Senhouse slip in the cable locker, and when that happened the anchor would either break ground and set him loose or the ship's head would be drawn down so that he would appear from the shore to command a diving duck. The other possibility would be to knock away all slips and stoppers and jettison the cable, and what would Captain Watkiss say then? Arrest would be his least pronouncement; anchors and cables cost a good deal of money and must be accounted for to the supplying dockyard, and many forms had to be filled in to explain why they had been cast adrift. Reasons and excuses had to be watertight or the officer responsible, which of course was always the Captain, might have to reimburse Her Majesty from his own pocket. It was such a worry ... and there was another worry too: Captain Watkiss' actual person. The Captain had adjured him to bear in mind constantly what was at stake – his very words. Beauchamp's hands shook: Captain Watkiss was very much at stake, he fancied. *Should* he bombard the port? And if so, should he bombard it now while he still had steady gun-platforms? If he left his decision too late, the gunboats might find themselves adrift upon the waters and being sucked willy-nilly downstream, for the current was immensely fast and Beauchamp foresaw the possibility that his engines would fail to breast it. A bombardment whilst being swept astern like a piece of jetsam would not carry much conviction or authority, and never mind that in any case the nine three-pounders distributed among the three ships of the flotilla were little more than popguns. Another consideration was whether or not such a bombardment would cause war; if it did, there would be no holding Captain Watkiss' wrath. On the other hand ...

Beauchamp straightened his shoulders. He must not fail, he must be firm one way or the other. When the time came, and it hadn't quite yet, he *would* be firm. A miracle could happen yet, and this awful nightmare be ended in the comparatively happy sight of Captain Watkiss strutting on to the wharf and waving his arms for a boat to be sent to bring him off.

*   *   *

'You appear to have been busy, Mr Erskine, and not only for the Lord.'

'Purely spare time,' the missionary said with a touch of reproof. Having picked all the pieces of rice-paper from his Bibles, he shuffled them into consecutive order. Each sheet was neatly numbered, Halfhyde noticed. The writing was in plain English, a rather large hand. Erskine handed the collected pages to the Consul, frowning and muttering to himself as he did so, still seeming uncertain as to the propriety of his action in making his messages available to anyone other than Bloementhal. This done, he excused himself and departed with his black bag and a comment that nature called. When he returned there was a smell of whisky. 'Well, Mr Carstairs?' he asked.

'Possibly helpful, but I'm not in a position to judge the whole situation.' Carstairs continued reading carefully while Erskine fidgeted about the room, and Halfhyde grew more and more impatient as the clock ticked on. Finally the Consul nodded and said, 'Thank you, Mr Erskine, you may leave this with me now.'

'That's all very well, but—'

'I'm sorry, Mr Erskine. These papers must not fall into the wrong hands if we come under attack either here or on our way to the gunboats. The contents are now in my head—'

'What are you suggesting should be done with the notes, then?'

'They must be destroyed, I'm afraid.' Carstairs raised an eyebrow, smiling at the parson. 'By eating, perhaps? Rice-paper—'

'Is not in fact made from edible *rice*, Mr Carstairs, but from *Fatsia Aralia papyrifera*, a Formosan tree. If you wish to eat, you

81

may do so, but *I* shall not risk it.' Erskine sat down looking angry. 'In any case, they're not your property.'

'Needs must,' Carstairs murmured, and brought a box of Lucifers from a pocket. He constructed a small bonfire in a metal waste-paper bin whilst the clergyman muttered crossly. Taking care that the last scrap was consumed by the fire, Carstairs said briskly, 'Thank you, Mr Erskine, you've been a great help and you may be sure I shall explain fully to Mr Bloementhal. Jacob's Tabernacle funds shall not suffer, I promise you, nor the Bishop in Peking if appropriate. If you will kindly join the others, I must now make plans with Mr Halfhyde.'

'Yes, but look here—'

'Thank you, Mr Erskine, your part is done, now if you please allow me to do mine.'

The missionary departed in a huff, clanking his black bag. (It contained, Halfhyde guessed, more than one bottle of John Haig.) When they were alone, Carstairs said, 'I could fall victim to the mob – I know that. If that should happen, others must know what Erskine's dug out so they can pass it to the right quarter. You, Halfhyde, and I, and Erskine – and you, Lord Edward—'

'You may rely upon me, sir!' Lord Edward said eagerly.

'Thank you—'

'Stinky was my friend, you see. I'd never let any pater of his down.'

'Decent of you. And my vice-consul here. That should be enough of us. One of us at least should get through. Now, here's the gist.'

They listened intently, conscious that any one of them might in fact become the sole conveyor to high authority or to Bloementhal. Much of the clergyman's labours were devoted to rambles about which areas were most anti-European and of those that were not wholly anti-European, which were the most likely to offer welcome to the Germans or to the Russians to the exclusion of the British, French and Americans; also which areas held murmurings of disloyalty towards the ageing Empress-Dowager. The pith lay chiefly in Erskine's estimate of the forces likely to be ranged against the British, French and American presence currently in Chungking. Szechwan province, it appeared, was fairly united in detesting all three equally, and the mandarins in the local seats of power could send many thousands of armed Chinese against the foreign devils in the consulates, of which only the British now remained intact. But the real heart of it all lay in a total indictment of the German, Count Hermann von Furstenberg, who was playing, at the very least, a double game that verged on being triple if not quadruple. Von Furstenberg's principal concern was von Furstenberg rather than his Kaiser and never mind that his Kaiser had provided him with a personal escort of Uhlan Lancers to intimidate the rustic Chinese in the provinces, much money, and personal introductions to the court at Peking. Von Furstenberg, as emerged strongly from the missionary's observations and subsequent committals to rice-paper, was doing the dirty on virtually everyone else concerned and arranging deals, and accepting vast bribes, on behalf of an armaments factory in the Austro-Hungarian Empire owned by his family. It was the intention of Count von Furstenberg to remain in China and set himself up in a position of power as a supplier of arms to the Empress-Dowager whilst at the same time maintaining through agents a supply line to certain interests hostile to the Empress-Dowager so that if she fell, von Furstenberg would still be indispensable to the new régime in China. All of this, obviously, would be of immense interest to the various European governments, not least to the German Kaiser, and to the old Empress-Dowager in Peking; and the knowledge of it was now, thanks to the Reverend Marchwood Erskine, a sword pointed at the disloyal heart of Count Hermann von Furstenberg.

'How in God's name,' Halfhyde asked in some astonishment, 'did Erskine acquire all this knowledge?'

Carstairs grinned. 'No doubt as you've just remarked – in God's name. He's a cunning old devil, you know. I dare say some of the Tabernacular funds have been handed out in bribes, too. He'd have repaid them from moneys received from Bloementhal, I think – he's basically honest. Anyway, there it is.'

'You believe it, sir?'

'For want of anything to make me *dis*believe it, yes. It ties up with what I've heard of von Furstenberg, and it's in the character of the German armaments manufacturers to put profit above all else.'

'Above patriotism?'

Carstairs pursed his lips. 'No ... not all of them, most certainly. Von Furstenberg's the black sheep.'

'And his Emperor wouldn't have known this?'

'Hard to say. It seems probably not. On the other hand, Kaiser Wilhelm hasn't his grandmother's moral outlook.'

'There may yet be something in it for him, you mean?'

'Yes, it's possible. A hit at the British Empire and its trading interests – you know the Germans and their aspirations, I'm sure, Halfhyde. They're a damned unprincipled lot when it comes to extending their spheres of influence.' He grinned. 'Or any other time when it suits them!'

'True. And now, sir? Time presses, and we should be away to the gunboats.'

'I still dislike retreat, Halfhyde. The attack may not come, you know.'

'But I believe it will, and I must make the assumption that it will. My orders were to evacuate the Consulate and escort all personnel to my flotilla – this I am bound to do.' Halfhyde responded with sympathy to the Consul's dejected look. 'You'll be back, sir, when all this is settled and times become happier.'

'I trust so, Halfhyde. I've spent much of my career in Chungking ... it's a sad business.' Carstairs gave himself a shake as though to clear away morbid thoughts. 'Well now, gentlemen, remember what you've heard. It's to be passed on by any one of you should I be unable to report. That apart, keep it under your hats.' He caught Cole's eye. 'Yes, Lord Edward, you've something to say?'

'Yes, sir. It's awfully underhand, isn't it? Count von Furstenberg, I mean. It's not *British*, is it?'

'Er ... no, it's not.'

'But it's all awfully exciting, sir. Stinky and I used to get up to all sorts of japes, but nothing quite like this, really.' Suddenly Lord Edward flushed, looking contrite. 'I shouldn't have said that – I'm awfully sorry, sir. I shouldn't have sneaked on Stinky and I hope you'll forget it, sir.'

Gravely, the Consul nodded.

'Mr Bodmin! Mr Bodmin!'

Bodmin broke off in full Chinese spate and turned. 'Ar, zur?'

'You are taking a devil of a long time over a simple order, Mr Bodmin. Just tell the buggers what I want, and leave it at that.'

'Ar, zur, but I can't, zur.'

'Can't? Why can't?' Watkiss rose to his feet and bounced towards the cage bars. 'No such word as can't, the Duke of Wellington said so, or was it Napoleon.'

'Ar, zur.'

'What? What d'you mean? I didn't ask a question, I made a statement.'

'Ar, zur, it were.'

Watkiss blew out his cheeks. 'What was?'

'Napoleon, zur. I remember the superintendent o' the foundling 'ospital, 'e—'

'Oh dear, dear, dear, does it matter, Mr Bodmin?'

'No, zur.' Bodmin seemed hurt. 'Point be, zur, they Chinks won't do what ee want. I asked 'em – told 'em like,' he added quickly, 'but they say no. I tried to argue like—'

'Good, good.'

'But they won't pay 'eed, zur, not to me.'

'Oh, balls and bang me arse, Mr Bodmin, they certainly won't pay heed to me since I don't speak their blasted lingo. Try again.' Captain Watkiss, not wishing to compromise his dignity by being stonewalled by dagoes, turned his back and retreated to sit upon the plank bed and Bodmin tried again as ordered. There was much talk but no success, and the former boatswain approached Watkiss to render his nil report.

'There be bad Chinks and good Chinks, zur, and these be bad. They threatened me, zur, that they did!'

'In what way?'

Bodmin wiped the back of a hand across his nose and looked indignant. 'They said, zur, if I went on like, they'd take it out on the old woman. Mrs Bodmin, zur.'

'I see.' Watkiss paused, then said stiffly, 'Your first duty is to the Queen, of course.'

'Of course, zur. But not afore Mrs Bodmin, zur.'

'Oh, balls, that's a contradictory statement if ever I heard one! Don't be browbeaten, my dear Bodmin – try again!'

'No, zur.'

'I beg your pardon?'

'No, zur. A man's wife is a man's wife, zur.'

'Yes, yes, I appreciate that, of course, but duty—'

'And I don't be in the Navy now, zur. And I tell ee summat else an' all, zur: Mrs Bodmin, you said yourself, she be a British subject now, zur, and you 'ave your duty as well as me, zur, and yours be to all British subjects in Chungking, and that includes Mrs Bodmin.' Bodmin stood with arms folded and a look of total obstinacy on his leathery old face. 'You can't 'ave it both ways, zur.'

'Oh, hold your tongue and don't argue, Bodmin, I detest argument.' Avoiding Bodmin's eye, Captain Watkiss glowered belligerently towards the bars of his cage.

*   *   *

In the British Consulate Halfhyde made his preparations for breaking out, taking charge over Carstairs as the sole fighting representative of the Queen. All the occupants were mustered with their arms and given explicit orders to stick together in a bunch, with the women and children in the centre; the men, including Mr Erskine, would form the guard and escort under the command of Halfhyde and Cole.

'I propose to leave from the rear of the premises,' Halfhyde told the assembly. 'The streets appear more or less quiet now, and we haven't far to go to reach the wharf. We'll not be unmolested, we must expect that, but no one is to use his weapon except under my orders. I shall try not to exacerbate the Chinese – my hope, frankly, is that they'll be glad enough to see us go and won't unduly hinder us. It'll look like defeat for the British, but I assure you that will be only temporary. In any case my orders are simply to extract all of you and embark you safely aboard the flotilla. Nothing else. I am not to be concerned with buttressing the British position. Are there any questions, ladies and gentlemen?'

'Yes,' Erskine said. 'May we take it that transport to the boats will be waiting at the wharf?'

'I doubt it,' Halfhyde answered, 'and our arrival there will be the tricky part. There will be a wait while Captain Watkiss sends away his boats to take us off, and we shall need courage and patience and steady tempers if the mob gathers, which I've no doubt it will. Now—' He broke off. A single shot had come from the back of the Consulate. Into the tense silence that followed, rapid fire broke with terrifying effect, and then a long-drawn scream was heard.

Halfhyde, with Cole behind him, ran for the exit into the garden.

EIGHT

From beyond the wall at the garden's end, a spatter of rifle fire came as Halfhyde appeared. Bullets zipped into the ground immediately outside the door from the kitchen quarters. Halfhyde stepped back quickly into cover, and ordered Cole to get back upstairs at the double and organize return fire from the rear windows. Outside, in the lee of a large and spreading tree, a man was trying to drag his wounded body along towards the building. He left a trail of blood and was crying out in pain, unintelligibly; by his clothing, he was a Chinese. Halfhyde waited tensely until the rifles were heard from the windows, then, bending his tall frame low, he made a dash for the wounded man. Bullets were still zipping across from the wall, but they died away under the impact of the return fire just as Halfhyde reached his objective. He lifted the man and took him in his arms and made back as fast as possible to the doorway.

Inside, he laid the Chinese gently on a kitchen table and put rolled-up towels beneath the head. Joined now by Cole, he sent his First Lieutenant back to fetch some women to tend the wounded man. 'Bring Carstairs too,' he added. 'He speaks Chinese.' As Cole went off, the Consul appeared in the kitchen doorway and Halfhyde said, 'A Chinese, sir, who must have come for a purpose.'

Carstairs approached. 'Is he alive?'

'He breathes yet. Ask him quickly why he came.'

'I know him,' Carstairs said. 'His name's Jing Bang, one of the Consulate servants. I was surprised when he deserted with the rest ... but these people are always subject to many pressures, of course.'

'Quickly, if you please, sir!'

'Yes.' Carstairs bent, and smoothed the man's forehead. There were a number of wounds in the body and the skull was bleeding freely. Carstairs spoke in rapid Chinese; the response was low and feeble. Carstairs seemed to be asking for a repeat, and for a moment, as if with a supreme last effort, the voice came clearer and stronger. Carstairs spoke again, and again there was an answer, and then, very suddenly, the body jerked grotesquely and the head fell aside with the mouth open and the eyes staring. Carstairs felt for the heart, then looked up.

'Dead?' Halfhyde asked.

Carstairs straightened. 'I'm afraid so. Poor fellow ... he was loyal after all. I'm glad of that ... it's a kind of testimony, as though my efforts haven't been all in vain!'

'Yes, indeed. And his message? Were you able to get that?'

'Yes. Quite clearly. Your Captain Watkiss has been taken, along with Bloementhal and Rear Admiral Hackenticker and poor old Bodmin. Taken by the Chinese authorities, not by the mob.'

'For what purpose, sir?'

'I've no idea.'

'Did Jing Bang say where they were?'

'Yes. In the town gaol, under lock and key. It's a pretty filthy place for anyone to be,' Carstairs added, 'let alone British and Americans.'

'Then I can sense my Captain's present feelings, sir. What's to be done now? Can some official complaint be laid?'

'At whose door?' Carstairs asked rhetorically. 'I'm afraid not, Halfhyde. I am the only British authority in the area, and I'm by way of being out of office to all intents and purposes. Likewise the Americans, and the French. We could appeal only to the mandarins, and they're against us to a man.' He ran a hand distractedly through his hair. 'This complicates the situation beyond all measure, I fear ... I take it you'll not leave Chungking with your Captain in Chinese hands?'

Halfhyde gave a grim laugh. 'One way of dealing with this would be to wait for Captain Watkiss to make such a nuisance of himself that the Chinese will hand him back thankfully and with apologies ... but you're right, of course. I shall not leave without him.'

'On the other hand, your orders are for the safety of British subjects, especially the women and children.'

'I know my orders, sir.' Halfhyde turned away, his face set hard, and stalked up and down the kitchen with his revolver still in his hand. What the Consul had said was in fact the simple truth. Watkiss himself might well say that the women and children came first, that the Commodore's orders, which derived from Whitehall, must take priority no matter what happened to the officer in command of the expedition. The decision was entirely Halfhyde's and he would have to stand or fall by it. He was about to utter when another diversion came: a pane of glass smashed, splinters flew about the kitchen area, and a heavy stone, heavy enough to have needed the cast of a sling from the garden perimeter, banged against the opposite wall. Tied to the stone was something wrapped in oiled silk. With long strides Halfhyde reached the stone and picked it up. Inside the silk was a parchment carrying Chinese characters, which he handed to Carstairs. The Consul studied it, his face hardening as he did so. 'It's a threat, Halfhyde,' he said, 'and a nasty one.'

'Of what nature, sir?'

'I'm called upon to surrender ... I'm to throw out all arms first, and then evacuate with everyone in the Consulate.' Carstairs glanced through the window and across the garden: rifles and bayonets were seen atop the perimeter wall, and Chinese faces stared back through the downpour. 'They're ready for us now – there'll be more in front, no doubt.'

'If you refuse to surrender, the attack will be mounted – is that it?'

'Not quite,' Carstairs answered grimly. 'No, the four men in custody – Captain Watkiss and the others – will be publicly executed outside the Consulate. I am given until midnight to decide.'

Halfhyde sent out a hiss of breath. 'Good God! I fail to understand ... why not an attack?'

'They know we're well armed, my dear fellow, and will give a good account of ourselves. We might even hold out – and "face" is vital to the Chinese character.'

'We'd not last long against artillery!'

Carstairs gave a humourless laugh. 'Even they don't trust

their guns, Halfhyde. More "face" would be lost by an explosion in their own ranks. They're strictly for show only, except in the very last resort.'

'I take your point.' Halfhyde remembered the ancient, trundling gun that had been ranged before them on the inward march that morning: that had had an antique look, and had given the impression that parts had dropped off it from time to time over the decades.

Carstairs said, 'I suggest we keep our heads down for a while, Halfhyde, and consider the position carefully.'

*   *   *

It was, it seemed, rain without end, without the smallest respite. Water sheeted down in angry torrents, hissing and drenching. The world, to Mr Beauchamp, was made up entirely of water and water was turning into his most vicious enemy. The terrible floodwaters swept down still from the upper reaches of the river and all Beauchamp's worst anticipations seemed about to take him over and swamp him and his command. There was a most threatening and alarming sound from the fo'c'sle as the darkness descended over China, the sort of sound never heard in the friendlier purlieus of Portsmouth or Devonport or Chatham or even Haulbowline in Ireland where things were never quite as they were in other ports of the naval command in home waters, the Irish being a funny bunch. Funny or not, their harbours didn't make the anchor cable hum angry songs, or scrape viciously in the hawse-pipe, or tug with steely fingers at the Blake slip and the stoppers. Clump, clump, yee-eeee, bang.

Mr Beauchamp shook beneath his oilskins and raised a cold wet hand to finger his jaw. Decisions, decisions . . . really it was no wonder that Captain Watkiss was short-tempered! Command was hard, a thing of much anguish. Mr Beauchamp turned for advice and comfort to his sub-lieutenant, a youth only just out of his midshipman's time.

'It's getting very nasty, Mr Pumphrey.'

'Yes, sir.'

'Very nasty indeed. Do you feel a slight dip, Mr Pumphrey, as though we're down by the head?'

'I don't think so, sir. Would that happen, do you suppose, sir?' The voice was earnest, hopeful of learning something. 'I mean, sir, wouldn't the anchor break ground if there was all that much strain?'

'Yes, I dare say it would, perhaps. Yes. However, we must be watchful. Kindly report at once if you notice any such inclination, in case I should miss it, Mr Pumphrey.'

'Aye, aye, sir.'

Mr Beauchamp, as a lieutenant of more than eight years' seniority and thus a wearer of the extra half stripe of rank, was a demi-god to a sub-lieutenant and was, moreover, a much kinder and less officious person than any lieutenant of more than eight years' seniority so far encountered by Mr Pumphrey, who liked him and wished to be of help. So Pumphrey diligently watched and felt for any dip of the bows even though he did not in fact expect to find a dip, being certain that, instead, the anchor would break clear of the mud as he had suggested. However, in due time he was confounded: Nemesis appeared to have struck after all. The bridge took a slant forward, almost imperceptibly at first, but it soon became quite noticeable as the bows of HMS *Cockroach* began to sink lower in the water, this being evidenced not by the tilt of the bridge alone but also by segments of filth that began to slop over on to the fo'c'sle to be seen clearly in the light from the anchor-lamp on the forestay. stay.

'Sir!'

'Yes, Mr Pumphrey, what is it?'

'Sir, I think we're now being drawn to the anchor, sir!'

They were indeed, and Mr Beauchamp had begun to notice it, but had prayed that it might go away again. Now he could delay no longer. 'Oh, dear me, Mr Pumphrey, pipe at once for the carpenter's mate, if you please. I fear we must take action immediately.'

'Yes, sir. What action, sir?'

Mr Beauchamp fingered his jaw. 'I shall await a report from the carpenter's mate, I think.'

'Aye, aye, sir.' The order was piped for the carpenter's mate and cable party to muster on the fo'c'sle. The men were there quickly and, watched anxiously from the bridge by Mr Beauchamp, the carpenter's mate, a wizened and taciturn petty officer, felt the cable with an expert hand, almost palpating it with a medical man's tenderness.

'Singing, sir,' he reported in a shout.

'I know, Petty Officer Thoms. What do you suggest?'

'Well, sir, the cable's out to its fullest extent and I'm surprised she ain't dragging by now.' The carpenter's mate turned his back upon the bridge and continued diagnosing, peering over the side as though attempting visually to penetrate the murky, rushing Yangtze water. The river was dappled with pits and spouts as the wicked rain drove down. Debris went past at great speed; so fast was the current moving that a small bow wave was giving the anchored *Cockroach* quite a bone in its teeth, and the groaning cable was stretched as taut as a triatic stay. The carpenter's mate scratched his nose, upon which the brim of his sou'wester was pouring a stream of water.

He turned back towards the bridge. 'Captain, sir?'

'Yes?'

'I reckon the anchor's fouled an obstruction, sir.'

'Oh, dear. That's why it's holding fast, I suppose?'

'Yes, sir.'

'We can't shake it free?'

Petty Officer Thoms sucked at his teeth and wondered if some officers ever learned. 'No, sir, not without putting divers down, and we haven't any divers and—'

'Yes, quite. I understand,' Beauchamp called back, his heart in his seaboots. 'What do you suggest, then?'

'Let 'er go, sir. Knock away the pin in the joining-shackle on deck, and then the slip. All right, sir?'

'Just one moment, Petty Officer Thoms, just one moment.' Beauchamp, now sweating like a pig beneath his oilskins, was almost frantic with worry and indecision. Suppose the obstruction was being caused by another mine or bomb, and he blew up Captain Watkiss' own command in succession to his own? But it couldn't be that, surely; all the straining and tugging would have detonated it already. Mr Beauchamp turned to the sub-lieutenant. 'Mr Pumphrey, I really don't know. It seems sensible, even inevitable perhaps . . . but the Rate Book value of an anchor and its cable must be high, I'm sure.'

'Yes, sir, I expect it is, but the angle's increasing all the time, sir.'

'Oh dear, oh dear!' Beauchamp paced the small bridge; the Rate Book value of a gunboat was certainly higher than that of an anchor and cable, but he could scarcely bring himself to believe that the vessel could actually founder. God alone could say what the obstruction might be if it wasn't a mine or bomb: a cable laid along the bottom, a sunken sampan or junk, even some sort of boulder perhaps; not that it made any difference, except that Captain Watkiss would demand a full and detailed report and was never pleased when an officer had to confess he didn't know all the answers. And if he should jettison unnecessarily . . . it didn't bear thinking about. Already he was hovering on the brink of re-arrest, his return to duty was merely temporary, and with another charge hanging over him . . . really, he didn't know what to do. Quite apart from anything else, an anchorless vessel carried a built-in hazard both to itself and other shipping upon the river, being unable to pull up sharply by letting go in an emergency. He might fall back upon *Bee* or *Wasp* or both and then two if not three of Her Majesty's ships of war would become seriously damaged . . .

Mr Beauchamp lurched, and slipped on the wet deck of the bridge. Yes, undoubtedly the vessel was going down further by the head, slowly to be sure, but inexorably. And then a shout from the fo'c'sle urged a speedy decision and Beauchamp took his courage in both hands.

He called down, 'Very well, Petty Officer Thoms, knock away the pin, if you please, and make sure all hands are aft of the slip.'

'Aye, aye, sir.'

'Mr Pumphrey, the yeoman must call up *Bee* and *Wasp*, informing them of what I am doing. Their Commanding Officers must take such independent action as they see fit.'

'Yes, sir.' Pumphrey turned to the yeoman of signals. On the fo'c'sle Thoms bent to tap out the pin in the joining-shackle. He tapped and banged and swore roundly, but nothing happened. Mr Beauchamp called down to him, and he paused in his labours and looked up.

'It's no use, sir, she won't budge. The wood plug's gone, but the pin . . . she's settled in like—'

'Is there no other way, a quicker one perhaps?'

'Well, sir, that pin, she's *never* going to budge. I reckon the

94

only way's to knock away the Blake slip, then go below to the cable locker and knock away the Senhouse slip.'

'Yes, very well then, Petty Officer Thoms. Please ensure that no hands remain in danger on the fo'c'sle when you go below.'

'That I will, sir.' Thoms spat on his hands and lifted his heavy blacksmith's hammer high and brought it down on the mousing-hook of the Blake slip. The hook fell away and the jaws of the slip came off the cable, leaving the vessel held only on the Senhouse slip in the cable locker. Shouting the hands off the fo'c'sle, Thoms led the way below, moving at the double. On the bridge, Beauchamp waited, biting his finger-nails and looking white about the gills. Now that he was committed, he should have felt better but did not. Captain Watkiss, when he came back aboard, would be sure to think of a better way. Soon from below came tremendous hammerings that clanged throughout the gunboat and seemed to make even the bridge reverberate. It was like a devil's orchestra, filled with foreboding. Beauchamp, passing the order to the engine-room to stand by to go ahead, waited tensely for the end of the cable to fly up from the navel-pipe, whip violently across the fo'c'sle plating, and speed down the hawse-pipe, thus leaving the *Cockroach* free upon the waters. Beauchamp gripped the bridge rail, his knuckles showing deathly white. Any moment now; but, instead, the hammering stopped and a moment later the carpenter's mate clumped to the upper deck and called to the bridge.

'Yes, Petty Officer Thoms?'

'Slip's stuck fast, sir, like that bleedin' pin.'

'You can't free it?'

'No, sir.'

'Oh, my God, now what will happen?'

'Likely we'll be arse uppards soon, sir.'

'Can't you do *anything*?'

'Well, sir, if things were normal like we could 'eave in another joining-shackle, an' try another pin, but now that'd only draw us down further, see, an' too far for safety. An' we've paid out so much cable, the shackle on deck's the only one left inboard. I'll just carry on 'ammering, sir.' Petty Officer Thoms vanished below once again, and Mr Beauchamp uttered prayers. He watched as river water lapped right over the stem; he watched as the lip of the hawse-pipe disappeared. The hammering was resumed. Mr Beauchamp, looking out towards the wharf where one or two storm lanterns flickered on the tops of poles to cast a dim and yellow light, saw a strange sight: Chungking appeared to be sinking below his own level, and water was streaming deep across the wharf and into the streets. From astern of *Cockroach* came a prolonged blast upon a steam siren, causing Mr Beauchamp to jump a mile, then another from a little further off: *Bee* and *Wasp* were under way while he, the acting Senior Officer God help him, was stuck fast like a dog tied to a stake.

*   *   *

For some time now the Chinese, the fellow prisoners of the British and Americans in the town gaol, had been restive and rude. They had continued to manifest hate for the non-yellow races by calling comments and were now rattling the bars of their cages and grimacing like monkeys. The comment was lost upon all but Bodmin, but its intent was clear enough and the constant rattling made Captain Watkiss' head ache intolerably. However, he set his teeth and endured it: the wretched dagoes would not be amenable to orders and he did not propose to make himself look foolish by issuing any. But his fury increased and, bottled up, threatened to suffocate him. By God, once he was free . . . but would he ever be? Would he ever again set foot upon a bridge? The noise was driving him insane and he shook all over like a tubby castanet . . . the blasted guards were taking no notice whatever and Bloementhal and Hackenticker were still throwing, or playing or whatever the jargon might be, their interminable craps, an appallingly pointless pastime. The Americans' impassiveness and ability to disregard the dagoes' din irritated Captain Watkiss immensely, and his mood grew worse. After a while he had tried turning his back upon the crap players and stuffing his fingers into his ears against the rattling of bars, but his arms had begun to ache badly and he had withdrawn his fingers. By now he had grown used to the dreadful Chinese smell and didn't really notice it much except now and again when a worse-than-usual waft struck him and he retched. Then, over the noise, rapid conversation came from a number of gaolers who suddenly entered the cage passage to speak to the sentry; and Watkiss noticed that Bodmin was pricking up his ears.

'What is it, Mr Bodmin? What are they talking about?'

'There be flood, zur.'

'I'm not surprised. Is the gaol threatened?'

'I believe it be, zur, yes.'

'Good! The water will clean it.'

'Aye, zur, and drown us more'n likely, zur.'

'Oh, nonsense.'

''Tisn't nonsense, zur, it's 'appened afore now.'

'And the prisoners?'

'Left where they was, zur, to drown.'

'Oh. Were they murderers, awaiting the death penalty in any case?'

'Not all on 'em, zur, no, but they Chinks, they execute all manner o' criminals, not just murderers, zur.'

'Well, Mr Bodmin, they'll rescue us you may be sure, since we're not criminals but prisoners of war for whom the blasted dagoes must have a use.'

'I 'ope you be right, zur.'

'I am. Admiral Hackenticker, do you not agree?'

'That depends, Captain.'

'Oh? On what, may I ask?'

'Whose hands we're in.'

'As I've said before, my dear sir, we must be in official hands since we're in the official town gaol—'

'That doesn't have to signify, you know—'

'No, I *don't* know,' Captain Watkiss interrupted in a temper, 'and it *does* signify, that's fact, I said it. Why look upon the black side?' He averted his face; both the Americans were looking sour, presumably because they knew very well he was right. It was the British way not to accept defeat or even to consider it, which was why the British had never been beaten in the field, except by – oh yes, the Americans, but that didn't count, it hadn't been a real war and the British had shown a natural and proper reticence when fighting colonists who, after all, were at that time basically British themselves. Had they extended themselves, King George's men would have had no difficulty in winning, no difficulty at all ... Captain Watkiss' thoughts came to a sudden end when a semi-naked Chinese strode

97

into the passage carrying an immense sword such as had been flourished during the march upon the Consulate earlier: an executioner's sword, and the idea, obviously, was to terrify. Captain Watkiss refused to be impressed, but made enquiries all the same.

'Mr Bodmin, what is this person's function?'

Bodmin was looking decidedly scared. He said, ''E be Shen Yun-wu, zur, the official executioner like.'

'*Official?*'

'Ar, zur.'

'Oh. Well, as I said to Admiral Hackenticker, we should not look upon the black side. Keep a stiff upper lip, my dear Bodmin. Remember we're British.' He gave the Americans a long, meaningful stare: Bloementhal was looking pretty sick, and very white, but all diplomats were yellow-bellies. A number of Chinese, gabbling away, advanced upon the door of the cage. 'What are they saying, Mr Bodmin?'

'Zur, they do 'int at trouble.'

'Kindly be precise, Mr Bodmin, I am not a young woman faced with rape, I can withstand the facts.'

'Ar, zur.' There was a tremble in the aged boatswain's voice. 'We be goin' to be took to the Consulate, zur, or rather outside it like...'

'Well, come on, man, come on! For what purpose? Why the Consulate?'

'I don't rightly know that, zur, but I think they Chinks be goin' to cut arf our 'eads, zur.'

*   *   *

Halfhyde stood by the window, broodingly. The onset of night had brought no stratagem to his mind. Morale inside the Consulate was by now low. To have broken out would still have been Halfhyde's wish, but to do so would have been to sign the death warrants of the four men held in the gaol, and that he was not prepared to risk; there had to be a different approach and sometimes procrastination paid off, allowing time for passions to cool and threats to be seen as dangerous to those who uttered them. To execute persons of importance must lead to certain retribution, and perhaps the Chinese could be made to see this before it was too late. Halfhyde turned from the window; outside the floodwater was deep, and appeared to be deepening more, but the mob had gathered again nevertheless, in sampans and anything else that floated, seeming to sense that matters were about to come to a head. Halfhyde, listening to the unlovely sounds from that mob, glanced for the hundredth time at the clock on the wall: eleven thirty-two, just under half an hour to go. Carstairs was sitting at his desk, gloomily drinking a glass of brandy. The Reverend Marchwood Erskine had already lowered the level of his John Haig and lay slumped in an easy chair with his black-trousered legs thrust out. A vice-consul was putting the finishing touches to the collection of all official documents and correspondence and the removal of it to the incinerator in the kitchen quarters. Other staff came and went, bringing reports of readiness to Carstairs, who received them with preoccupied nods of his head. In the main the women were bearing up well; there had been some hysterics, mostly from the French contingent, but these had been calmed with brandy. Some of the children were weepy, but the prevalent feeling among them was excitement; they knew nothing of the threat of public execution – nor indeed did any of the sheltering community. Carstairs had thought that best, and Halfhyde had agreed.

At eleven forty Lord Edward came into the room, having made rounds.

'All's well, sir.'

'Thank you, Mr Cole. What's the feeling now?'

'They're being awfully brave, sir, awfully strong. I'm sure we could make a fight of it, sir.'

'Mr Carstairs thinks otherwise.

'Oh, well, sir, orders are orders.' Lord Edward lowered his voice and spoke confidentially into Halfhyde's ear. 'Does Mr Carstairs mean to surrender, sir, d'you think?'

'Events will shape themselves, Mr Cole. There'll be no surrender without guarantees of safety for the people who took shelter here.'

'Yes, quite, sir.' Cole paused. 'Guarantees, sir. Can we accept the word of the Chinese? I mean—'

'Yes, Mr Cole, I know very well what you mean, and I fear the answer must be no.'

'It'd be awfully rotten to leave the women and children in the lurch, sir.'

'I know. That makes the question of surrender highly doubtful.'

'In which case the Captain and the others will die, sir.'

'Yes.'

'That's rotten too,' Cole said glumly. 'Simply rotten.'

'Many things are rotten in this world, Mr Cole, and you are beginning to learn the strains of command and of the need to make life and death decisions, sometimes instantly.' Halfhyde paused, looking Cole in the eye. 'Mark the word *instantly*, Mr Cole!'

Cole frowned and lifted an eyebrow quizzically, then nodded. 'I believe I see what you're driving at, sir. You think we may have a sudden opportunity of turning the tables on the Chinese?'

'I hope, that's all! Stranger things have come to pass before now, and you may be sure I shall be ready to take full advantage of any shift—' Halfhyde broke off as the mob sounds came louder through the rain. He strode back quickly to the window and looked down. The mob was really howling now, a sound of bitter and intense hate and lust for blood and killing, and in a moment Halfhyde saw why: a weird boat with an upthrust dragon's head for a prow was approaching under the impulse of oarsmen, and in the light from the many storm lanterns rigged along its length and in the hands of the boat-borne mob, he saw the hostages. They were heavily guarded and behind them stood the massive, naked-chested figure of the official executioner, his hands resting upon the hilt of his great curved sword whose tip pricked into the deck planking of the prison boat.

NINE

There had been much indignity in the act of removal from the gaol: into the mind of Captain Watkiss had come a vaguely remembered term used by the law – General Gaol Delivery, and that just about summed it up even if in reverse. They were delivered, like sides of beef or common convicts, into the boat waiting upon the flood-waters, and only just in time. Although the building was raised well off the ground in order to cope so far as possible with the vagaries of the Yangtze, it reposed not upon a hill but on low ground, and the water had already reached the level of the doorway and was slopping in. A number of Chinese officials were already making off in other boats, the rats deserting the sinking ship and leaving the remaining prisoners to their fate. For a happy moment Captain Watkiss managed to convince himself that his rank was responsible for rescue from drowning and all was well after all, but the moment, bearing in mind the presence of the executioner and his sword, did not last long. Watkiss instructed Bodmin to inform the guards that he did not propose to embark in the boat, and Bodmin did so, but Watkiss was at once seized and lifted bodily and conveyed, with legs kicking helplessly, through a slop of dirty water to the exit and dropped to the bottom-boards. As they cruised subsequently through the streets, cries and yells came down from windows on either side and filth was hurled at the foreign devils.

'What abominable people, Mr Bodmin.'

'Not *all* on 'em, zur.'

'I suppose,' Watkiss said disparagingly, 'you refer to whatever her name is, your wife.' Mrs Bodmin would, he suspected, in fact follow her native Chinese custom and put her surname first, making her Bodmin Ling-Fung or whatever. 'I don't know how you could bring yourself to marry a Chinee, frankly! Did you obtain your commanding officer's consent at the time?'

' 'Twere after I retired like, zur.'

'Then your senior officer in Chinese Customs?'

Bodmin shook his head and looked obstinate, as though he had had enough of Captain Watkiss by now. 'No, zur, I'd 'ad years an' years o' asking permission about all manner o' things in the Navy, zur, so I didn't ask no more I didn't.' He paused, then went on solemnly as though making a death-bed confession, 'As a matter o' fact, zur, she bain't be my *wife*, not strictly speaking like, zur.'

'What?'

'We do co-'abit, zur, that be all.'

'Goodness gracious!'

'I know 'tain't right, zur, in the sight o' the Lord, and I do be very sorry.'

'She's not Mrs Bodmin at all, then? Not a British subject?'

'On'y by custom like, zur, by common law as they do say—'

'But your principles, man!' Watkiss was outraged; Bodmin had told him, as he had told Beauchamp, of his high moral tone, the one that permitted no drink or foul language. 'I must say I'm most surprised.'

'Ar, zur, I confess my wickedness now before the Lord, zur, and ask His mercy upon an 'umble sinner like, but I do be yuman, zur.'

'At your age, Bodmin?'

'It be the last thing that dies in a man, zur.'

Watkiss made no response to that; there was a great deal of truth in it, in fact, as he was himself aware. Naval service, the service of Her Majesty, was hard in more ways than one and Captain Watkiss, in Her Majesty's interests, had passed many deprived years at a stretch. But – and here was one of the many differences between the wardroom and the lower deck or even the warrant officers' mess – he had never fallen so low as to seek solace with dagoes. West Africa, the East Indies, South America, Bermuda, Malta, Gibraltar, the Red Sea, India: all these places and no hanky-panky. If the Pope could do it, then so could a Post Captain of the Royal Navy. It followed that a mere boatswain could too; Watkiss felt a keen sense of disappointment in Bodmin who had let the side down. Yet every cloud had a silver lining and his brooding on Bodmin's sins and weaknesses had the effect of occupying his mind during his journey to the exclusion of the menacing manifestations of the Chinese *en route*; and he was surprised when the rowers of the dragon-prowed boat held water with their oars. The way came off and they drifted below the windows of the British Consulate.

Bodmin spoke again, and lifted an arm. 'There be parson, zur.'

'What?'

'There be parson, zur. If it be possible, zur, I'd like a word with parson so as—'

'Oh, bugger the parson, Mr Bodmin, I've just seen Mr Halfhyde.' Standing up dangerously in the boat, Watkiss raised his voice and called loudly, *'Mr Halfhyde, your Captain is here!'*

*   *   *

Two arms had come swiftly around Watkiss and he had been plumped back upon his thwart and a dagger thrust against the back of his neck: all this Halfhyde saw from the Consulate window. Beside him the missionary said, 'I fear they have not long upon this earth, poor fellows, unless we concede defeat.'

'We're not done for yet, Mr Erskine.' An idea of a sort struck Halfhyde. 'Could you not intercede?'

Erskine looked surprised. 'With heathens, my dear sir?'

'Presumably some have been converted by your efforts.'

'Not, I fear, in Chungking itself. Besides, it's been my experience that when mob passions become aroused, then primaeval man takes over—'

'And Christ is forgotten?'

Erskine nodded. 'In the case of the recently converted, yes. They revert to earlier instincts and persuasions.'

'Yet as a man of God you may carry weight even in the eyes of those who worship Buddha ... may you not?'

'No,' the clergyman answered crossly. 'I think you fail to understand. God is poles apart from Buddha. God brings hope for the spirit, the creed of Buddhism is one of hopelessness since

Nirvana is virtually unattainable except through utter perfection. God, you see, is forgiveness – Buddha is not.'

'Yet I've heard it said that life is important to those who follow Buddha, Mr Erskine. Even the life of an insect is precious – to kill the humblest creature is accounted murder. Is there not some way through to their hearts?'

Erskine said no, there was not. Thoughts of Buddha had not noticeably prevented any killing in China's past and there was no reason why they should do so now. Erskine turned from the window and approached his black bag, which was beside the easy chair he had vacated; an association of ideas reminded Halfhyde that Buddha had also proscribed inebriation, but that had not prevented the fermentation of rice by the godless Chinese ... Buddha was perhaps out.

Watching again from the window and awaiting the Chinese move, Halfhyde saw the approach of another boat, a boat whose crew pushed arrogantly through the packed sampans and took no notice of the wails of protest from their occupants as the sampans rocked and banged together. It was an extraordinary sight and a Germanic one: the rowers wore the uniforms of the Empress-Dowager, all very official, but the passengers were heavily-armed men of the Uhlan Lancers and in their midst sat Count Hermann von Furstenberg, large, smug, and military, for all the world as though he were issuing from the royal palace of his Kaiser in distant Berlin to progress in state down the Under den Linden to the triumphal arch of the Brandenburg Gate. There was even a fanfare of trumpets as von Furstenberg barged alongside the boatload of gaol prisoners. Disregarding these, the German bellowed towards the Consulate in English.

'I wish words with the British Consul.'

Called by Halfhyde as the boat came into view, Carstairs was already at the window. He called back, 'Carstairs here. What do you want, Count von Furstenberg?'

'Speech.' The German lifted an arm and pointed towards a Chinese in a sampan floating about behind the prisoners' craft. 'The man you see is Lim Puk-Fo – he leads the mob. It must be obvious to you that the British and Americans will be executed if you do not surrender, is this not so?'

'Yes,' Carstairs called back. 'How do you know this?'

'I have sources, Herr Carstairs. Now I am going to enter your Consulate, please.' He gave an order to his Chinese rowers and was propelled closer to the main entrance; along with the kitchen quarters, the steps were now under water. Above, Carstairs turned to Halfhyde.

'He'd better come in, I think, though God knows what he's up to!'

'He may be on our side, sir.'

'Perhaps, but if so, why?'

Halfhyde shrugged. Carstairs went down to the ground floor, where flood-water sogged greasily, to meet von Furstenberg. Halfhyde remained at the window, watching. He saw the German leave the boat, saw the movement of the Chinese craft towards the entrance to the Consulate ... there was an air of unease, of suspicion, amongst them. Lim Puk-Fo conferred with his henchmen. The British and American prisoners were watching closely and all of them, even Watkiss, were silent. The mob was mainly silent too, though there was a background murmur of discontent, as though the delaying of the execution was unwelcome. Over all, the rain teemed down still, the cascade visible in the light from the many lanterns. Water poured down the motionless bare body of the executioner, standing immediately behind Captain Watkiss with his hands still resting on his sword-hilt.

Carstairs came back with von Furstenberg and an escort of two Uhlans. He introduced Halfhyde and his vice-consul; von Furstenberg clicked his heels and bowed his head. 'Lieutenant Halfhyde of the British Navy – I have heard of you. I am well acquainted with Vice-Admiral von Merkatz, who is no friend of yours!'

'Indeed, sir.' Halfhyde had twice outwitted Paulus von Merkatz, once in West African waters and again in South America, and could well understand the lack of friendship. 'Perhaps his unfortunate experiences may serve to underline the fact that Britain, not Germany, tends to rule the waves!' He swept a hand towards the window. 'Waves of a kind now lap our doors, Count von Furstenberg, and—'

'Yet you are helpless, Lieutenant Halfhyde, in the face of the mob.'

'That will—'

'Pray be silent, Lieutenant Halfhyde.' The German turned his back and addressed the Consul. 'Herr Carstairs, I come with an offer of help, and I come because my instructions have been ignored by the Chinese under the man Lim Puk-Fo. I did not intend that prisoners should be taken. All naval persons were to be allowed to board the British gunboats, and sail away in peace and safety. And I intended no interference with your Consulate.' He looked smug. 'My Kaiser is a humane man, and he does not wish war.'

'No one wishes that, Count von Furstenberg.'

The German smiled. 'Except Lim Puk-Fo. There is much danger from his direction. This danger I shall deal with. You see, I am the good friend of the British Empire!'

'One moment, if you please.' Hearing the voice, Halfhyde turned. The Reverend Marchwood Erskine, drunk though speaking without slur and walking with extreme care, approached Count von Furstenberg and tapped him on the chest. 'You are a scoundrel, sir—'

'Thank you, Mr Erskine, kindly return to your black bag and keep silent.' Halfhyde took the clergyman's arm in a tight grip and dragged him away protesting: this was scarcely the moment to look gift horses, however intrigue-ridden, too closely in the mouth; that could come later. Halfhyde dumped Erskine back in the easy chair and told him in a hard whisper that if he emerged again he would be reported to the Foreign Office and the American State Department. Then he went back towards Carstairs and von Furstenberg. The German said that he wished to incur no blame from Kaiser Wilhelm for disturbing the amicable state of British and German relations. He repeated that his orders to the Chinese had been misinterpreted and he was here now to wipe the slate clean; and his suggestions to this end were practical enough.

'To wipe it clean I shall protect your Captain Watkiss, and Rear Admiral Hackenticker of the so-great United States Navy also,' he announced.

'How?' Carstairs asked.

'I shall speak to Lim Puk-Fo through an interpreter among my Chinese crew. I shall tell Lim Puk-Fo that the dragon-headed boat is to be allowed to move alongside the Consulate, and the British and Americans allowed to enter freely. If this is not done, then my Uhlans will open fire and kill first Lim Puk-Fo. Then many others.'

'And you, afterwards?'

'I have the support of the Empress-Dowager, and I shall remain in the Consulate with your permission until loyal soldiers reach Chungking from Peking.'

Carstairs said, 'I have no communication left, Count. My cable links have been cut.'

The German waved a hand. 'It is of no consequence. Already soldiers are on their way and it is a question of time only. You accept my assistance, Herr Carstairs?'

'Very gratefully,' Carstairs answered, with a glance at Halfhyde, who nodded his agreement. 'But perhaps you'd indicate what you wish in return?'

Von Furstenberg spread his hands. 'But nothing, nothing! Only the wiping of the slate, Herr Carstairs, that is all, believe me. Germany is the good, good friend of Britain and Queen Victoria, my Kaiser's most beloved and revered grandmother!'

Halfhyde raised an eyebrow. 'A family matter, Count von Furstenberg?'

'Yes, yes! A family matter, yes!' Von Furstenberg rubbed his hands together and smiled a lot. 'That is good, a family matter, it so much sums up my feelings and reasons!' He was, Halfhyde thought, as wily and dishonest as any Borgia of old, but his offer of present help seemed genuine enough.

*　　　*　　　*

'Admiral Hackenticker, kindly, if you please, allow me room to move.'

'Sorry, Captain.' Hackenticker shifted a little.

'I wish my shoulder-straps to be *seen*! I have not been acknowledged by Halfhyde, and it's important my rank is seen from the Consulate, you understand.' Captain Watkiss shifted his right shoulder so that a lantern struck brilliant gold from his four Post Captain's stripes. 'That German.'

'What about him?'

'I don't trust him. Now he's gone inside the Consulate he'll be telling all manner of blasted lies, won't he, to justify putting us in that wretched prison?'

107

'I don't see what he'd expect to gain from that. It's your Consulate, Captain, when all's said and done—'

'Yes, yes, yes – don't let us waste time in argument. None of these buggers appears to speak English, so I feel free to say this, Admiral: I propose to make a dash for it shortly.'

'Don't you mean a plunge, Captain?'

'Yes, exactly, a plunge, you have it! A fast swim for the Consulate. You'll be with me?'

Hackenticker nodded. 'Certainly. I was about to suggest the same thing.'

'Really. Mr Bloementhal?'

Bloementhal nodded, but without enthusiasm, evidently fearing death *en route*.

'Mr Bodmin, you are a little elderly, but depend upon it, I shall not leave you behind. Mr Bloementhal is the youngest of us all, and will assist you, and that is an order, Mr Bloementhal.'

'Look, I don't happen to be a strong swimmer, and anyway I—'

'Please don't argue, Mr Bloementhal, I detest argument, and if you are about to say you come under Admiral Hackenticker's orders, then I say you don't, since you boarded my ship off Woosung, thus placing yourself under the orders of the Royal Navy. Now then: when I'm ready I shall give the word, and the moment I do so all hands will plunge in and swim. I admit the danger, but we are men not mice. Speed's the thing – speed and the element of surprise. And good luck to you all.'

Captain Watkiss sat back, shifting his shoulder again into the best advantage of the light as the lantern was moved a little. His head was back and his jaw out-thrust, but he gave an involuntary shiver as his eye caught the light gleaming on the execution sword. He could imagine the horror as that blade was lifted, and flashed through the air with the speed of light in powerful, muscle-rippled arms to detach his head from his body. He had read somewhere that executed heads had been known to live on for a brief while in some cases – that was historical fact, he believed, some story of the French Revolution when the accursed proletariat, after guillotining one of their victims had smacked the cheeks of the severed head, which then registered anger and humiliation. In case of accidents, Captain Watkiss composed his mind not to register fear in death, that would never do. He was British, a naval officer, and the blasted dagoes must see no flinching. It would also be a good example to the Americans. If his face registered anything, it must be devotion to duty and loyalty to the Queen.

'Now,' said Captain Watkiss loudly, and at once tipped himself face first over the side into the smelly flood. Behind him leaped Bodmin, who sank like a stone.

* * *

'Sir, sir!'

Cole shouted from the window, and Halfhyde went towards him. 'What is it, Mr Cole?'

'The Captain's gone, sir!'

'Executed?'

'I don't know, sir! I saw him one moment, and the next he was gone.'

Halfhyde swore and stared down. Then he saw the kerfuffle in the water, the movement of a man swimming in ungainly fashion. At the same time he saw Chinese hands seizing Hack-enticker and Bloementhal, who had failed to jump from the boat in time, and the official executioner bringing up his sword. Calling for von Furstenberg's Uhlans to open fire immediately, he ran down the stairs for the main entrance and plunged into the flood-water. As he swam fast towards the dragon prow, the German rifles opened above his head, volley after volley smashing into the Chinese. Pandemonium broke out. There were yells and cries and the sampans tried to press back and away from the rifle-fire, and many were upset. As Halfhyde reached the floundering Watkiss and seized him by the neck-band of his white tunic, a muddy figure rose from the depths and staggered about with his face above the water-level: Mr Bodmin, on tip-toe. The water was not especially deep, but was negotiated the faster by swimming. Halfhyde, drawing his Captain back towards the Consulate entrance, saw that the executioner was lying face down across the gunwale of the dragon-prowed boat and Rear Admiral Hackenticker was laying about himself energetically with the execution sword, the Chinese keeping well outside range of the flashing blade. Halfhyde called to him

109

to jump in and swim while he had the chance, but the American took no notice: he seemed to be enjoying himself and to hell with diplomacy. Meanwhile there was a considerable jam of sampans all trying to escape the German fire, and soon the Chinese were seen in many cases to be abandoning ship and swimming for it, a mode of escape which had the twin advantages of more speed and a low profile against the German rifle-sights.

Reaching the Consulate steps, Halfhyde dragged Captain Watkiss clear of the filthy water and handed him over to Cole. Then he turned his attention back to the busy figure of Rear Admiral Hackenticker, who in fact seemed to be tiring now. He called out again.

'Admiral Hackenticker, I believe you've made your point now!'

Hackenticker flailed on, but suffered a misfortune: his aching arms had caused the sword to droop a little, and on the next flail the tip took the dragon's head and jarred its wielder so severely that the weapon was wrenched from his grip. It went over the side.

'Heck!'

'I suggest you leave it, sir!' Halfhyde called.

'I guess you're right, Lieutenant. I'll jump and join you.' The Rear Admiral poised himself on the gunwale, but was held back by another shout from Halfhyde.

'If you'll stay where you are, sir, I'll join you rather than you join me—'

'Why? What's the idea, Lieutenant?'

'We need a fleet, and you and I can ensure that we have one.' Without waiting for an answer, Halfhyde plunged back into the flood and swam strongly towards Hackenticker. Still the German fire was being maintained and the Chinese were being kept nicely at arms' length; their return fire was wild, although directed mainly at the Consulate windows. Even so, when Halfhyde reached the boat where Hackenticker stood four square like Custer's Last Stand, and heaved himself over the gunwale, shots sang uncomfortably close to his head.

'Well?' Hackenticker asked.

'Let us get under way, sir, and round up as many of the empty sampans as we can—'

'To take us to your flotilla, Lieutenant?'

'Yes—'

'Good idea!' Hackenticker seized one of the oars that lay slack in the crutches, and sank down upon a thwart. Halfhyde followed suit. As the oars took the water and both men bent their backs to it, the dragon-prowed vessel moved towards the log-jam of sampans, but somewhat sluggishly. More speed was necessary. 'Bodies, sir,' Halfhyde said to Hackenticker, and gestured at the Chinese lying dead on the bottom-boards. The oars were shipped, and the bodies were lifted and dumped over the side. When all but one had been disposed of Halfhyde was surprised to find Bloementhal, covered with blood. The blood turned out to be Chinese; Bloementhal appeared totally unhurt, though angry. He said, 'Whoever opened fire will have a lot to answer for. I suppose you two gentlemen realize that?'

Hackenticker said belligerently, 'You and your God-damn diplomacy!'

'Diplomacy's vital, Admiral, very vital.'

'We should have talked our way out from under that executioner's sword?'

Bloementhal said, 'We should have *tried* at least. Killing doesn't help.'

'Rowing does,' Hackenticker said unkindly. He lifted a third oar and jabbed the blade into Bloementhal's stomach. 'Just you pull your weight on that, Mr Bloementhal, and row like the Secretary of State's waiting—' He broke off as a tremendous roar was heard and a sudden demoniac explosion came from behind the Consulate to spread a red light like that of some hellish inferno over the whole area, making everything stand starkly out for a brief moment until the light departed to leave a great blackness: even the storm lanterns on the boat had been blown clear away in a tremendous rush of air that almost sent the rowers themselves toppling. At the same time there was an eerie whistle overhead and as they heard this the upper storey of the Consulate seemed to take fire. Roofing materials and chunks of masonry splashed into the water all around.

Halfhyde caught Hackenticker's eye.

'They're throwing in the big battalions, I fancy, sir. The artillery!' He plunged his oar into the water. 'We may not have long now.'

TEN

There was now nowhere to dry Captain Watkiss; the fires were out in the flooded kitchens, and he had perforce to suffer. 'I shall take a chill,' he announced pathetically. 'I suppose it's too much to expect the services of a leech, Carstairs?'

'There are Chinese medical men in the town – if they were available – who practise acupuncture, Captain.'

'Oh, no, no,' Watkiss said, sounding disagreeable. 'I refuse to be stuck with quills like a blasted porcupine.' He gave a realistic shiver. 'I shall have to put up with it, that's all, Carstairs, my dear fellow.'

Carstairs said, 'I doubt if you'll come to harm. As a sailor you must be used to wet clothing.'

'That's quite different. Seawater's salt, and it harms no one. Where's that Customs man, Bodmin?'

'I be 'ere, zur.'

'Oh, for God's sake ... however, I'm glad you're safe, Bodmin. What about your ... er, wife?'

'Well, zur, I 'ope she'll be all right, and I fancy she ought to be, zur, what with all them relatives like—'

'Yes, yes, but what I'm getting at is this: we have reached the Consulate in accordance with my orders, and now it's my duty to escort all personnel to my flotilla.' Watkiss paused. 'Are you listening, Carstairs?'

'Yes, I am—'

'Good, you didn't appear to be paying attention to me, but since you are, I shall go on. Boats must be commandeered since we can scarcely march through the flood – perhaps you'll be good enough to see to that at once—'

'Admiral Hackenticker and Halfhyde are already doing so,' Carstairs interrupted.

'Oh, are they? I'm glad.' Watkiss swung back to Mr Bodmin. 'That is why I enquired about your ... er, wife. I take it you'll accompany me to Shanghai. You'll not be popular with the dagoes after this, I suppose you realize that?'

'Ar, zur, but this be 'ome now, zur—'

'Oh, nonsense, Chungking can't possibly be home, home's England, and I shall expect you to be sensible and come out with my flotilla for your own good. There's still the question of your—'

'Ar, zur. The old woman, zur. I'll go an' get 'er, zur. Might be better, like you said, zur, and they Chinks, they might take it out on 'er like, so—'

'Do you know where to find her, Bodmin?'

'I reckon I do, zur.'

'But all those relatives!'

'Some on 'em she don't like, zur. I'll find her, zur.'

Watkiss nodded. 'Be quick, then. I shall give you half an hour from now. And positively none of her kin. What about your own person? Will you not be attacked?'

'No, zur. I'll be safe for long enough ... I got along well with they Chinks for many a year, and they'll not turn all that fast, zur.'

'I hope you're right. Off you go.' Watkiss turned his back on the former boatswain. 'Where's Lord Edward? Oh, there you are.'

'Yes, sir.' Lord Edward beamed politely, and came to attention.

'Fall in all hands, Lord Edward, women and children included. Have them ready to embark in the boats when Mr Halfhyde and that American ... what exactly *are* they doing, Carstairs?'

The Consul was about to reply when the great shattering roar that had interrupted Rear Admiral Hackenticker caused Carstairs to miss a heart-beat. The building shook like a rat in the mouth of a terrier, and everywhere things fell to the floors. Red light flickered across the windows and in that bright light Hackenticker and Halfhyde were momentarily seen urging the dragon-headed Chinese boat across the flood towards the massed, deserted sampans. Captain Watkiss, his balance interfered with by the enormous blast and the vibration, spun like a top and then collapsed on the floor.

Lord Edward bent and heaved his Captain back to his feet. 'Upsadaisy, sir!' he said cheerfully.

'Don't be impertinent.' Watkiss breathed deeply. He heard crashes and splashes as shattered masonry fell from overhead. Carstairs had vanished with his vice-consul, and Bodmin too had gone, presumably in search of his paramour as ordered. Apart from Lord Edward Cole, only Watkiss and the clergyman remained, the latter once again lying back in the easy chair with his legs stuck out and an empty bottle of John Haig by his side.

'You there!' Watkiss called sharply. 'Can you not lend a hand?'

There was no answer. 'Who and what is he, Lord Edward?' Watkiss demanded.

Lord Edward explained.

'Oh, I see, a missionary.' Watkiss sniffed. 'All missionaries are a blasted nuisance, they give the natives ideas. Wherever you find missionaries, you find incipient rebellion. I can't stand parsons of *any* kind. I hope that damn gun doesn't go off again. Go and get everyone mustered, if you please, and we'll make our getaway before it does.'

'Yes, sir. Er ... what about Mr Bodmin, sir?'

'He must take his chance, Lord Edward. I can't put women and children in jeopardy because of an old fool who fails to appreciate his age.'

Twice more the Chinese artillery thundered and the Consulate seemed in imminent danger of disintegrating. But with the second blast the gun was put out of action, having done what Captain Watkiss had fancied earlier it might do – blown itself to fragments, along with many Chinese, when its charge exploded in the muzzle. For a moment all hell was let loose and fragments of gun-metal embedded themselves in the broken Consulate walls or were projected through the gaps that had previously been windows. A sliver of jagged metal cut a neat line across the shoulders of Captain Watkiss' once-white tunic. Watkiss gasped and staggered, felt behind himself, and then put on a noble expression as Lord Edward hastened solicitously to his side.

'Are you all right, sir?'

'Yes, yes, I think I am. In any case I shall continue and not cause a fuss. Is there much blood?'

'I can't see any at all, sir.'

'None?' Watkiss' face reddened dangerously. 'Oh, nonsense, there must be!'

'Just a very little, sir,' Lord Edward, bred to tact, said.

'Ah! Well, I must endure.'

'Yes, sir. When we get back aboard, sir, the po bosun—'

'Sick berth attendant.'

'Yes, sir. He—'

'Yes, yes, yes, it's gallant enough of you to be so concerned, Lord Edward my dear fellow, but I'm not too seriously wounded, and I shall carry on with the action. Thank God we shall not have to endure more heavy gunfire. Now, get everyone mustered at once, Lord Edward.'

'Aye, aye, sir.' Lord Edward hastened away while Captain Watkiss followed more slowly down to the Consulate entrance. Cold and fearful, the civilians assembled under the sheepdog efforts of Lord Edward assisted by a vice-consul who had once been attached to a volunteer battalion of infantry of the line. As they all waited at the top of the flood-washed steps, Hackenticker and Halfhyde were seen advancing towards them with a string of sampans tied head to tail behind the dragon-prowed boat with an assortment of makeshift lashings found from socks, boot-laces, braces, handkerchiefs, long pants and strips torn from Halfhyde's white uniform jacket. Captain Watkiss despatched Lord Edward with a band of volunteers from the Consulate staff to help the progress of the strange rescue fleet by swimming and pushing. At the entrance the Reverend Marchwood Erskine sat in a puddle with his head in his hands and his black bag by his side. Watkiss, outraged, stirred at him with a foot.

'How dare you!' Watkiss said indignantly. 'Sitting about doing nothing!'

Erskine looked up. 'Who are you?' he asked.

'I am Captain Watkiss of the Royal Navy and you are as drunk as a fiddler's bitch. Had I not more respect for your cloth than you appear to have yourself, damme if I wouldn't kick your backside into the damn water and leave you to the dagoes. What an example! *Missionaries* ... you're all tarred with the same brush.'

'I am not *drunk*, I am—'

'Oh, balls and bang me arse, don't argue with me. You are drunk, and that's fact, I said it.' Watkiss turned away distastefully and stood out in the downpour to await the berthing alongside of his sampan fleet. He expected some onslaught from the Chinese, who assuredly would not let them go without further attempts at restraint, but so far at any rate there was no more manifestation from the enemy, for which Watkiss gave heartfelt thanks to God. His fleet would be at some distinct disadvantage in any attack. A moment later he heard heavy sounds behind him, a clump of boots and a loud, hectoring voice shouting out monotonously in what Watkiss took to be German, and he remembered that Carstairs had said something about Count von Furstenberg being present and on their side, an unlikely thing, surely.

He turned.

A posse of dismounted Hun cavalrymen was marching out from the hall with a sergeant shouting the step. In rear was von Furstenberg himself. The men were halted just inside the doorway and stood at ease; von Furstenberg then advanced upon Captain Watkiss, halted, clicked his heels and dipped his head. Just like a blasted Hun, Watkiss thought angrily, but of course the fellow *was* a Hun....

'Where have you been skulking, may I ask?' Watkiss demanded.

'Skulking? I do not understand, Captain?'

'Her Majesty's Consul told me you were present, but I failed to find you. I assume you to have been skulking with your men where you were safe from the dago artillery – just like Huns.'

'I think you are rude, Captain—'

'So do I, and I meant to be,' Watkiss broke in energetically. 'You had the damned effrontery to have me arrested and thrown into that stinking gaol—'

'A misunderstanding, Captain, I assure you—'

'Misunderstanding my left tit. You are a blasted scoundrel. I shall seek your arrest the moment I reach Hong Kong.'

'But I am sorry—'

'Oh, nonsense, Huns are never sorry for anything—'

'And I offer redress by way—'

'Hold your tongue, my dear sir.'

'I shall accompany you, Captain, all of my men spread out among the sampans to help in your defence, with carbines and sabres!'

'You ... oh. Ah. Well, you have a point, perhaps. Yes, I accept your offer and indeed I would expect no less. You will remember, of course, that you're under my command, Count von Furstenberg, and you and your men will obey my orders immediately and without question.'

'But there is an Admiral, an American—'

'Exactly. As you say, an American. I am British.' Watkiss turned away to find his fleet approaching the Consulate entrance, rather more rapidly now. He bounced along the wide frontage, shouting berthing orders like a piermaster at Clacton-on-Sea, orders that both Hackenticker and Halfhyde found it expedient to ignore as they skilfully brought the ramshackle collection of sampans into position for the embarkation. As each boat came alongside, Lord Edward Cole ushered the waiting persons aboard one by one, ensuring that the children all embarked with one or other parent and that they, with the women, were settled down as safely as possible beneath the straw canopy in the midships or after parts of the boats. As Captain Watkiss, last to embark as befitted both his responsibilities and his rank, put a foot aboard his flag-sampan, there was a shout from the darkness where by now all but one of the storm lanterns had disappeared:

'Zur, zur, zur! Cap'n Watkiss, zur, it be me and I be 'ere!'

Into view of the last lantern dangling above the steps, there swept a curious vessel like a tub, the kind of thing from which an early-morning sportsman would shoot wild duck at home in England, only in the latter case stationary and not with way upon it; from this vessel, propelled round and round in giddy circles by a single oar, waved Mr Bodmin whilst a Chinese girl wielded the means of propulsion. Captain Watkiss looked in some astonishment: Bodmin's 'old woman' was certainly a good deal less than half his own age – a good deal less – and was really very pretty. In truth the former boatswain could be called a baby-snatcher ...

*   *   *

'It's most unfortunate, Petty Officer Thoms, most unfortunate.'

'It is, sir, I agree, but—'

'Is there nothing more you can do?'

'Not as far as I can see, sir. Not without divers.'

Mr Beauchamp looked grey, weary and close to tears. 'But this – this *sawing through* the cable ... it could take days!'

'It could, sir, but the 'ands are doing their best.' The carpenter's mate drew a thumb across the stubble of his chin and studied Beauchamp's face. The officer looked like cracking up. A fine fellow to put in charge of sailors, but it couldn't be helped; everyone was doing his best, except maybe Beauchamp himself who had nagged without cease, like a woman. God help sailors on a night like this, thought the carpenter's mate as he left the bridge and returned downhill to the fo'c'sle and the ear-piercing screech of the saw on the metal link of the cable. Time would do it, but how much time it was hard to say. . . . On the bridge Mr Beauchamp consulted once again with the sub-lieutenant, assuring himself that nothing had been left unattended to.

'The movable gear, Mr Pumphrey, it's all secured?'

'Yes, sir.' Pumphrey steadied himself by clinging to the after guardrail of the bridge. It was like a precipice; the stern was lifted high and the screw was visible if one cared to look with a lantern.

'Mess stools, wardroom and cabin furnishings, paint shop, main stores?'

'Yes, sir.'

'The Captain's ice-box, Mr Pumphrey?'

'Yes, sir.'

'Good, good, well, that's a relief I must say.' Mr Beauchamp turned to look out into the blackness that covered the still-rising Yangtze Kiang. Navigation lights of red and green and white, slowly and aimlessly moving about, indicated that Her Majesty's gunboats *Bee* and *Wasp* were safe and that, too, was a

118

great relief. Two ships safe out of three – Beauchamp dared not think in the true terms of two out of four – perhaps Captain Watkiss would consider that not too bad in the circumstances and really he should not cast blame for acts of God like underwater obstructions that gripped anchors like vices, but he most probably would. It was very unfair, very unfair indeed. Mr Beauchamp had been a lieutenant of more than eight years' seniority for far too long; he was really a lieutenant of almost fifteen years' seniority, and he feared that tonight's ill fortune might well cut him off for ever from the prized brass hat of a Commander in the Royal Navy. It would take a miracle ... Mr Beauchamp suddenly praised God, for he believed that the miracle had occurred when a loud shout came from the carpenter's mate beneath him on the fo'c'sle.

'Mr Beauchamp, sir!'

Beauchamp was eager. 'Yes, Petty Officer Thoms, is the anchor free?'

'No, sir, it's not that, sir. Fact is, we've been boarded as you might say.'

'Boarded, Petty Officer Thoms?'

'By a dead bullock, sir. Very dead ... floated down from upstream and wrapped itself round the forestay.' There was a burst of laughter from the fo'c'sle, but Beauchamp didn't find it at all funny. Once again, God had let him down. It was becoming a personal vendetta.

*   *   *

The sampan fleet drifted in unwieldy and unseamanlike fashion through the apparently deserted city of Chungking. The inhabitants of the low-lying areas along the river banks, and farther inland as well, had mostly taken themselves off to the higher parts of the town. The houses by the quays were under water right up to the level of the top storeys; many of the shops and dwellings were totally submerged, which made navigation extremely tricky, and at one stage the head of the line deviated under the guidance of Mr Bodmin into what he said was the Street of the Prostitutes.

'How do you know that?' Watkiss demanded.

'It be a guess, zur.' Bodmin pointed towards a high-set

clothes-line from which dozens of pairs of ladies' silk pyjama trousers dangled into the flood-water, visible in the boat's lantern. 'I takes bearings from that, zur.'

'Oh, it's scarcely positive, is it?'

'No, zur.'

'Then you can't be *sure* we're in the Street of the blasted Prostitutes, can you?'

'No, zur. But I be fairly sure all the same like.' There was a hint of stubbornness in Bodmin's voice. 'I reckon we'd best execute a ninety-degree turn, zur, an' come out clear into the main stream.'

Watkiss breathed hard down his nose. 'I'm responsible for the safety of a large number of persons, Mr Bodmin, and I need more precise information. Be more explicit.'

'Ar, zur.' Bodmin looked down momentarily at the young Chinese girl: she had only a word or two of English, and it might be all right. Bodmin coughed and cleared his throat, then spoke to the Captain behind the cover of a hand. 'Some o' they drawers, zur. They pyjamas like. There be a rare quantity of 'em. I recognizes whose they may be!'

Watkiss glared. 'What a disgusting old man you are to be sure, Mr Bodmin.' He passed orders for the turn and the long line of sampans came round in very unfleetlike fashion, but made it safely back into the main stream or street without grounding upon brothel premises. Throughout the manoeuvre there was a look of something like awe in Bodmin's face: he was thinking it was about time to leave Chungking ... it would be a good long while before those sunken premises would be fit for trade again. The sampans were pulled onward by the oarsmen, with Count von Furstenberg's waterborne Uhlan Lancers staring to right and left behind their carbines and sabres, Count von Furstenberg himself sitting in solemn state in the rearmost sampan sharing a bottle of John Haig with the man who had revealed all, though this he did not as yet know. Erskine was keeping his own counsel, saying little between nips and hiccups. After some while of safe and steady progress, with no attack from the Chinese other than a few verbal insults hurled from marooned upper rooms, the leading boat grounded upon some sharp obstruction and Watkiss found himself sitting in a deepening puddle.

'Damn it, we've sprung a leak, Mr Bodmin. Abandon ship!'
Watkiss and Bodmin together shepherded the sampan's occupants into the second boat of the line, which was brought neatly alongside by Rear Admiral Hackenticker. Hackenticker's boat became overcrowded to a possibly dangerous extent, and there was a General Post whilst the extra persons were farmed out into the following craft and Watkiss' sampan gradually filled and sank. It was while all this was in progress that a single shot was heard from close by, then a number of others.

Captain Watkiss shook a fist towards the pinprick ripple of fire. 'Damn dagoes! It's not gentlemanly . . . taking advantage of us at such a time!' He cupped his hands around his mouth and shouted to the tail of the line. 'You there, Count von Furstenberg! Get your blasted soldiers into action at once, if you please! Mr Halfhyde!'

'Sir?'

'Open fire, can't you, why do I have to think of everything myself?'

On the heels of his words, rapid fire was opened from both sides. One by one the storm lanterns set in the bows of the sampans went out, the invisible enemy taking them as their first points of aim. There were shouts and cries and splashes, and then from the blank darkness Chinese craft surged in, cutting the British line like Nelson at Trafalgar putting his ships in amongst the French and Spanish; and hand-to-hand combat began.

ELEVEN

A sword whistled past Watkiss' right ear and he flung himself so far to the left that he very nearly went overboard and indeed would have done so had he not collided with Mr Bodmin, who was knocked flat to the bottom-boards. Watkiss himself was badly winded, and curled himself into a gasping ball. As he gasped and groaned, rifles opened from the rest of the sampan fleet; the fire from the Uhlans and the armed traders was well sustained and had the effect of fighting off the attack and then keeping it largely at a distance. In his own sampan Halfhyde made a quick count of casualties so far as he was able in the darkness, which in fact was tending to lighten just a little now: there were some sword and bullet wounds and one of the vice-consuls lay dead.

Halfhyde shouted to his Captain: 'I believe we're not far from the wharf, sir. I suggest we strike out across the river, and hope to meet the flotilla.'

There was an indistinct sound from Captain Watkiss, one that could have been an affirmative or a negative, and Halfhyde chose to regard it as the former. He shouted down the line in a carrying voice, ordering the sampans to alter course ninety degrees to their port hand and steer through the chasms of the buildings whose upper storeys stood clear of the flood, and which were visible as darker shapes looming through the night. Each sampan was to take the street nearest to it and then all would rendezvous on the river side. A voice came back excitedly from Lord Edward Cole.

'We're coming under attack from the rear of the line, sir!' A moment later Halfhyde heard a renewal of the rifle fire.

'Fight them off, Mr Cole,' he called, 'and beat retreat as ordered.'

'A rearguard action, sir?'

'Don't waste words, Mr Cole.' Halfhyde lost no time now; he gave his orders to his rowers to get way upon the sampan and headed his craft through the gap between two high buildings close upon his port side. Swiftly the sampan was pulled through; close behind now was Captain Watkiss, shaking a fist astern. A faint loom of light was positively starting to come into the sky now: dawn was approaching, though full daylight in such weather conditions would not be for some hours yet. Then, as Halfhyde's sampan reached the river end of the canyon-like floodway, he saw lights ahead, a half-dozen cables'-lengths away by his estimate – lights of red and green and white which must be the flotilla, under way for safety's sake but remaining on station. He was about to call back the good news to Captain Watkiss, when all of a sudden something erupted; there was a great boom and belch of flame from the flotilla, and an eerie whistle went overhead accompanied by a gale of wind. Halfhyde had the feeling that Beauchamp had avoided taking his head off by a mere matter of inches.

There was a bellow from Captain Watkiss. 'That blasted idiot Beauchamp ... he'll blow us all to kingdom come, Mr Halfhyde!' His voice had scarcely died away when a further explosion occurred somewhere above, and a sizeable chunk of masonry toppled into the water and descended upon the after gunwale of Watkiss' sampan.

*   *   *

Beauchamp had been in a quandary upon hearing the earlier sound of the rifles from the shore. He had peered through the dreadful rain, using his telescope, but had seen nothing except the pinpricks of flashes that seemed to be widely scattered along an extended line.

'What do you think, Mr Pumphrey?'

'It's an attack, sir!'

'Yes, indeed it is, but by whom and upon whom? Do you suppose Captain Watkiss is the objective?'

'I don't know, sir. He could be. Perhaps we should open fire, sir.'

'Bombard the town? Yes, I believe that was in Captain Watkiss' mind in certain circumstances.' Beauchamp shook his head and felt a surge in his stomach: the worry was dreadful and was making him queazy. 'We *can't* open fire, Mr Pumphrey – except upon the bottom of the river, such is our angle.'

'No, sir, *we* can't, but *Bee* and *Wasp* should be able to.'

Beauchamp nodded. 'Yes, very true. But all the same I fear Captain Watkiss might be hit if he's in the vicinity.' He wrung his hands. 'If only I knew the facts, Mr Pumphrey, the state of things ashore!'

'Yes, sir.' The sub-lieutenant gave a discreet cough. 'May I make a suggestion, sir?'

'Yes, yes, do.' Beauchamp sounded much relieved.

'Suppose we – or rather *Bee* and *Wasp* – were to open in the direction of where we saw the fire from the rifles, sir, but elevate the guns so as to make certain they fire over the Captain's head if he's there?'

'Yes, a good idea, I think! Thank you, Mr Pumphrey, we shall do as you say.'

'It should scare the Chinese off, sir.'

'Certainly it should, yes. Be so good as to pass the orders by megaphone to *Bee* and *Wasp*, Mr Pumphrey, will you?'

*   *   *

'I shall have his guts for garters, Mr Halfhyde, you may be sure.' The filth-plastered face of Captain Watkiss appeared at the gunwale of Halfhyde's sampan, patchy white in the lightening darkness. Halfhyde reached down and with assistance dragged his Captain aboard, and after him Bodmin and Bodmin's common-law wife. Farther along the gunwales, the rest of the upset passengers clambered aboard. All were accounted for, but the sampan itself had sunk to the street below. Watkiss continued. 'Feller's the most consummate ass I've ever had the blasted misfortune to sail with, and that's fact, I said it. Too much damn money, that's the trouble, no incentive left! Father's a blasted tradesman, very wealthy. I shall have him court martialled the moment I reach Hong Kong.'

Halfhyde said, 'I believe his gunfire will have a good effect, sir, and that he should be commended.'

'Oh, nonsense, commended my backside, he nearly blew me up, and he's sunk my sampan, hasn't he?'

'Purely by chance, sir. I'd have done the same myself – opened fire, I mean.'

'Then you're a blasted idiot as well, Mr Halfhyde, and an argumentative one into the bargain.'

'Sir, I merely—'

'Hold your tongue, if you please, Mr Halfhyde.' Watkiss peered around, looking this way and that as more three-pounder shells zoomed overhead – safely this time. 'Oh, God, why doesn't he stop? Where's von Furstenberg, do you know?'

'Four sampans astern, sir, and now no doubt heading to his port flank as ordered—'

'Well, I hope for your sake he is,' Watkiss said belligerently, 'because according to someone or other – Hackenticker, right at the start, I think it was – I'm supposed to arrest him and bring him in. You do realize that, don't you?'

'I do now, sir. I don't anticipate much difficulty – he'll scarcely wish to linger in Chungking now, I fancy.' Halfhyde paused. 'Do you notice anything, sir?'

'No. What?'

'An absence of fire from the Chinese pursuit, sir.'

'Oh.' Watkiss lifted his head as though listening. 'Yes. Curious!'

'Not curious, sir: Mr Beauchamp.'

'*Beauchamp?*' Watkiss repeated in astonishment.

Halfhyde said, 'His gunfire has had its due effect, sir. I think we can now head direct for the flotilla after we've rendez-voused.'

'Oh. Yes, well.' Watkiss breathed down his nose. 'I suppose by the law of averages Beauchamp has to make the right decision sometimes.' He sat huffily silent in the sampan's stern as Halfhyde passed the orders to continue riverwards; and once beyond the building line there was just enough faint light for Watkiss to see the other craft converging upon them, whilst well out in the river steaming lights and three blurs indicated, presumably, the three gunboats – although one of them was showing a curious silhouette, most ungunboatlike ... Watkiss turned his attention from his flotilla for the moment and searched again for Count von Furstenberg as Beauchamp continued to rain shells upon Chungking; from astern came plops and waterspouts, or explosions and crashes as buildings were hit above the waterline. Then Watkiss noticed one of his sampans turning round in a circle and beating it back into the maze of flooded alleys. That must be von Furstenberg, who had probably spotted the flotilla. Watkiss rose from his seat.

'That Hun bugger's making off! Get him, Mr Halfhyde! Get him, I say!'

'I think he's being pursued already, sir, by a craft nearer than us.'

'By God, he'd better be! Who's pursuing?'

'I believe it's Admiral Hackenticker, sir.'

'Is it, by God!' Watkiss jabbed a finger into Halfhyde's ribs. 'I'm not having the Americans taking the initiative and the credit, Mr Halfhyde, you will give chase immediately and overtake, d'you hear?'

Halfhyde shrugged but obeyed. Under his orders the sampan turned and headed fast towards the fleeing German, the oars moving like the legs of an urgent centipede. Von Furstenberg vanished after a few moments, but Hackenticker was still behind him. Back into the alleys ... Watkiss' boat swept into the mouth just as Hackenticker put himself alongside the German. There was some exchange of fire and shouts were heard, then a heavy body was seen to leap from one sampan to the other, then more bodies. Hand-to-hand combat raged, and a body was seen to fall overboard from the German's craft as Watkiss hastened up importantly. Admiral Hackenticker, breathing hard, reached down into the water and tugged at the collar of a tunic. Count von Furstenberg rose into view, his face furious as he was brought aboard like a landed fish. Hackenticker grinned across at Watkiss, which was damned cheek.

'Beat you to it, Captain!'

'Illegally so, my dear sir. Von Furstenberg's my prisoner, not yours.'

'You're wrong, Captain. I was given certain information by the reverend gentleman—'

'You mean the missionary. Missionaries are never gentlemen, Admiral Hackenticker, and—'

'Well, gentleman or not, and it's not important, he works for the US State Department, not your Foreign Office. That makes von Furstenberg mine, I think.'

Watkiss, furious, turned his back. 'We shall return aboard my flotilla, Mr Halfhyde, and Admiral Hackenticker and the Hun are to be escorted aboard. I am taking them both into arrest, as is my privilege when representing Her Majesty Queen Victoria on foreign soil.' He added, 'The tradespeople with rifles and revolvers are to cover the Uhlans and ensure that there's no interference.'

Watkiss sat stiffly, glowering, head held back, a hand tapping on the gunwale as he resumed the lead and headed out for the river. Americans were quite impossible, always somehow contriving to put one in the wrong: Watkiss himself had strong doubts as to his right to arrest an officer of the United States Navy, but was damned if he was going to climb down. As the sampans came closer to the three blurs ahead, and the night lifted still more towards the dawn, Watkiss, peering through the rain, saw a sight that almost paralysed him. His own ship, the *Cockroach* itself, was apparently standing upon its head and diving down towards the muddy bottom of the Yangtze. Hackenticker saw it too, and gave a rude laugh and slapped his thigh, both abominable sounds sweeping forward towards Captain Watkiss, accompanied by a stupid remark about duck's arses.

* * *

'Words fail me, Mr Beauchamp.' Captain Watkiss, who had clambered aboard his command with great difficulty and now had more difficulty in maintaining his equilibrium upon a deck that was not far from the vertical, spat his words out, words not in fact failing him entirely. 'God give me strength to endure you as far as Hong Kong!'

'Sir, I believed it better to open fire rather—'

'Great God above us all, Mr Beauchamp, I am not referring to your blasted gunfire, although I shall certainly do so presently – I am referring to *this*!' He swept a hand round from lofty bridge to sunken fo'c'sle.

'Ah, yes, sir, this,' Beauchamp said carefully.

'Kindly explain, if you can.'

'Yes, sir.' White-faced and shaking, Beauchamp did so. 'The anchor became obstructed, sir.'

'By what?'

'Well, sir ... an obstruction.'

Watkiss seemed to vibrate. 'Yes, Mr Beauchamp, an obstruction. *What bloody obstruction?* You don't damn well know, do you?' He thrust his stomach forward threateningly. '*Do you?*'

'Er ... no, sir.'

'Then allow me to make a guess, Mr Beauchamp.' Watkiss whirled an arm about his head, slipped a little on the sloping deck, and swore. 'When you paid out your blasted cable to an unreasonable extent, you dropped astern on the flood – did you not?'

'I – I expect so, sir—'

'You expect so! And you wrapped a bight of your blasted cable round the blasted wreckage of the *Gadfly* which you yourself had sunk earlier! We are now being held fast, Mr Beauchamp, by the result of your blasted stupid seamanship in losing Her Majesty a ship of war! God help you, for I shall not!'

'Sir, I—'

'You have made me look foolish, Mr blasted Beauchamp, in front of a damn Hun and an American, to say nothing of all those wretched tradespeople I've rescued! What will they all think of Her Majesty's Navy I'd like to know! Hey? Do you know what you are, Mr Beauchamp? *Do you?*'

'No, sir—'

'Then I'll tell you. You are a blasted *lunatic*, Mr Beauchamp, a total disaster afloat ...' Captain Watkiss seethed to a stop and brandished a fist at his First Lieutenant, seeming to be about to choke. '*What are you, Mr Beauchamp?*'

'Sir, I – I ...' Beauchamp's voice tailed away and he wrung his hands. A hunted look came into his face; he had suffered similarly in the past and knew only too well what was expected of him now. He had to go through with it or he would be threatened with court martial ... in a strained voice he said, 'I'm a blasted lunatic, sir, and a total disaster afloat. I'm very sorry indeed, sir.'

*　　　*　　　*

128

Captain Watkiss was faced with two alternatives: either he delayed his departure from Chungking for God knew how long until the flood-waters receded and thus automatically lowered his stern, when he might be able to send men down in short spasms to try to free the links of his cable from the sunken *Gadfly*, or he could continue with the painfully laborious business of sawing through the cable with tools that had proved woefully inadequate and for the supply of which some damn civilian popinjay in Hong Kong dockyard would be sent home in disgrace. At first there had been a third possibility but this had been rejected when Captain Watkiss went down most dangerously to the tip-tilted cable locker to examine personally the Senhouse slip: it was as solidly set in place, and as immovable, as a seventy-year-old maidenhead. Ascending to the upper deck, Watkiss told Halfhyde to set all available hands to the saw.

'Aye, aye, sir.' Halfhyde paused, lifting an eyebrow. 'Would not Mr Beauchamp—'

'Beauchamp? Beauchamp's back in arrest. Did I not make that quite plain?'

'No, sir.'

'Well, I'm making it plain now. You will take over again as my First Lieutenant, Mr Halfhyde – oh, and one more thing: Bodmin.'

'Yes, sir?'

'He's to be berthed, if a berth can be found at all, away from the woman, Song Tso-P'eng I understand her name is. They're *not married*, Mr Halfhyde.' Unusually, his voice had dropped to a whisper. 'I shall not allow hanky-panky aboard my ship and if they have contact I shall see to it that his boatswain's pension is withdrawn. The charge will be immoral conduct – you'd better warn him, he's not a bad old fellow, and must have been a damn sight better seaman than that fool Beauchamp. That's all, Mr Halfhyde.'

'One moment, sir, if you please—'

'Oh, what is it now, Mr Halfhyde? I'm exceedingly busy.'

'Quite, sir, and I apologize. But how is the woman to be berthed where she'll not be molested by the ship's company?'

Watkiss clicked his tongue. 'Do use your initiative, Mr

Halfhyde, and refrain from bothering me about every little detail. I have much on my mind . . . if any of the ship's company molest Song whatever it is, then they'll have me to deal with and I'll not be merciful.'

'Indeed not, sir. But—'

Captain Watkiss, now re-united with his telescope, waved it threateningly. 'Oh, I don't know! Rig a canvas shelter on the upper deck where she can be under the supervision of the Officer of the Watch.' He turned about and bounced away, then suddenly stopped and came back again. 'The question of bunkers, Mr Halfhyde. Damn steam propulsion . . . if only I had sails! Tell the engineer I wish words with him at once.'

*   *   *

Many more hours went into the slow and tedious business of sawing through the cable beneath the teeming rain. Captain Watkiss grew more and more frustrated as the swollen river swelled even more and the filthy waters of the Yangtze rose higher up his fo'c'sle, bringing stench and debris, and no doubt disease, closer to his person. Among other things he was plagued by the two Americans, who kept urging speed; at any moment the Russians, Hackenticker said, might enter the Yangtze from Port Arthur and seal the British flotilla into the river.

'Oh, nonsense, I shall not be sealed in by anybody, Admiral Hackenticker, who do you think I am?'

'But if the Russians enter, you'll not be able to help being sealed in, Captain.'

'I shall fight my way out,' Watkiss responded with truculence. 'In any case, don't forget there's a squadron of first-class cruisers lying off Foochow under Commodore Marriot-Lee. He'll use his initiative and move in at once, sooner than he originally intended, you may be sure.'

'Maybe, but Foochow's a long way south of Shanghai. Marriot-Lee may not have knowledge of Russian movements.'

'Really?' Watkiss raised his eyebrows. 'I was under the impression you brought word from your legation in Peking. Will they not have thought fit to inform the British naval command at Hong Kong?'

Hackenticker shrugged. 'I can't say, Captain. Maybe yes, maybe no. With the legation out of contact by the cable links, which've been cut, it'll take a hell of a long while to get word through to Hong Kong or anywhere else.'

Watkiss shook his telescope in frustration: Americans were quite impossible. He was about to utter strong words when very suddenly the world turned upside down. There was a loud shout from the carpenter's mate on the fo'c'sle and the next split second, after a dreadful banging noise, Captain Watkiss was jerked from his chair and thrown to the deck of his cabin. The Americans were similarly assailed. The *Cockroach* was shaken violently from stem to stern, rocking and pitching at the same time. Noise came from everywhere: the remaining coal rattled about the bunkers, woodwork creaked and groaned under massive strain, and the wire rigging twanged like an orchestra. Small objects rained down upon Watkiss and the Americans – all Watkiss' personal gear: toothbrush, shaving tackle, a tin of solidified brilliantine for the hair, tumblers, *Burke's Landed Gentry* from the bookshelf, the latter very heavy when flung. As his ship settled herself, Captain Watkiss rose from the wreckage like a phoenix, red, rattled and angry. There was a polite knock at the doorpost of his cabin and the curtain was drawn aside. The sub-lieutenant stood there at attention.

'Sir, Mr Halfhyde's compliments. The cable has now parted and we are under way.'

*   *   *

The carpenter's mate had been flung overboard with two men of the cable party, but all were drawn from the river unharmed. Many of the ship's company had suffered bruising and one man had a wrist broken. Some stokers had been burned but not seriously and there was nothing the sick berth attendant couldn't cope with. Though angry that his ship had come free without warning, Watkiss was only too thankful to be under way and able to project his mind towards the future and a successful dash with his overcrowded flotilla past Shanghai and out into the East China Sea and the safe arms of Marriot-Lee's cruiser squadron. Once again upon his bridge, Watkiss passed the orders for the flotilla to form into line ahead and proceed out of Chungking. They set off at immense speed, borne along on the flood-waters racing for the gorges and the open sea; and they proceeded with some navigational difficulty since the actual course of the Yangtze was totally invisible beneath them. The question of bunkers was much upon Captain Watkiss' mind as what was to be seen of Chungking dwindled away behind, still shrouded in rain. What a country. Thank God he was British! Looking over the forward guardrail of his bridge he saw Bloementhal hovering by the canvas prison in which a wet Song Tso-P'eng was sitting disconsolately; and he called down sharply.

'Mr Bloementhal!'

Bloementhal looked up and waved a hand. 'Yeah?'

'Kindly leave the woman alone, if you please.'

'It's one hell of a way to treat a lady, Captain.'

'I'd be obliged if you'd leave the conduct of my ship to me, Mr Bloementhal, thank you.'

'Anything you say . . .' Bloementhal walked aft and vanished. Watkiss simmered silently for a few moments, then turned his mind back to bunkers. Having topped up initially off Foochow from Marriot-Lee's cruisers, and having steamed subsequently at slow and therefore economical speed, he should have had enough coal for the return voyage to Shanghai where he would be able to replenish for the haul south to Hong Kong. However, although *Cockroach*'s supply of coal appeared to be adequate, the reports from *Bee* and *Wasp* were less happy: they had each consumed extra quantities, not much to be sure but possibly enough to embarrass them, whilst maintaining steam for steerage way after weighing when the waters rose. And Watkiss was, of course, responsible for the whole flotilla, or what that fool Beauchamp had left of it, and he could scarcely steam on and leave *Bee* and *Wasp* behind if their bunkers should empty. It was possible he could obtain coal at Nanking, but everything would depend upon the political situation, and also upon the movements and general chicanery of the Russians . . . pondering upon the Russians led Watkiss to thoughts of Count von Furstenberg, presently under close arrest in the paint store . . . and a blasted nuisance he was, with his wretched military Uhlans! Certainly they had proved of value in the fighting, but now they were cluttering up his ships along with the wretched tradespeople and Consulate staff, and Watkiss, who disliked civilians as much as he disliked foreigners, but liked a tidy and shipshape flotilla, had been much put out to find his storerooms and alleyways chock-a-block with riff-raff. But von Furstenberg now: currently Watkiss couldn't see how, but he might in some way prove a handy bargaining counter if the Russians should be encountered before the flotilla had cleared away from Shanghai. One never knew. It was worth bearing in mind. Hackenticker had indicated quite positively that von Furstenberg must not fall into Russian hands. But Captain Watkiss gave not a jot for any blasted Hun and if there was no *British* requirement for von Furstenberg's immunity from Russian arrest, then he could perhaps be jettisoned to them in return for a safe conduct out of the Yangtze.

'Mr Halfhyde, a word in your ear, if you please.'

Halfhyde bent towards his Captain, courteously, keeping an eye upon his navigation at the same time. Briefly, Watkiss revealed his thought processes, and Halfhyde shook his head dubiously. 'I don't like it, sir.'

'What d'you mean, don't like it? Why not, may I ask?'

'Count von Furstenberg fought on our side after leaving the Consulate, sir.'

'Yes, yes, I know! All honour to him. But I don't suppose for a moment he did it for us, do you? Jiggery-pokery, my dear Halfhyde, the Huns are stuffed full of it! He must have had an ulterior motive, don't you see?'

'Possibly, sir. But to hand him over to the Russians ... it's very extreme.'

'No it isn't!'

'I can think of nothing *more* extreme, sir.'

'Oh, blast you, Mr Halfhyde, you're as bad as Beauchamp.' Watkiss' voice rose and he brandished his telescope. 'Wars are never won by namby-pambyism – extreme measures are often called for, and they are now, or may be. I thought I could count upon your support.'

Halfhyde said, 'I shall obey your orders, sir, that goes without saying—'

'Yes, it does.'

'But I dislike your suggestion. It's not British, sir.'

'Oh, balls and bang me arse, Mr Halfhyde, don't become

unctuous, I dislike unctuous people, dislike them intensely. I shall have a word with Admiral Hackenticker.'

'I've no doubt he'll see it my way, sir. Admiral Hackenticker strikes me as an honourable man.'

'And I don't, I suppose? I think you are damned impertinent, Mr Halfhyde, if not downright insubordinate, and I shall report as much to the Commodore-in-Charge at Hong Kong.' Furiously Captain Watkiss turned his back and bounced towards the ladder from the bridge, which he descended rapidly only to find his way blocked at the bottom by Mr Bodmin.

'Zur—'

'Oh, dear, what is it now, Bodmin?'

'It be my wife, zur—'

'Don't call her your wife. She's not.'

'No, zur, that be quite true, zur.' Mr Bodmin drew a hand across his nose, sniffing. ''Cept like I said, zur, by common law—'

'Which for all I know doesn't pertain in China – but go on, what is it, I'm in a hurry.'

'Ar, zur. I've just 'ad words with 'er like, over the canvas dodger, not inside it, zur—'

'Good.'

'It be that Bloementhal, zur.' Mr Bodmin dropped his voice conspiratorially and clutched at Captain Watkiss' arm, a gesture that Watkiss shook off impatiently. 'She do say, zur, she's clapped eyes on 'im afore now. An' she do go on to say, zur, she don't trust 'im.'

'Goodness gracious me! In what way, Bodmin?'

'Well, zur, she be truly British and never mind she's one o' they Chinks. I brought 'er up proper like, zur, like she was a ratin' in the Navy. It be natural to me, zur, if you take my meanin'. When I were in the old sailin' Navy, zur—'

'Yes, yes, Bodmin, do keep to the point. What about Mr Bloementhal?'

''E don't be one o' they Yanks at all, zur. Nor do 'e be Bloementhal.'

'He don't – isn't?' Watkiss' ears were now a-cockbill: he had never trusted Bloementhal, not an inch, and by God he'd been proved right! 'Who is he, then?'

'Well, zur, she do say 'e be someone different like. Mind, I dunno if she do be right, but that's what she says, an' swears it be the truth like.'

'I see. And his true identity, in her view?'

'Ar!' Mr Bodmin gave an impertinent movement of an eyelid – a wink. Watkiss didn't like that: Post Captains were not to be winked at. But he held his peace and waited for Bodmin to go on. 'She be cold an' she be terrible wet, zur, out there on the upper deck, zur. 'Tisn't right.'

Watkiss glared. 'Surely you're not attempting to blackmail me into bringing the woman below decks, Bodmin?'

'No, no, zur, no,' Mr Bodmin said at once. 'Course not! 'Twouldn't be my place like. But she be too shivery and shaky, zur, to tell me the name, see? She be taken sick, zur, I do believe. Now, if she were to be put in a cabin like, and cosseted up proper – why, then, zur, she'd find 'er tongue.'

'Would she indeed? Suppose I were to take action of a different sort, Bodmin, and place you in arrest until your – until the woman talked? What then, hey?'

Bodmin gave a throaty chuckle. 'Ar, zur, I've told ee afore, I bain't in the Navy now, zur, I be retired. And I tell ee summat else: Song Tso-P'eng, zur, she be fair sick. Ar – fair *sick* she be! And she do be sort of British.'

'Yes, that's all very well, but—'

'China's a funny place, zur. All that rain an' damp clothin', zur. If she be left in the open like, she could take the cholera, zur, an' that be bad aboard a ship, zur.'

TWELVE

The urgent need to find out more, allied to his sense of duty, won a victory over rage, and Watkiss turned and shouted up the ladder to the bridge. 'Mr Halfhyde!'

'Sir?'

'I'm sorry, but you'll have to give up your cabin.'

'I have already, sir. One of the women from the Consulate, with two children—'

'Oh, hold your tongue, Mr Halfhyde, what a blasted nuisance everything is.' Watkiss turned and seethed along the deck, cogitating, the terrible rain finding its way down the neck of his oilskins. God damn and blast! Then he bounced back towards Bodmin, who was watching him hopefully yet cautiously. 'Oh, very well, Bodmin, I suppose she'll have to have my cabin and I'll put a sentry on the door, which will remain under guard until you and she disembark in Hong Kong.'

Bodmin touched his cap-peak. 'Thankee, zur, thankee!'

'She must reveal all, Bodmin.'

'Ar, zur, that she will, zur.'

Watkiss gave an angry grunt and began to contemplate the paint store, out of which von Furstenberg would have to be ejected to make room for him, and where the Hun berthed thereafter Watkiss gave not a jot so long as he was under guard. It was all a most dreadful nuisance, but the woman's story had to emerge, and Bodmin was an obstinate old fool who knew very well when he held the upper hand – and of course there was the threat of the cholera, which would be too terrible to contemplate in a close community. Watkiss knew little or nothing of medical science, but he did believe it possible that continual wet and exposure could weaken persons and lay them open to the scourge of cholera. He couldn't possibly take the risk. He went below to take his leave of his cabin and have his gear shifted out by his servant to the paint store; and whilst there he tracked down cholera in a copy of *The Ship Captain's Medical Guide*, a Board of Trade publication left behind by his predecessor who had presumably filched it from a merchant ship. His worst fears were confirmed: cholera went with the rainy season, the wretched *comma bacillus* flourished in conditions of damp but was killed by long drought, of which there was none in prospect. The sufferer descended through acute diarrhoea, vomiting, feeble circulation, coldness and cramps to total collapse. In China, and especially, God-damn it, along the Yangtze, cholera appeared every year without fail. It was a water-borne disease, and if rain wasn't water then what was, and the first victims were those who were already exhausted. Death could strike within twelve hours from the onset. And the disease could spread like lightning.

Watkiss closed the book with a snap. Yes, his decision, though it had been a kind of surrender, had been right. He could not reach Hong Kong with all his ship's company dead or dying.

*　　　*　　　*

'Mr Halfhyde, I have given orders that the sentry on my cabin is to prohibit all entry.' Watkiss bounced up and down on his heels. 'There will be no fornication aboard the *Cockroach*, Mr Halfhyde, and I shall hold you responsible that it does not take place. And there's one more thing.'

'Yes, sir?'

'The paint store. I'll not be using it after all, so von Furstenberg can remain. I've just thought ... I don't know why it didn't occur to me earlier. I shall take over the wardroom, and the refugees berthed in there must be re-allocated to somewhere else – the Captain must be able to avail himself of proper accommodation and privacy.'

'Very good, sir.'

'My officers will be allowed in for their meals, and for no other purpose, Mr Halfhyde.' Watkiss paused. 'Kindly send for

Mr Bodmin and arrange for Mr Pumphrey to relieve you on the bridge. You and Bodmin are to report to my cabin for the interrogation of Bodmin's woman.' He left the bridge, aware that his flotilla was being borne along still at a somewhat risky pace. He proceeded below to his cabin where already the sentry was posted, gaitered and with a rifle. When the man failed to prevent his entry, Watkiss halted, turned and stared into his face.

'My orders were that no one should be allowed entry. Were they not?'

The seaman swallowed. 'Yessir.'

'Then may I ask why you have not prevented me going in?'

'Well, sir, you're the Captain, sir. It's your cabin, sir.'

Watkiss flourished his telescope. 'No, no, no – it's not my cabin now, it's Mr Bodmin's – er – the Chinee woman's. You should have stopped and questioned me. Do you understand?'

'Yessir, I do now, sir,' the man answered obligingly.

'Good. Because when a man acting as sentry is in dereliction of his duty, it is an offence punishable by warrant and could lead to the detention quarters in Hong Kong. On this occasion, I shall say no more, but next time will be different.'

'Yessir, thank you, sir.'

Watkiss bounced into his cabin. The sentry sucked at his teeth and reflected that there was no knowing with the old bugger; like as not, had he been stopped, the heavens would have fallen and himself told that no one but a blasted lunatic would fail to recognize his Captain. Inside the cabin, which was hot and stuffy, Song Tso-P'eng sat in Watkiss' basketwork chair with her hands demurely in her lap and eyes cast down before the splendour of a Post Captain of the Royal Navy. Watkiss, having no Chinese, was somewhat at a loss when the girl stood up politely, and he made a sit-down-again motion with his hand. She appeared to understand, and sat. She was, Watkiss realized, extremely good-looking, dark and slim. As with all Chinese women her chest was flat: Watkiss liked breasts, but the woman was nonetheless attractive.

He made conversation in English whilst he waited for Halfhyde and Bodmin to report. 'You are dry now,' he said. The girl smiled at him, very pleasantly indeed, almost invit-ingly. Well, of course, he was a good deal younger than Bodmin

... since she seemed not to have understood, he tried again, laboriously digging into his pidgin. 'Make not wet,' he said, then realized that this could be misunderstood. 'Water go way from Song Tso-P'eng ... oh, never mind.' Feeling at a loss again, he frowned, turned in a circle and made a pretence of ferreting about in his roll-top desk. He had a suspicion the girl had recovered pretty quickly from her ills, but of course that was just as well really. Some minutes passed and Watkiss grew fractious under the girl's scrutiny, which was upon him every time he turned round. However, some ten minutes after entry there was a commotion in the alleyway outside the cabin, and Watkiss put his head through the curtain and snapped at the sentry.

'Oh, for goodness' sake, man, let them in, I should have thought it obvious I wish to speak to them.' Halfhyde and Bodmin entered and Watkiss told the sentry to move away out of earshot, threatening him with all manner of punishment if he should dare to eavesdrop. Then he turned back into the crowded cabin, pushing past Mr Bodmin towards his desk. 'Now, Bodmin. The woman doesn't look as sick as you led me to expect,' he said accusingly.

'P'raps not, zur, but 'tis better to be safe than sorry, zur, and the cholera be terrible nasty, zur. Vomit an'—'

'Yes, I'm aware of all that, thank you. Now if you'll kindly be quick, I have much to do. Kindly extract her story, in English, if you please.'

'Ar, zur, I'll do that.' Bodmin advanced towards his woman and sat on Watkiss' bunk alongside the basketwork chair. He reached out and patted the girl on the cheek, his face wearing a thoroughly stupid expression of lust that made Captain Watkiss feel quite sick, it was all most undignified at the old goat's age and he would have expected a better standard from a boatswain whose position as a warrant officer demanded responsible behaviour at all times. Caressing her cheek still, his veined hand trembling as he did so, Bodmin began speaking in Chinese, words that Watkiss – since the woman's eyes melted at her preposterous old lover – suspected of being ones of endearment and suggestion rather than of interrogation.

'Do get on with it!' Watkiss snapped.

'Ar, zur, I be doing that.'

'I'm relieved to hear it.'

The conversation continued, and after what seemed like an immense time, Bodmin looked up at Watkiss and reverted to English. 'She do say, zur, that she's seen Mr Bloementhal afore—'

'Yes, yes, you've told me that, also that she doesn't trust him. I want to know *why*.'

'Ar, zur, so ee do, so ee do.' Bodmin paused, touched the girl's cheek again, then went on, 'She says she's seen 'im, zur, some while back it were, in the company of some of they local mandarins from the country districts like—'

'In Szechwan province?'

'Ar, zur, that be right. In Szechwan province.'

'All right, Mr Bodmin, go on.'

'Ar, zur. They mandarins . . . they be the enemy like, zur, the opposition.'

'Yes, yes. But to what in particular?'

'Why, zur, to us. And to the Yanks, zur.'

'I see. That's interesting. Do you mean Mr Bloementhal's playing a double game, Mr Bodmin, double-crossing his own countrymen as well as us?'

Bodmin pursed his lips. 'Why, zur, I dunno as to that. She didn't say that, but—'

'Understandable,' Watkiss said, nodding vigorously. 'She wasn't to know the ins and outs of diplomacy I don't suppose. It would be beyond her class, naturally. However, a wink's as good as a nod to a blind horse, and I am well able to make my own deductions.' Suddenly he remembered something. 'Mr Bodmin, did you not tell me earlier that Bloementhal was *not* an American according to your – er – to your woman? If he's not, then he can't be accused of traitorous atrocities exactly, can he? At any rate in regard to the Americans?'

'That be true enough, zur.'

'Then who is he, for God's sake?'

'She don't know 'is name like, zur, but she do reckon 'e's a German.'

'A *Hun*? A Hun, in the American Legation at Peking, which is where he came from according to both Admiral Hackenticker and Mr Carstairs, isn't that so, Mr Halfhyde? *And* that missionary, who was quite drunk.' Watkiss pondered. 'If a Hun

managed to make himself *persons grata* in the American Legation, it doesn't say much for the Americans, does it, but I'm
certainly not in the least surprised I must admit. They're a
woolly lot and they don't understand diplomacy or foreign
countries, never really had the experience, of course – I suppose
you can't blame them. There's another point too, is there not?'

'What point, sir?'

'Isn't it obvious, my dear Halfhyde? If he was vouched for by
Hackenticker, does not that fact implicate Hackenticker in the
jiggery-pokery?'

'Possibly, sir, but I don't believe so.'

'Oh? Why not?'

'Because Admiral Hackenticker strikes me as a very genuine
American naval officer, sir.'

'I take your diplomatic experience with a grain of salt, Mr
Halfhyde, I doubt if you'd know a spy when you saw one.'

'He fought with us, sir, on the way from the Consulate.'

'So did that Hun von Furstenberg! All Huns together if you
ask me!'

Halfhyde gave a cough. 'Perhaps it would be as well to ask
Mrs Bodmin – Song Tso-P'eng – how she deduced that
Bloementhal was a German?'

Watkiss scratched his jaw. 'Bloementhal could be a Hun
name as much as American ... clever of him in a way, I suppose
he'd have claimed German ancestry if anyone had got suspicious, and thus disarmed them. Don't you think? However, I
take your point – all that wouldn't have occurred to a Chinee
woman.' He turned to Mr Bodmin. 'Kindly ask her, if you
please, unless she's already told you.'

'Ar, she 'as that, zur. She were told like. One o' they ninety-
seven relations, zur, is butler to one o' they mandarin fellows in
Szechwan province. And—'

'And she saw Bloementhal when she was visiting this rela-
tion?' Watkiss asked perspicaciously.

'Ar, zur. And 'e did tell her that Mr Bloementhal spoke
German all the time, zur, and Germans was there as well,
suppin' and dinin' and winin' with that there mandarin, zur.'

Watkiss nodded. 'I see. He could, of course, speak German
even as an American citizen, I imagine, but what you tell me
sounds pretty conclusive – the Hun guests, you see. I'm most

141

grateful, my dear Bodmin, most grateful. I shall see to it that your services are reported in Hong Kong. Now, Mr Halfhyde, we must ponder the facts we've learned.' An ungallant thought sprang into his mind: Song Tso-P'eng had done her talking and could now be removed from the comfort of his cabin, but that would be churlish and it was un-British to go back on one's word. 'We shall go to the wardroom, Mr Halfhyde,' he said. 'All right, Mr Bodmin, that'll be all, thank you.'

Bodmin looked peeved and disappointed. 'If I might ask a favour, zur, she do be awful lonely like, and I—'

'No, Mr Bodmin, I'm sorry.'

'But, zur—'

Watkiss snapped, 'I said no and I mean no. How many times have I to tell you, she's not your wife!'

*　　*　　*

Before seeking Halfhyde's views, Captain Watkiss conferred within himself so as to clear his mind towards decision. Seated at the tiny wardroom table, he tapped his fingers on the wood whilst he pondered, a sound that soon began to drive Halfhyde to the verge of insanity. Watkiss' mental processes were in fact simple: he resented Hackenticker's presence and was half inclined to see him as a wicked intriguer who could now be clapped in irons, but he felt a need to be cautious all the same. And then there was the damn parson: surely he was now shown to be an evil man? Had not Bloementhal been sent to meet him? Watkiss mentioned this to Halfhyde.

'He's not necessarily evil, sir, in my view—'

'Why not?'

'Clergymen are seldom intriguers—'

'Oh, balls and bang me arse, of course they are!' Watkiss sounded indignant. 'Look at parish work, it's all intrigue, and as for bishops – how do they obtain their dioceses in the first place?'

'It's outside my province, sir. But considering the information Erskine parted with, I scarcely see him as working against us.' Halfhyde frowned. 'On the other hand ...'

'Yes, Mr Halfhyde?' The tapping, which had thankfully ceased, started again. 'What other hand?'

'It's possible Erskine's information about the Kaiser's intentions was false—'

'False? How, false? And why?'

'False simply in the sense that it wasn't true,' Halfhyde answered patiently. 'And for the reason that Bloementhal and Erskine *could* have been working together with a view to discrediting von Furstenberg.'

'Oh, nonsense, von Furstenberg's a Hun and you're obscuring the issue. I don't know what you're talking about, frankly. It's the very fact that Bloementhal hob-nobs with Huns that has made us suspicious, isn't it, except that *I* was always suspicious of him from the start, if you remember.' Watkiss sniffed. 'A rascally face, don't you know.'

'Perhaps, sir. But von Furstenberg, at any rate, was of much assistance in saving your neck.'

'My neck, yes, that's true, certainly.' As if instinctively, Watkiss felt the folds of his short, bull-like neck, so recently adjacent to the executioner's sword. 'Well, I really don't know, all this is most tiresome for simple sailors, Mr Halfhyde, who are happiest when upon the clean sea. Good, clean winds and—' Suddenly he broke off. 'I think we had better have words with Hackenticker – you're probably right that he's honest; I feel I must take the chance. Send for him, if you please, Mr Halfhyde.'

'If you remember, sir, you placed him in arrest.'

'Of course I remember, and it was *open* arrest not close arrest. In any case I've changed my mind and I'm taking him out again.' Watkiss paused. 'Better get the parson, too, I think. Missionaries! That's another thing about parsons, or missionaries anyway – *all* missionaries are unctuous, and unctuous people are generally blasted liars, so there may be something in what you say.'

*   *   *

Mr Erskine was, in fact, thoroughly drunk. He was found in the stoker's messdeck wrapped in a blanket inside a hammock, where a kindly stoker had placed him when he had been discovered beneath the mess table. The fumes of John Haig were immensely strong, and the clergyman could not be woken, so

Halfhyde left him where he was. Rear-Admiral Hackenticker was easily found, being positioned beneath the lee of the bridge overhang where he was to some extent sheltered from the rain. He preferred the upper deck, he said, since the fug below was terrible in the overcrowded conditions. Some of the traders and their womenfolk had even managed to be seasick, or anyway riversick; and it was true that the progress of the *Cockroach* was somewhat wild as she sheered from side to side under the torrent's thrust.

Halfhyde said, 'My Captain is taking you out of arrest, sir, and wishes words with you in the wardroom.' He kept his face straight, but the American burst out into laughter.

'Arrest is Watkiss' panacea, I think,' he said. 'Not to be taken too seriously, Lieutenant?'

'Not always, sir.' Halfhyde smiled. 'When it becomes awkward ...'

'He backs down?'

'I prefer to say he puts the safety of his ship first, sir.'

Hackenticker chuckled. 'Loyally said!' He clapped Halfhyde on the shoulder. 'I guess I've been humouring your Captain Watkiss, but the time could have come to stop.'

'I don't quite follow, sir?'

'Why, he seems to me to be kind of whacky – no offence intended, but that's the way I see him. I've heard it said, Captains in your Royal Navy get like that because there's no one dares say boo to them except Admirals ... and they often don't see too much of Admirals when they're away on detached service.' Hackenticker paused. 'Tell me, Lieutenant, has Captain Watkiss done a lot of detached service in his time?'

'*Mostly* detached, sir. Possibly the Admirals preferred it that way ... but my Captain is all right at heart and has an uncanny knack of achieving a kind of success.' Halfhyde, not wishing to elaborate on that, suggested that the Rear Admiral might accompany him below. Hackenticker assented, and down they went for the wardroom, passing on the way a somewhat furtive Mr Bodmin making his way forward below decks. As Hackenticker and Halfhyde went through the curtained doorway of the wardroom, Mr Bodmin vanished into the messdecks. He was looking for the Reverend Marchwood Erskine who was reputed to be somewhere in the fore end of the gunboat. Mr Bodmin picked his way past civilians sitting upon the decks, past marines from Commodore Marriot-Lee's squadron, past off-watch seamen in their hammocks. Enquiring after the parson, he was told he could be found billeted with the stokers; and thence Mr Bodmin continued zealously, and at length found his quarry. Mr Bodmin gently rocked the hammock to and fro. He said, 'Parson?'

There was an indistinct sound and Mr Bodmin repeated, 'Parson?' before realizing that the missionary had entered the hammock in an unseamanlike fashion and was the wrong way round in it. He had been addressing the feet. Shifting to the head end, he tried again, but now got the full bouquet of the John Haig and made the appropriate deductions. Mr Bodmin shook his head sadly and went back the way he had come, muttering to himself. A fat lot of good it would be to ask the forgiveness of the Lord from a drunk parson even when he became sober again. Two sinners never could make a repentant, 'twasn't within nature, and Mr Bodmin rated drunkenness a longish way more sinful than going with women of easy virtue, or co-habiting. That was no more than answering the call of a nature given to mankind by the Lord Himself; the Lord had never made it natural to imbibe the wicked potions distilled in the world's dens of yeast and alcohol.

*　　*　　*

Full information now imparted as to Bloementhal, Captain Watkiss sat back at full arm's-stretch from the wardroom table, so that the tail of his tattooed snake emerged colourfully from the screen of his uniform cuff. 'Now, Admiral Hackenticker, what's your view of all that?'

Hackenticker shook his head and looked baffled. 'That's hard to answer, Captain. I've no reason to doubt Bloementhal's loyalty myself, that's for sure, but then I don't know the man, I only knew *of* him, if you follow, until you brought him up to Chungking.'

'But you had orders to contact him, had you not?'

'Yes, I had—'

'From your Peking Legation?'

'Yes. I signed his authority to—'

'To request passage up river aboard my ship – I know. But do I take it you didn't know him in Peking?'

'No, I didn't, that's correct, the passage chit was signed in his absence and on-forwarded.' Hackenticker leaned across the table. 'I'd not been long in Peking, I was hoicked away from a US squadron off Weihaiwei and told to report. Much against my will, I can tell you. All the time I was there, this Bloementhal was kind of out on field work – he had a sort of roving commission to keep contact with the American business community all over. And that's all I know about him.'

'From what you've seen of him, do you trust him?'

'I say again, I have no reason not to. I don't like him, let's be honest – but that's different.'

Watkiss sniffed. 'It's evidence of a sort, Admiral. Traitors are never likeable people.'

'Sure, but something more tangible is called for, isn't it?'

'Yes. Now then: Bloementhal told me, not long after he embarked off Tsingkiang, that there's a question of a treaty, though in my view everything has gone a long way beyond treaties now. Anyway, this treaty was a bone of contention between America, Germany and Russia – their trading interest, you know. None of the three wished the other two to conclude an agreement with the Empress-Dowager. And, I suppose in all fairness I might add, nor would Great Britain.'

Hackenticker looked faintly puzzled. 'So what are you driving at, Captain?'

Watkiss snapped, 'My new information suggests to me that Bloementhal could be in negotiation with the blasted Huns, don't you see! We must stop his little game, sir, you and I between us, and perhaps at the same time show up that bloated von Furstenberg before the world ... show him up for an intriguer and a potential traitor to his blasted Kaiser! Do you not agree?'

'Why, I can't yet say, Captain—'

'Why not?'

'I suggest we send first for Bloementhal, and carry out a probe. If he's playing a double game, I think we between us all can break him down, gentlemen. Then we'll have something more concrete to face von Furstenberg with.'

'Yes, that sounds reasonable. Mr Halfhyde?'

146

'Very reasonable, sir.'

'Yes. Then I shall see to it at once, or rather you will, Mr Halfhyde. Send a messenger—' Watkiss broke off as the voice-pipe from the bridge whistled eerily at him. He seized the flexible tube and placed the end of it against his ear. 'This is the Captain. Yes, Mr Pumphrey, what is it?' Listening, his face grew red, then redder. Wordlessly, he hurled the tube back towards its hook, which it missed and thereafter dangled like a serpent. Halfhyde got to his feet and replaced it.

'What was that, sir?' he asked.

Watkiss waved his telescope in the air and his spare monocle flew from his eye. 'That bloody fool Pumphrey . . . it's as bad as having Beauchamp back on the bridge! He has a feeling he's lost his way and we're off course!' The telescope was waved again, vigorously. 'I damn nearly said, how do even *you* manage to lose your way in a blasted river . . . then I remembered the flooding. By God, I'll give him off course!'

Watkiss, with Halfhyde, went at once to the bridge; Hacken-ticker, exercising tact, remained blind. Emerging from the head of the ladder, Captain Watkiss attacked the wretched sub-lieutenant.

'Mr Pumphrey, may your Captain enquire what makes you think you may have lost your way?'

'Yes, sir.' Pumphrey pointed over the side: Watkiss and Halfhyde stared down to see a highly curious sight. The *Cockroach* was sailing past the tops of small trees and close upon the starboard bow was seen what looked like the roof of a cottage with a goat perched upon it the better to avoid the deluge; on the port bow the upper reaches of a pagoda thrust through the waters of the flood, a flood upon which Captain Watkiss was certainly most mightily adrift.

He brandished his telescope at Pumphrey. 'Get away from the binnacle, you fool, you're utterly useless. Mr Halfhyde, get my ship back on her course immediately, if you please. I do not propose to turn the *Cockroach* into a blasted Ark, nor to assume the role of Noah.'

THIRTEEN

Truant, as it were, in a watery wilderness, Watkiss seethed from side to side of his bridge. Obediently behind *Cockroach* came *Bee* and *Wasp*, who had followed in the leader's wake throughout. 'Like damn sheep!' Watkiss said vengefully. 'Did it occur to no one to question Mr Pumphrey's course into the blasted countryside?'

'It would have been taken as *your* course, sir,' Halfhyde said, pouring oil on troubled waters.

'Well?'

'No one would care to question your course, sir. It would smack of insubordination ... would it not?'

'Possibly, yes.' Watkiss gave a sage nod. 'Nevertheless, each Commanding Officer is responsible for the safe handling and navigation of his own ship. Yeoman!'

Barefoot despite the wet, the yeoman of signals hastened to his side. 'Yessir?'

'Make to *Bee* and *Wasp*, you are to report the name of your Officer of the Watch by alphabetical flag hoist.'

'Aye, aye, sir.' The signals made, the unfortunate officers saw their names spelled out in full by the coloured bunting, draggled beneath the rain. Watkiss stared down over his ship's side: the flood-water was not especially deep in his view – any blasted idiot should have been able to pick up shoaling water. He stared down again and fancied he saw waving grass, or possibly it was a paddy field, or even wheat beneath him, just visible through the disturbed silt. He had no wish to ground upon a farm gate or some religious shrine and he said as much to Halfhyde.

148

'We shall soon be back in the stream, sir.'

'I trust we shall, Mr Halfhyde.' Watkiss glared as terraced hillsides swept past farther away to port and starboard, hills that were holding the flood-water back from spreading, thus keeping it sufficiently deep for his progress. Not far ahead, so said the chart, the Yangtze took a wide north-easterly sweep towards the Chutang Gorge, and before they reached the gorge the flood-waters must surely be contained within the river bed even though ships might pass through at a great height and the current would be fast to the point of extreme danger. . . . After some fifty minutes of acute anxiety, Halfhyde reported that the Yangtze was once again beneath them and that they were set upon their course for the Chutang Gorge. As *Cockroach* took the river and the main stream of the current, her speed increased rapidly and she seemed to hurtle along like an express train, with *Bee* and *Wasp*, dead bullocks and general debris hurtling after her.

'Damn it, Mr Halfhyde, we're not under control, are we?'

'Not fully, sir—'

'Then hoist your balls, man, hoist your balls!'

'Aye, aye, sir.' Halfhyde gave an order to the yeoman of signals and the Not Under Control balls, black-painted, tar-stiffened spheres of canvas, were hoisted to the starboard upper yardarm of *Cockroach*'s single mast. This, after an interval, was repeated by both *Bee* and *Wasp* as they rushed along similarly hell-bent.

'This is a pretty kettle of fish, Mr Halfhyde.'

'No more than was to be expected, I think, sir.'

Watkiss bounced on the balls of his feet. 'But what about the gorges, Mr Halfhyde? I cannot make the passage of the gorges whilst being hurled along like an arrow from a bow!'

Halfhyde smiled. 'It will be difficult, I agree. However, it's an ill wind that blows nobody any good, sir, is it not?'

'What do you mean?' Watkiss asked suspiciously.

'Why, sir, the Russians out of Port Arthur. They'll make no progress up river against such a current and I'd not now expect to see them before Kiukiang at the earliest.'

'Yes, perhaps, but I didn't expect to find them so far up as this anyway, Mr Halfhyde, anyone would be a fool if they did.'

Watkiss moved back and forth along his bridge while rain bounced off his oilskins. There was still the matter of Bloementhal: that must of course be settled before there was any encounter with Russian vessels, but for the moment, and indeed for some hours to come, the safety of his flotilla must be Watkiss' first concern and Bloementhal must wait upon that. Watkiss announced his intention of remaining upon the bridge until all three gorges had been safely negotiated, and that at their current speed the Chutang should be reached a good deal earlier than had been expected.

Halfhyde concurred. 'By nightfall, I estimate, sir, and possibly sooner.'

'Yes. I suggest you put the telegraph to stop, Mr Halfhyde. We have still to conserve fuel, have we not?'

'We have, sir, but the saving will be very small so long as we keep steam on the main engine at all, whilst we can't risk shutting down the boilers entirely.'

'Precisely so, Mr Halfhyde, I am not a fool, but every little helps, does it not?'

Halfhyde shrugged. 'Yes, sir—'

'Then the telegraph to stop, Mr Halfhyde, and kindly inform *Bee* and *Wasp* accordingly.'

Halfhyde passed the orders somewhat reluctantly. There was risk in it: to 'coast' down upon the gorges would mean that each ship would lose its ability to respond on the instant to any changing situation – perhaps not for long, but for long enough to cause trouble while the engine-room put the silent engine back into gear so that the screw could turn again. However, it was perhaps less of a risk than running out of coal.

The flotilla sped on upon its long voyage to Shanghai and the open sea.

*   *   *

'Ah, Mr Bloementhal, just the very man I wanted to see.' Rear Admiral Hackenticker had been having a good think about Bloementhal, who sure looked like being the villain of the piece if Watkiss was right, or if that Chinese girl was right, to be more accurate. Hackenticker had a strong feeling she wouldn't have risked inventing the whole thing, and anyway she looked honest as the day was long, though it sure could be hard to read a Chinese face. Anyway, she couldn't have any axe of her own or Bodmin's to grind. Meantime, Watkiss was busy on his bridge, so it wouldn't hurt to have a word himself with Bloementhal who was, after all, his own countryman. After a search, Bloementhal had come to light taking some sort of shelter beneath the *Cockroach*'s cutter griped-in to the davits abaft the bridge. He looked thoroughly damp and dispirited, suffering badly from the overcrowded conditions.

'Hi there, Admiral,' he said, waving a hand morosely.

Hackenticker squatted on his haunches for easier speech. 'You look pretty miserable. Aren't they feeding you, or something?'

'I had some breakfast, Admiral, what I need's a drink.'

'Scotch?'

'Sure!'

'Come along with me, then. I have a flask.' Hackenticker resumed an upright position and Bloementhal crawled out from under the davits and followed him below. Hackenticker went by way of the paint store, outside which stood an armed marine as sentry on the arrested German. The sentry made no difficulties about admitting the Rear Admiral, and obligingly unlocked the door.

'What the heck,' Bloementhal said.

'Bear with me a while,' Hackenticker said. He went in. Count von Furstenberg was reclining in a deck chair, eating a wrinkled-looking apple, taking great bites with big yellow teeth and munching the results. 'Good morning, Count.'

The apple-eating was held in abeyance. 'A good morning to you, Admiral.' The German grinned. 'See, I am so polite to my captors, to my enemies!'

'Why be enemies all the while, Count? We can all be civilized in between times, can't we? We're all gentlemen—'

'I am a von.' The apple was bitten again.

'Yes, indeed. No reason why we shouldn't take a drink together that I can see.' Hackenticker produced his whisky flask, a vast affair of pewter, more like a bottle. The German's eyes gleamed. 'May we come in and join you, Count? Your *pied-à-terre* is rather bigger than mine.'

'But of course.' Von Furstenberg heaved himself from the

deck chair, and gave a small bow and a heel-click. 'You are most welcome, gentlemen, but be careful of the paint which is everywhere in profusion.'

They went in, found seats wherever it was possible to obtain bottom-hold, and Rear Admiral Hackenticker unscrewed the stopper of his flask.

*   *   *

This time Mr Beauchamp was not in open arrest but, since his crime had been so heinous, in close arrest, which meant he was now confined to his quarters. His quarters were not his own cabin, which had been required for the accommodation of some of the unfortunate passengers from Chungking, but a windy and wet compartment situated on deck immediately above the paint store – a compartment normally reserved for the various items of deck-cleaning gear such as scrubbers and squeegees, mops, holystoning equipment and caulking materials like tar and oakum. Outside in the rain shivered Mr Pumphrey as Mr Beauchamp's warder. Normally an officer in close arrest was entitled to become the personal responsibility of an officer of his own rank, but Watkiss had felt unable to waste his more senior officers upon such a task when danger threatened, and this inability had forced him initially to accept Beauchamp's word that he wouldn't escape. However, after Mr Pumphrey had lost his way upon the flood-water, he had become better fitted for such a task than to be allowed upon the bridge; and had been so detailed, even though he was a mere sub-lieutenant.

As Pumphrey shivered and grew more and more depressed as to his future *vis-à-vis* Captain Watkiss, a tap came upon the door he was guarding, and it was opened from within. Mr Beauchamp looked out nervously as though half expecting to be sprung upon by Captain Watkiss. 'Ah, Mr Pumphrey.'

'Yes, sir?'

'I feel a little sick. The smells of tar and oakum and so forth.'

'I'm sorry, sir—'

'If you would be so kind, Mr Pumphrey.' Suddenly, Mr Beauchamp came out at the rush and Pumphrey stepped quickly aside. Beauchamp flew for the rail and bent over. When he had finished he felt quite washed-out and cold, and was indeed shaking all over as though with the ague. As he turned he saw that Pumphrey had been joined by ex-Boatswain Bodmin, who was wagging his head and clicking his tongue.

'Well, I never did, zur. Seasick like, zur?'

'No. Tar and oakum, Mr Bodmin.'

Bodmin raised his shaggy eyebrows, then understanding dawned. 'Ar, zur, I see what ee means. The whole ship be topsy turvy like, with people livin' in – in unsuitable places, zur. 'Tis the luck o' the draw, like, zur.' He peered into the deck store. 'All the same like, ee 'ave a better place 'n what I 'ave, though that's nothin' but right an' proper, o' course, seein' ee be a wardroom gentleman, zur.'

Beauchamp wiped his mouth and continued shaking. He turned sad eyes upon Bodmin. 'I'd appreciate your company if you can spare the time, Mr Bodmin. Won't you come in?' He indicated his abode.

Bodmin nodded, 'Ar, zur, and thankee.' He walked in, followed by Beauchamp, and Pumphrey, somewhat hesitantly, closed the door upon them, whereat Mr Bodmin registered some alarm, for stirrings in his memory reminded him of the interpretations that could be placed in Her Majesty's service upon the proximity of two male persons in a deck store. However, it was not for him to give the orders and certainly the door kept out the rain and the chill air.

Mr Beauchamp came out with it bluntly. 'I'm in arrest, Mr Bodmin, that's why you see me in this place.'

'In arrest, zur?' Mr Bodmin held his head back, pursed his lips, and frowned. 'In arrest ee be, zur? Accused o' some crime or other, zur?'

'Yes, Mr Bodmin, and most unfairly. I've been very poorly treated by Captain Watkiss!'

'Ar, zur. Well, zur, Cap'n Watkiss, 'e do be a short tempered man, zur, was even as a nipper, but 'arf the time 'e don't mean it like, zur. 'E be full o' bullshit, zur, if ee'll pardon the expression.'

'Yes. You've served with him before – I remember. Did he put people in arrest in those days too?'

'No, zur, 'e warn't senior enough, zur, 'e were no more'n a midshipman what relied upon 'is cox'n to 'andle 'is boat for him, zur, an' if 'e'd 'ave tried to put the cox'n in arrest, why zur, cox'n 'd 'ave died laughin', zur.' Bodmin paused. 'Just you try thinkin' o' that, zur, next time 'e torments you like.'

'Yes, I will. Thank you, Mr Bodmin.'

'That be all right, zur.' Bodmin hesitated. 'This crime, zur, you're not guilty do I take it?'

Beauchamp said with extreme bitterness, 'How does anyone know whether or not they're guilty in Captain Watkiss' eyes? I did my best, but Captain Watkiss thinks I did it wrong.'

'Ar, zur. So it's to do wi' duty like, zur, not summat *grave* in the sense o'—'

'No, no. My handling of the ship in his absence.'

Light dawned, and Mr Bodmin nodded. 'Oh, ar, zur, I do understand now. Like when we found the ship standin' on 'er 'ead and the cable all fouled up, and—'

'Yes, yes!'

'Ar, zur, yes, I do understand. Yes, reckon I do ...' The sympathy seemed to be leaving Bodmin's tone somewhat; after all, he was a boatswain of the old school, of the sailing navy, and probably in his day keel-hauling would have awaited any officer who had held a ship down by her snout to drown while the waters rose around her. Beauchamp was willing to accept a degree of blame but still felt very hard done by: surely *open* arrest would have been enough – he was used to that and it was no great inconvenience once you'd acclimatized ... all at once he became aware of a change in Mr Bodmin's expression: the old fellow was in an attitude of listening and his starboard ear was being gradually pressed closer and closer to the inboard bulkhead of the smelly deck store.

'What is it, Mr Bodmin?'

Bodmin placed a tobacco-stained forefinger against his lips. 'Voices, zur. Talkin' like.'

'Where?'

'Somewhere below, zur. There must be a pipe or summat comin' up the bulk'ead t' other side.'

'Whose voices?'

'One o' 'em's that there American, zur, Admiral Hackenticker. I 'ear the 'Un too, zur, Count von Furstenberg, I reckon.'

'Do you think it's right to—'
'*Sssssh*, zur, with respect like.'

*   *   *

Count von Furstenberg had taken a fairly large quantity of
Scotch, and had taken it neat. So had Bloementhal. The
German, with his head against an ascending ventilation shaft,
was taken by surprise when the shaft hissed at him suddenly,
and he gave a loud belch and reached out his hand for Hackenticker's flask. The American passed it over. Von Furstenberg
took a gulp, wiped his lips with the back of his hand, and passed
the flask on to Bloementhal. 'Good spirit, very good. Not much
drunk in my country.'
'You drink beer, I believe, Count?'
'Lager from Pilsen and much wine, yes. Much wine. A little
schnapps. I am a lager man.' Von Furstenberg patted his noble
stomach in proof. He belched again, and smiled.
'We were saying,' Hackenticker said meaningly, and
watched Bloementhal's face without appearing to.
'Yes, yes, we were saying.' A few words of German were
gobbled out like a turkey with a sore throat. 'This is my time of
relaxation. Arrest does not worry me – the stupid British Captain will get his deserts from my Kaiser, who will complain
much to his grandmother in Windsor Castle. Politics, work . . .
no, I shall *not* discuss more.' The Count waved his arms
around the paint store, dangerously, and only just missed
a can of turpentine. 'We are all good, good friends, no?
Yes?'
'I guess so,' Hackenticker answered. 'Some of us more than
others, maybe.' He paused, and sat well back beneath a shelf
bearing what seemed to be hundreds of cans of white paint and
a few dozen pounds of putty. He gave an appearance of the
relaxation desired by Count von Furstenberg; he yawned
largely and said, 'The Peking Legation, Mr Bloementhal.'
'Uh-huh?'
'When you were there . . . did you ever meet an old guy by the
name of Colonel O'Flynn?'
'O'Flynn?'
'Right. Mickey O'Flynn.'

Bloementhal considered. 'No,' he said at length. 'No, I never met anyone of that name in Peking.'

'You must have heard of him? That old guy Bodmin now ... Mickey O'Flynn is kind of Peking's Bodmin with a difference. O'Flynn was once a colonel in the US Eighth Cavalry. Flamboyant, likes his Scotch. Irish immigrant family settled in Texas. One of the pioneers who opened up the West. Always around the Legation and known to all.'

'Yes. I do remember something, Admiral.' Bloementhal was being off-hand, casual.

'Thought you would. Mickey wasn't attached to the Legation, not officially. He has trading interests around Peking, as I recall, but he keeps in touch a lot.'

'Sure.'

'You heard of him, then?'

Bloementhal said dismissingly, 'Oh, sure, sure. They talked about him ... when you mentioned Texas and that, well, I remembered.'

'Thought you would,' Hackenticker said again, then went on, 'Where in the States do you come from, Mr Bloementhal?'

'Upstate New York. Watertown.'

'You'll know Sackets Harbor?'

'Sure.'

'Good sailing ... Lake Ontario.'

'I'm no sailing man, Admiral.'

Hackenticker laughed. 'Neither am I. Funny, that, for a sailor! I was always a big ship man, a battleship man for preference. I go for solidity.'

'Not a bad thing to go for, Admiral.'

'No. Mickey O'Flynn is like that, too. Likes things big, did you ever hear that?'

'I don't know.' Bloementhal answered shortly. He was, Hackenticker saw, becoming restively cagey. That was interesting. 'I don't know how he likes things. Should I?'

'Well, now, I suppose not. Only he was such a great old character around the Legation and that was one of the things they talked a lot about. How Mickey O'Flynn liked things big. How he built the biggest barn, grew the biggest grapefruit, wore the biggest hat.' A number of other bignesses emerged. 'Big in all things little, Mr Bloementhal. Have another Scotch.'

'Thanks.'

Once more the enormous flask was passed and there was a silence whilst Bloementhal drew from it. Then Bloementhal laughed and said, 'Tell you one thing about Mickey O'Flynn, and that is, he doesn't exist.'

Hackenticker's eyebrows went up. 'Now, if that's the case, why in heck have I been talking about him, Mr Bloementhal?'

'Let's say, trying to catch me out on something?'

'Why should I do that?'

Bloementhal shrugged. 'You tell me, Admiral. But that's what it's been sounding like to me . . . describing this big-liking Irish Texan who seems to me very considerably larger than life—'

'Just what Mickey O'Flynn is. He exists all right, Mr Bloementhal, as is well-known to anyone who's been within a hundred miles of our Legation in Peking. Which means you haven't. Maybe it's not a lot to go on, but added to other things it grows and grows.'

Bloementhal remained calm and sardonic outwardly, but there was a new tension in the air of the paint store and he seemed to be holding himself ready to jump someone, coiled like a spring. He said, 'So how do you explain your own signature on my authority to ask British transportation, and how do you explain the fact that the Legation got you to countersign and onforward what was an official document?'

Hackenticker grinned. 'That raises other interesting points, Mr Bloementhal, since I don't deny there was indeed a Bloementhal attached to the Peking Legation. Maybe we'd better talk about that.'

*   *   *

'Zur, zur!'

'Yes, Mr Bodmin?'

'Did you 'ear that, zur?' Both Bodmin and Beauchamp had their ears to the bulkhead now, eavesdropping without shame. 'I reckon it were a blow, zur, fisticuffs.'

Beauchamp listened more intently. 'Yes, I think you're right.' Sounds of violence came up the ventilation shaft, bone upon flesh, sharp cries, curses, and then a terrible racket as of an ironmonger's shop being ravaged by a wild animal, and finally the sharp sound of a revolver shot. Beauchamp lost no more time. 'Mr Bodmin, you must inform the Captain at once.'

'Beg pardon, zur, but I be a mere passenger aboard—'

'And I'm in arrest, Mr Bodmin, and should I break out, no matter what the reason, I fear it would go ill with me. At once, Mr Bodmin!'

'Ar, zur, I'll do as ee says, zur.' Bodmin pushed open the door of the deck store and came out, as he had expected, into the rain. He went as fast as he could for the bridge ladder, noting as he moved the immense speed of the *Cockroach* in the grip of the fierce torrent that propelled her on for the Chutang Gorge. Grasping the handrails he climbed the ladder and emerged on to the bridge.

'Cap'n, zur!'

Captain Watkiss, standing with his stomach wedged against the forward guardrail as though he were his own figurehead, did not turn. 'Go away, Mr Bodmin, I am conning my ship and the river is full of danger.'

'But, zur, Mr Beauchamp, 'e—'

'Mr Beauchamp's in arrest and doesn't exist. Kindly make yourself scarce.'

'Zur, zur, I—'

'*Go away*, Mr Bodmin, or you'll be in arrest too.'

'But zur, there was a shot—'

'Oh, hold your tongue!'

It was no use; that there Watkiss, he were as stubborn as a mule, as stubborn and foolish as Bodmin remembered him being as a midshipman – no real change, he'd just worsened with the passing years. Sulkily, Bodmin turned to go back down the ladder and when he was half-way down there came the sound of rifle-fire – several shots from somewhere near the Captain's cabin as he judged, right below where he stood poised on the bridge ladder. He went down in a brace of shakes, very nimble for old man. Watkiss had had his chance and now Mr Bodmin had other things to do, and one of them was to see to the physical safety of Song Tso-P'eng.

FOURTEEN

There was quite a crowd at the head of the Captain's alleyway when Bodmin reached it: men and women, seamen, marines, and that Lord Edward Cole. Farther into the alley Bodmin saw Hackenticker, who seemed to be taking charge. Bodmin tried to push through, but was prevented by Lord Edward.

'I wouldn't if I were you, Mr Bodmin. There's a lot of blood. It's awfully messy and you'll only be in the way.'

Bodmin quivered. 'Blood did you say, my lord?'

'Yes, but don't worry, your good lady's perfectly all right thanks to Admiral Hackenticker. And the sentry.'

'That be an immense relief, zur.' Mr Bodmin brought out a huge handkerchief of spotted red silk and mopped his face. 'And the blood, my lord?'

'Bloementhal's. I don't know yet what happened, Mr Bodmin, but it appears Bloementhal was attempting to get at your good lady, and Admiral Hackenticker, who was in pursuit, called to the sentry to stop him, and the sentry very sensibly shot him.'

'I see, zur, my lord. Now I'd like to go through and comfort Mrs Bodmin, if you don't mind—'

'Oh, I'm sure Admiral Hackenticker will do that, Mr Bodmin, and you needn't worry—'

'No, zur, young fellow-me-lad, you don't understand, and I'm not 'avin' no Hadmiral 'Ackentickers comfortin' Mrs Bodmin. I'm about to go through, zur, my lord, don't you try an' stop me.' Mr Bodmin thrust at the back end of the crowd and burrowed his way vigorously in, shouting out aloud in the stentorian voice that he had used when, as a boatswain on the active list in days long past, he had hazed the common seamen aloft to the masts and yards of a sailing line-of-battleship.

*   *   *

'Thank you, Admiral Hackenticker, you've done well and I'm obliged.' The American's report of the shooting rendered, Captain Watkiss remained staring belligerently ahead, four square beneath the drenching rain, looking in his sou'wester and obliterative oilskins like a miniature Buddha set immovably in unlikely surroundings. However, the time for consultation and movement had in fact come and he turned to Halfhyde.

'Mr Halfhyde, I am now required to attend to urgent matters of state. We are at last well on course in the river and the banks will prevent wandering.' This was true: the banks had deepened as the run-in to the Chutang Gorge began, and the Yangtze was now contained, but rushing along at an even greater pace than before now that it was channelled again. 'Kindly take over my ship, and report when you have the gorge in sight, Mr Halfhyde. I shall be in the wardroom.'

'Yes, sir.'

Watkiss turned away and preceded Hackenticker down his bridge ladder. Coming forward along the upper deck was Beauchamp, eyes wide and earnest, with Pumphrey behind him.

'Captain, sir!'

'Good heavens, Mr Beauchamp, what's this I see? What the devil are you doing out of the deck store, may I enquire?'

'Sir, I—'

'Go back in this instant. Mr Pumphrey, I shall have words with you later, when you shall give your reasons why you allowed Mr Beauchamp to emerge contrary to my orders.'

'Sir,' Pumphrey said, 'Mr Beauchamp had important matters to communicate.'

'What matters?'

'It was I, sir,' Beauchamp said eagerly, 'who sent Mr Bodmin to report to you—'

'Bodmin, Bodmin. I was not aware of any report, and you should know better than to *send messengers* to your Captain, Mr Beauchamp, it's not done when you can come yourself—'

160

Beauchamp broke in desperately, 'I was in arrest, sir!'

'Yes, you were and are.' Watkiss lunged towards him with his telescope. 'Kindly stop all this chatter and get back to the deck store.'

'But I heard what was taking place below in the paint store, sir, and I thought—'

'Never mind what you thought, Mr Beauchamp, I have been informed of events already by Admiral Hackenticker and your thoughts are superfluous.' Captain Watkiss turned his back and went below to the wardroom, where he cast his sou'wester from his head and sat down. 'Now, Admiral. Some filling-in of detail would be in order, I fancy.'

Hackenticker nodded. Bloementhal, he explained, or whatever his real name might prove to be, had gone berserk when he, Hackenticker, had faced him with the fact that there had been a Bloementhal attached to the Legation staff in Peking but that he was not that man: the inference had been plain enough for all present to see – the real Bloementhal had been disposed of somewhere along the line, which taken to the extreme could implicate the fake Bloementhal in murder. When this had been put to him, Bloementhal had hit back in no mean fashion. He had hurled himself upon Hackenticker, who had drawn his revolver, but had been unable to use it before Bloementhal's movement had brought down a large number of paint cans and the putty, most of which, in fact, had fallen upon Count von Furstenberg. Much angered, the German had retaliated upon the deluge of cans by snatching Hackenticker's revolver and firing it at Bloementhal, by which time the sentry on watch outside had entered the paint store and had his rifle torn from his grasp by von Furstenberg's bullet, which had missed Bloementhal. Hackenticker had managed to seize his revolver back and having done so had struck Bloementhal hard upon the back of the neck with the barrel; the fake Bloementhal had gone down gasping, but had quickly got up again and sped out of the door, knocking down the sentry in the rush, whilst von Furstenberg, taking a gallon can of paint on his head, had fallen heavily upon Hackenticker, pinning him down for a while. Hackenticker had caught up with his adversary as he was running for the Captain's cabin and had shouted ahead to the sentry. Bloementhal, whose name in fact was Kurt Schmultz, was now dead; and he had been a German.

'I had a word with von Furstenberg,' Hackenticker said. 'He saw no reason not to come clean, since it was all blown anyway.' He added with a grin, 'He's turning what you might call Queen's evidence in your country, having an eye to the main chance for himself, of course!'

'Of course,' Watkiss said distantly. 'I always knew Bloementhal was not an American, I might add.'

'You did?'

'Yes.' Watkiss glowered at the note of astonishment, but preened himself upon his perspicacity. He recalled duty not dooty, coffee not carffee, and a lack of nasality. 'I never trusted the man, don't you know. Shifty. And not very efficient, moreover – he must have learned his English in England, not America. He spoke quite well. It didn't take me long to see through *that*. But what about that Hun?'

'What about him?'

'I suppose I'd better see him. You say he's in a mood to talk – that may not last.' Watkiss reached out for the voicepipe to the bridge. 'Where is he at this moment, Admiral?'

'Back in the paint locker, Captain, and under arrest again. I wasn't taking any chances!' He paused, lifting an eyebrow. 'I trust I didn't intrude on your prerogative?'

'Oh, no, no, no, that's quite all right.' Watkiss sounded huffy nevertheless. He blew down the voice-pipe. 'The Captain speaking,' he said. 'Mr Halfhyde, kindly send your bridge messenger to fetch Count von Furstenberg to the wardroom under the guard of the marine sentry to be found on the paint store.' He put the tube back in its clip. 'There! In a few moments I shall be in a position to make my plans, Admiral Hackenticker.'

'To which I shall need to be party, Captain, since United States interests are concerned as much as those of Great Britain – and we have still to remember the Russians.'

Watkiss gave an irritable grunt and jerked his monocle from his eye. He had not forgotten the Russians, but they were a fairly tinpot country when set against the Empire; they were always seething with discontent, and discontent always sapped the guts of a nation. Also, they were dreadfully backward, like

162

all peasantries. Surging towards the Chutang Gorge upon a tide of flood-water and victory – for had he not successfully brought out all the civilians and Consulate staff? – Captain Watkiss was in the full flush of bounce. When Count von Furstenberg entered the wardroom ahead of the marine sentry's rifle and bayonet, Watkiss felt in a fine position of dominance. He pointed at a chair. 'Be seated, if you please, Count.'

Ungraciously, the Hun thumped into a seat. The whisky had subsided a little now, and he announced that nothing had changed in regard to the wishes of his Kaiser.

'What do you mean?' Watkiss demanded.

'Because of the man Schmultz, alias Bloementhal.'

'Yes, yes. But the wishes of your Kaiser! For whom do you work, Count – for your Kaiser, or for yourself?'

Von Furstenberg glared and answered stiffly, 'Captain, I think you speak in most insulting terms. Never have I, never would I, act against the interest of my Kaiser. In all I do, my thoughts and my duty are for my Kaiser. I am an honourable man.'

'I see.' Watkiss was looking flummoxed: the German's words had somehow held the ring of truth.

'But I think you do *not* see, Captain. I think you doubt what I say. At Shanghai you will learn different, and I say this, that if you have behaved improperly towards me, then the wrath of your Queen will fall upon you!' Count von Furstenberg raised a beefy fist and brought it down with a crash upon the wardroom table. 'Already you have insulted me with arrest—'

'That was Admiral Hackenticker,' Watkiss said, sounding smug.

'The second time yes, the first time no. The first time the arrestor was you, Captain Watkiss, but it matters not who did it. It is the principle. Gentlemen,' von Furstenberg went on passionately, 'I represent my Kaiser, who is an honourable—'

'Ha!'

'—and peace-loving Emperor—'

'What balls!'

'—and for him I do my duty as you do for your Queen and President respectively. This is fair and aboveboard and though perhaps we try to outwit one another, we should have respect for each. No?' Von Furstenberg sounded hopeful, and when agreement was reached upon the point, he went on, 'I believe you are being too much swayed by lies told to you by the renegade Schmultz. Has this man told you that I, Count Hermann von Furstenberg, act against my Kaiser?'

Hackenticker lowered an eyelid fractionally at Watkiss. 'Yes, that's what we understood from—'

'And you believed him?' There was amazement in the German's expression, and in his tone. 'Why was this? A man of Schmultz' type and class, to be believed before a Count of the German Empire, a Prussian, one of the German officer corps? What madness is this?'

Watkiss' face was a deep red and he squirmed in his chair. He had been guilty of not behaving as a gentleman, perhaps. He had believed scandal too readily in the first place, as a result of the utterances, the repeated utterances, of that blasted missionary. Yes! The blasted missionary! He cleared his throat and began to eat humble pie. 'My apologies, Count. The word of the cloth, don't you know ... should I take it that you were the genuine dealer, and Bloementhal – Schmultz – the one who was seeking personal gain at his Kaiser's expense?'

'*But of course, of course!*' Once again, the fist crashed down. 'A case of wrong identity! You speak of the cloth. Do I take it you mean that ragbag missionary who drinks whisky like fishes?'

'Yes, yes—'

Von Furstenberg gave a roar of deep belly-laughter and again smote the table, an action that was beginning to irritate Captain Watkiss, who was financially responsible for the good maintenance of ship fittings and furnishings. 'You are such damned fools, such idiots! In the cloth of that man there is little guile, little dishonesty as such, truly, but always he sells his wares to the one who bids the highest in whisky bottles! Oh, such fools, such idiots!'

The German rocked, holding his sides. Tears ran down his face. He laughed for a full two minutes, and then was brought up sharp by a question from Hackenticker. 'Tell me, Count, why did you not turn Schmultz in earlier if you knew what he was about?'

'Aha,' von Furstenberg said, sounding cunning, 'because we have still to face and outwit the Russians! It was for me better that you should believe Schmultz to be Bloementhal until we were past the Russian danger, do you not see?'

'Why so?' Hackenticker asked. 'I don't see it.'

The German wagged a finger. 'I am still against you, as my duty dictates – this you are men of the world enough to understand. I foresaw a greater chance of success in dealing with the Russians if you believed me to be a featherer of personal nests, for I could so easily prove that I am not, and the Russians would know you to be liars after that—'

'But my dear sir,' Watkiss broke in angrily, 'that presupposes that there is some intent upon our part to deal with the Russians, does it not, whereas that is not *my* intention at all events! I can't speak for Admiral Hackenticker. I consider my own duty to be done – or that it will be the moment I have steamed through the blasted Russians and taken my flotilla out to sea!'

'But the diplomatic considerations, Captain—'

'Oh, balls to the diplomatic considerations,' Watkiss said loftily. 'I'm a British seaman, not some damn – some damn dago,' he finished lamely, having intended to say Hun. The blasted German! He looked like a sausage, but a sausage that he, Watkiss, could do little about now. Watkiss was a very angry man inside; Halfhyde had said, had he not, that the missionary's information could prove to be false and that Erskine and Bloementhal could have been hand in glove – Halfhyde had been right again! Captain Watkiss ground his teeth. However, all was not lost and someone could be made to suffer. As bitter thoughts revolved in his head, Captain Watkiss became aware that the German was addressing him again.

'What is it now, Count?'

'I am no longer in arrest? I am now discharged?'

Watkiss glared. The bugger, he felt sure, was laughing up his blasted sleeve. 'Oh, go to the devil!' he snapped rudely, and bounced out of the wardroom, back to his bridge. Reaching it he found, to his immense pleasure, that the rain was at last stopping, the clouds were rolling away and the sky was blue though now tending towards night.

'Just in time, sir,' Halfhyde said.

'For what, may I ask?'

Halfhyde pointed ahead and Watkiss placed his monocle in

165

his eye. Ahead now lay the great pale orange limestone cliffs of the Chutang Gorge. Watkiss rubbed his hands together and nodded. 'Excellent, Mr Halfhyde. First, however, there's another matter: send a messenger to find that missionary, Erskine.'

'He's still where he was, sir – in a hammock in the stoker's messdeck and he's still drunk.'

'Just as I expected. Have him sent for, if you please, Mr Halfhyde, and muster the side party with hoses. Before I talk to him, Mr Erskine's to be hosed down and rendered sober.'

'Aye, aye, sir.'

*   *   *

Erskine was not extracted from his hammock until it was too late for an immediate hosing down: the Chutang Gorge appeared to be rushing to meet them at breakneck speed, and Captain Watkiss gripped the guardrail ahead of his stomach and stood with chin thrust forward as he entered the narrows like a charioteer and about as fast. With the engine now put full astern in an attempt to check her way, the *Cockroach* was gripped by a torrent that seemed entirely disrespectful of engines whether they be put ahead or astern, and sent surging into the gap between the cliff faces. Captain Watkiss remained aloof and left the handling of the ship to Halfhyde. The speed was tremendous, but the much increased depth of water gave the vessels safety, protecting them from the scattered boulders that sat dam-like across the river bed to ensnare voyagers at times of normal depth. The principal danger was that they might be swung across, beam on, if the head should fall off, and then they could be smashed willy-nilly against the sheer sides of the cliffs that formed the gorge. But the hands of the quartermasters were steady on the wheels, and Halfhyde in the lead kept his own ship on an iron-set course as if by exercise of his will alone. All three gunboats came through in record time and unscathed, and rushed on towards the thirty miles of the Wu Gorge not far ahead, the gorge that would lead them out of Szechwan province and into Hupei. Hawks flew above, wheeling high, as the mighty current swirled the flotilla into the grip of the next array of cliffs. The passage of the Wu was behind them within some ninety minutes, leaving only the Hsiling yet to be traversed; and some three and a half hours from the first entry into the Chutang, all the gorges had been safely navigated and they were steaming out into the Central China plain for Ichang. So strong was the current still that they emerged almost like a champagne cork into more uncontained flood-water spewing from the Hsiling Gorge.

Captain Watkiss removed the uniform cap that by now had replaced his sou'wester, and mopped at his forehead. 'Thank God that's over, Mr Halfhyde.'

'Amen, sir.'

'You did well.'

'Thank you, sir.'

'I was watching most carefully throughout, ready with advice.'

'It was a comfort, sir. And now—'

'First, that blasted missionary.' Captain Watkiss had not forgotten. The orders were passed and the Reverend Marchwood Erskine was taken by two able-seamen to the fo'c'sle, where his garments were removed behind the canvas screen rigged originally for Bodmin's woman, and the wash-deck hoses were turned most vigorously and coldly upon his dancing body until he was both clean and sober. Captain Watkiss personally ordered the vomit-covered clothing to be cast into the Yangtze; the clergyman, he said, was to be re-dressed from whatever might be found available aboard, and when rendered respectable was to be brought to the wardroom for words with himself. Watkiss conducted the interview in the presence of the British Consul from Chungking, who had been firmly told not to interrupt; his advice would be sought if and when required.

Watkiss started off baldly. 'You are a disgrace to your cloth, Mr Erskine.'

'My dear sir, you have no right—'

'Oh, yes, you are and I have, that's fact, I said it. I detest drunkenness, detest it. For a clergyman it's unforgivable, but that's between you and your God and I shall not pre-empt His decisions. It's your dreadful chicanery in other directions that is of the first concern to me in the execution of my duty. I demand an explanation.' Watkiss sat back with arms folded and his eyes raised to the deckhead as though he could no longer abide the sight of wickedness. 'Produce it.'

Erskine, still a little damp from his hosing, was shaking like a leaf; it could be the dregs of alcohol, or it could be guilt. He mustered speech and a touch of dignity. 'If you'd be so good as to inform me of what I'm supposed to have done, Captain, I might be able to satisfy you that I have nothing to be ashamed of.'

'Rubbish. You know perfectly well what I'm talking about and you know you've been rumbled and you know you're a blasted traitor and a liar.' Watkiss' gaze came down from the deckhead to fasten, monocle-aided and a-glitter, upon the parson. 'Your information was utterly false and intended to mislead. Thanks largely to Admiral Hackenticker, you have been unmasked, and next you shall be unfrocked. A word to your bishop . . . but that will not be necessary, since you'll face public trial in England – kindly hold your tongue, Mr Carstairs, I told you not to interrupt—'

'Captain, I'm sorry, but a word would be advisable in your own interests.' The Consul leaned across and spoke into Watkiss' ear: Watkiss frowned and grew restive. Carstairs seemed to be suggesting that for the missionary to utter untruths about a German to another German masquerading as an American just might not be a crime pursuable through the British courts, but Watkiss took no notice of that. Once the facts had been established they would form part of his report to the Commodore in Hong Kong, who would thereafter report to the Admiralty, and that would be that. Erskine would be for it. Watkiss turned back to the parson to continue the interrogation and saw, to his astonishment, that Erskine was weeping. Tears were streaming down between the fingers that covered his face, and his shoulders were jerking like a reciprocating steam engine. Watkiss was about to utter a strong rebuke to unmanliness when he was interrupted by the wail of the voice-pipe. He snatched at it forbearingly. 'Yes?' he snapped. 'The Captain here.'

The voice was Lord Edward's and it was excited. 'Signal from *Bee*, sir. She's running short of coal.'

'Oh, God damn and blast, Lord Edward, what am I expected to do about it? I'll not be able to bunker before Nanking, if then!

Tell them—' Watkiss broke off. There had been a clang from above, and now there were two more clangs, indicating that the bridge end of the voice-pipe had been dropped by Lord Edward and that Watkiss' voice, issuing up it, was being unattended to. And the voice-pipe was picking up sounds of confusion and chaos. Watkiss, enraged, lifted his voice in a bellow through the flexible tube: '*Lord Edward, kindly pay attention to your Captain—*'

'This is Halfhyde now, sir—'

'What the devil—'

'The Russians are in sight ahead, sir.'

FIFTEEN

Watkiss was on his bridge in no time, furious that his flotilla should go and let him down at a time like this by running out of coal. He shook a fist towards the *Bee*, then rounded upon Halfhyde.

'Mr Halfhyde, sound for action if you please.'

'Is that wise, sir?'

'Oh, balls to wisdom, Mr Halfhyde, there's a time and place for everything and I'm not to be intimidated.'

'They've not yet tried to intimidate you, sir. I see no reason to suppose they will do so. We are carrying none of their nationals and they have no right to stop us—'

'I know, I know, you fool—'

'Then do not exacerbate the situation, sir! Remember we have women and children aboard.'

'Yes, exactly, and I must get them out of the Yangtze and into safe waters!'

'Sir—'

Watkiss brandished his telescope in Halfhyde's face. 'Stop this damned argument, Mr Halfhyde, and sound for action or I shall place you in arrest. We happen to have marines embarked, so they shall beat to quarters – that should put the fear of God into the buggers!' Watkiss glared out ahead towards the Russians: four gunboats of a class he recognized as superior to his own in speed, gun-power, and general fighting capability – for one thing, they carried torpedo-tubes. Long and low and sleek, they appeared as greyhounds to his hedgehogs. Again he addressed Halfhyde. 'Make to *Bee* and *Wasp*, they too are to beat to quarters and are to feed their fires with anything that will burn. Woodwork, furniture, anything. They are to maintain steam at all costs.'

'Aye, aye, sir.' Halfhyde passed the orders. There was a martial sound of drums more fitting to a battle squadron than the little gunboat flotilla. As his three-pounders were manned and armed, Watkiss waved his telescope energetically at the Russians.

'Scum!' he cried loudly. There was a step upon the ladder: Rear Admiral Hackenticker, who asked permission to join him on the bridge. Watkiss nodded: the more brass upon his bridge today the better, and better still, in the circumstances, that it was international. He said, 'A serious situation has arisen, Admiral.'

'If you remember, Captain, I forecast that you might be sealed into the Yangtze—'

'Yes. And if *you* remember, Admiral, *I* said I would fight my way through.'

Hackenticker raised an eyebrow. 'All that darned racket on the drums ... you really mean to do just that?'

'Of course!'

'You must be crazy, Captain.'

'Get off my bridge.'

'Just one moment, Captain ... now look, I was speaking in jocular vein as you might say ... I don't believe those Russians'll offer resistance, I really don't—'

'I said, get off my bridge.' Captain Watkiss bounced angrily and waved his telescope. 'I am not mad and I shall not be addressed as a common seaman.'

Hackenticker grinned. 'So there!'

'Kindly leave.'

The American shrugged and turned away for the ladder. What the heck. Watkiss *was* mad, say what he liked. He vanished, while on the bridge Captain Watkiss seethed with anger, turning his thoughts towards Count von Furstenberg who, it had been clearly stated, was not to be allowed to fall into Russian hands, a fact that surely indicated that the Russians, for their part, would like him to; indeed, that also had been stated. Captain Watkiss was damned if he was going to bring Hackenticker back to his bridge for consultation; he would make his own decision and the devil take Hackenticker. He was hamstrung by the lack of coal; in truth, he needed an alternative to engaging in action, since if he did, his fuel would run out in the course of it. He would therefore, if the chance arose, make good use of von Furstenberg as he had suggested earlier to Halfhyde. He would make untrue signals to the Russians indicating where von Furstenberg could be found if they would allow the gunboats free passage out. He lifted his telescope: the Russian vessels must have him within their range now, though they themselves were still out of reach of his three-pounders. Well, in any case, he fully intended to leave blatant aggression to the Russians, stupid popinjays, he wasn't anybody's fool. Once they had opened upon him, that would put him in the clear and no one would blame him for opening fire then. Below now, all the civilians had been ordered off the upper deck. Along with the wretched Beauchamp, Mr Pumphrey had been released from guard duty to go to his action station; and as the two flotillas swept inexorably closer together, Mr Bodmin climbed to the bridge to make representations about his woman.

'She's as safe in my cabin as anywhere else, Mr Bodmin.'

'Ar, zur. But she'd be a sight safer with me there, zur—'

'Oh, nonsense, what use would you be?'

'Well, protective like, zur, and I've no action station to go to, see.'

'Oh dear, Mr Bodmin, action station or no, surely she'd expect you to play a man's part in a fight? Or is it the custom in China to retire to the boudoir?'

'Well, zur, I don't know about that, zur, but it do be a fact that they Chinks do think some of *our* customs be right daft, zur—'

'How stupid. Why?'

'Because they be different like, zur.'

'Oh, nonsense, it's they who are different, not us. Oh, go to her if you wish, Bodmin, do.'

Mr Bodmin touched his cap. 'Thankee, zur, thankee.' He clambered back down the ladder. The *Cockroach* plunged on, still flood-borne and going at a smacking pace. A flashing light was seen ahead, winking from the Russian flotilla-leader's bridge.

'Yeoman!'

'Yessir.' Already the yeoman of signals was reading the message, and within half a minute had reported: 'You are requested to heave to, sir.'

Watkiss sniffed. 'Am I, indeed. What balls. Make, no.'

'Just no, sir?'

'Just no. Wait a moment. Perhaps I should settle this affair from the very start and leave the blasted Russian in no doubt as to my intentions. Write this down, Yeoman. Make, From Senior Officer of Her Britannic Majesty's First River Gunboat Flotilla detached from the naval command at Hong Kong: I regard myself as being upon the high seas and any attempt by you to obstruct my passage will be deemed an act of war or piracy against Her Majesty the Queen. Doubtless you understand that the Royal Navy does not stand idly by when opened fire upon. That's all, yeoman.'

'Aye, aye, sir.' The yeoman padded to his signal lamp and began sending rapidly. The two flotillas were no more than a mile apart when the yeoman reported the reply. 'Who said anything about opening fire, sir.'

Watkiss' face reddened. 'Damned impertinence!' He turned to Halfhyde. 'Warn my gun's crews, if you please. Action may be imminent – I don't trust dagoes.' As he finished speaking more signalling was observed; Watkiss waited impatiently for the yeoman, who reported, 'Please disembark Count von Furstenberg, sir.'

'That's all?'

'Yessir, message ends there, sir.'

'H'm.' Captain Watkiss took a turn or two up and down his bridge, his long shorts flapping in the beginnings of a breeze. Now he would put his master plan into execution and fool the stupid Russians, who were all gaudy uniforms of light blue and gold and red and had no brains to speak of. 'Yeoman, tell the Russians that Count von Furstenberg is not aboard my ship and why the devil should he be, but I am prepared under certain circumstances to reveal his whereabouts.'

'Aye, aye, sir.' The opposing flotillas closed more; the Russians had deployed to either side of the river, two to port and two to starboard. Clever ... Watkiss saw that his flotilla could be raked from stem to stern as each ship passed by, caught by fire from both flanks with their own guns forced to fight on two sides at once. What bloodthirsty fiends the Russians were to be sure, a dreadful race! Watkiss sweated as he tried to judge the exact split second when, if von Furstenberg should fail as a bargaining counter, he should open, and the wisdom of doing so at all if the Russians did not. The buggers might leave it too late for him to answer with his popguns, while they for their part could go on pumping shells into his rear for quite some time. He would have but one hope: sheer speed, for so long as *Bee* and *Wasp* could keep their fires fed anyway.

He looked astern. He fancied his ships were facing difficulties – they were tending to drop a little behind, and smoke of a curious texture and colour was coming from their funnels as unusual items were fed into the furnaces.

Down swept Captain Watkiss; there was silence on the bridge of *Cockroach* now, a very tense silence. Watkiss watched narrowly, ready upon the instant to order his guns into flame and explosion if his telescope should show the smallest movement to indicate hostility. He felt vindicated in his act in beating to quarters when he saw without doubt that the dirty Russians had manned their guns and were just as ready as he was. And the buggers hadn't damn well bothered to reply to his second signal.

*   *   *

Much earlier, word of the Russian presence had spread amongst the civilians crowding the messdecks and alleyways and this word had reached the paint store, where Count von Furstenberg, though no longer under arrest, was still being accommodated for want of anywhere better to put him. Von Furstenberg was cogitating: it was true, very true, as he had done his best to indicate to the British Captain, that he was no ally of the Russians who all along had been set to grab the all-important treaty from under his nose. On the other hand, he was now being swept away out of Chinese waters by the British Captain, who, he was becoming more and more convinced, would refuse to land him at Shanghai when he asked him to. It did not suit von Furstenberg to be withdrawn like a sack of potatoes from China and deposited with the stupid British in Hong Kong, whence it might take him months of cable and

174

argument to be drawn back again. By that time, the Russians would have consolidated their position, so far as at the moment they had any at all, with the old Empress-Dowager, and he, Count von Furstenberg, emissary of his Kaiser, would have achieved nothing. The wretched British had kidnapped him in the first place, even though the exit from Chungking had been a collaborative lifesaving expedition in basis, and they couldn't be trusted. Nor could the Russians, but in many ways they were easier to deal with than the British, having much more worldly ideas about international dealings . . . more amenable were the Russians! Oh, so much more amenable . . . von Furstenberg sat in the paint store and considered the advantages to be gained by the sharing of gold and concessions with the Czar of All The Russias so that at least his Kaiser would gain something if not all. With much care, all was in fact yet there to be gained. Yes, most certainly! Von Furstenberg, seeing positively on which side his bread was buttered, removed his polished leather Uhlan knee-boots and, barefoot, stepped out from the paint store into the alley.

'Excuse please . . . excuse . . . *Himmel*, such dolts to get in my way!' He pushed and shoved. He reached the open deck, somewhere aft where the fool on the bridge would not see. Ahead were the Russians, so sinister-looking, but no matter the sinisterness. 'Pardon me, please get out of my damn way, such stupid dolts.' Count von Furstenberg reached the gunboat's bulwarks and without more ado climbed them. He stood teetering dangerously for a moment, then plopped in.

The shout of 'man overboard port' went up but Watkiss took no notice, his whole attention being riveted on the Russian guns as he swept so close between them that he could almost read the expressions on the faces of the seamen behind the breeches of the main armament. Some of those expressions were odd: men were laughing. Watkiss fumed and projected his telescope to the bridge of the flagship, where the Russian officers were also laughing, and laughing heartily. In the instant that his ship was abeam of the Russian flagship, he saw the Russian Captain lift his gold-braided cap and give a solemn bow in his direction. Very soon upon the heels of this the signal came, plain for all his ships to read: FROM CAPTAIN SUVAROV TO BRITISH CAPTAIN. YOU ARE SUCH A LIAR.

Watkiss bounced about his bridge, shaking a fist back towards the Russian flotilla. As he looked, he saw a dripping wet figure, large and fat, being hauled like a whale aboard the flagship and he turned upon Halfhyde.

'Did I hear man overboard, Mr Halfhyde?'

'You did, sir—'

'And who was that man? No, don't tell me, I can't bear it! My God, now what's the Admiralty going to say? I've a damn good mind to put the whole blasted ship's company in arrest, surely to God *somebody* could have stopped the bugger!'

*   *   *

They sped downriver, disconsolately on the part of Captain Watkiss. Nanking could or would provide no bunkers and no notice was taken of Watkiss' peremptory tones. They continued on at the most economical speed, all vessels now burning smashed chairs and tables, officers' wash-hand cabinets, wooden bulkheads and anything else that would take flame and eke out the small remaining coal stocks that as yet provided a nucleus. In the end it was Mr Bodmin who saved the day when there was nothing left to burn at all: he busied himself with all the canvas he could find stored aboard the three gunboats, and a sailmaker's palm he found hidden away in the deck store now vacated by Count von Furstenberg; eventually Watkiss' flotilla made its way through the channel off Shanghai under sail of a sort and, with a distant view of the just-arriving cruisers of the China Squadron, entered Woosung to take, at long last, bunkers. At Woosung the somewhat smelly and decomposing body of Kurt Schmultz alias Bloementhal was landed into custody of the police authority; and word came through from United States sources that the body of the real Bloementhal from the Peking Legation had been found in a sleazy alley in the back streets of Shanghai. In Woosung Rear Admiral Hackenticker also took his leave and was piped over the side into a gasoline gig of the United States Navy. Captain Watkiss heaved an almighty sigh of relief as he speeded the parting guest.

'Nice to have been aboard your vessel, Captain,' Hackenticker said.

'Delighted to have you, sir. Delighted.'

176

Hackenticker gave a final grin. 'I'll bet,' he said, and stepped into the gasoline gig. Captain Watkiss gave a perfunctory salute and turned round on Halfhyde.

'Now, Mr Halfhyde, those blasted Uhlans and the parson. I propose taking the parson aboard the Commodore's ship if he's sober enough, and he'll be accompanied by my report and submissions as to his conduct, the bugger. But what about the Uhlans?'

'They've given no trouble, sir—'

'I didn't say they had, and anyway they can't do much without their blasted horses, can they? I'd better leave that to Commodore Marriot-Lee, I think. He may wish to take them into Hong Kong for questioning, or something.' Captain Watkiss gave a brisk rub of his hands. Things were not too black – why, they were not black at all really. Good heavens, no! He summarized his virtues to Halfhyde: 'Well, Mr Halfhyde, I've done my duty, I fancy.'

'Yes, indeed, sir.'

'I took off the Consulate staff and the blasted civilians, I achieved what I was sent to do, I believe. I outwitted the Americans, too!'

'Outwitted them, sir?'

Watkiss glared angrily. 'Well, *dealt* with them, then. Hackenticker had rather a hang-dog look, I thought. One of them was a German anyway.'

'Yes, sir.' Halfhyde coughed. 'And the treaties, sir? They're not yet—'

'Oh, balls to treaties, Mr Halfhyde, I'm a sailor not a blasted diplomat, and as I said, I've done my duty, what more could be expected I'd like to know! One day the British Consulate in Chungking will re-open, and then the dagoes'll know they can't cock snooks at British power and get away with it, won't they?'

'Yes, sir.'

'And talking of damn diplomacy,' Watkiss went on with a belligerent look in his eye, 'if I hadn't allowed that blasted Hun to make a dash for the Russians there would have been a very nasty incident and what would have happened to diplomacy then, may I ask? I avoided that quite neatly, I thought.'

'Very neatly indeed, sir.'

Watkiss bounced up and down on the balls of his feet. 'Obstinate bugger's probably been shot by now I shouldn't wonder, or on his way to the Siberian salt mines.'

'Perhaps, sir.' Halfhyde paused. 'The signal, sir?'

Watkiss looked blank. 'What signal, pray?'

'The Commodore. You had not yet decided what to make when we raised the flagship off the estuary—'

'Oh, yes, yes. Well, now I have decided, Mr Halfhyde, so kindly take a note and inform my yeoman of signals. He's to make, to Commodore China Squadron from Senior Officer First River Gunboat Flotilla, mission accomplished in every particular in accordance with your orders. I am able to report complete success and propose to board you shortly with twelve Uhlan Lancers and a clerk in Holy Orders.'